Camp Redemption

Winner of the 2011 Ferrol Sams Award for Fiction

I don't get how Raymond Atkins does it. Here's a book that is at once funny and sad and silly and wise. Here's a book as irreverent as any book can be, hilariously poking holes in the wind-baggery, Bible-thumpery, holy-rollery, cant, hypocrisy, ignorance, and willful narrow-mindedness of organized—and disorganized—religion, and yet, undeniably, through it all, a divine unseen hand is working out its plan through the lives of these flawed, ridiculous, and all-too-human characters. A marvel.
—Man Martin, author of *Paradise Dogs* and *Days of the Endless Corvette*

Raymond L. Atkins once again reflects the South and all its beloved contradictions in his new novel *Camp Redemption*. Beautifully crafted. His storytelling is an art form only found in the best Southern literature.
—Ann Hite, author of the award winning
Ghost on Black Mountain

Camp Redemption is the best novel yet by award-winning Raymond Atkins, one of the most original new authors in the South today. Atkins is a brilliant writer who captivates the reader with his quirky yet lovable characters. Ivey and Early Willingham draw us into their lives, as they draw other characters, like the runaway Jesús and the honorable bootlegger Hugh Don Monfort, into Camp Redemption, as they have dubbed their Georgia home place. Ivey is something of a mystic whose visions consist of visits from the beyond, mostly dead relatives whose forewarnings and advice are spot-on, however bizarre they may sometimes seem to her "brother" Early. As a result of her visions, they convert their family land into a summer Bible camp and then, as the economy collapses, into a place of refuge for worthy folks in need. I simply couldn't stop reading. The book is at once funny, ironic, poignant, tender, and lyrical.
—June Hall McCash, author of *A Titanic Love Story:*
Ida and Isidor Straus, Almost to Eden, and *Plum Orchard*

This book has soul. Raymond Atkins has weaved together layer upon layer of brilliant writing with strands of wisdom and humor, creating a unique texture of plot development guaranteed to satisfy any reader. The story, which takes place in a rural Georgia community, touches contemporary issues of religion, immigration, racism, economic hardship, and domestic violence, through the pitch-perfect Southern cadence of rich dialogue and character development. I enjoyed every minute of reading this book.
—Catherine McCall is the author of *When the*
Piano Stops and *Never Tell*

Camp Redemption showcases the best of Raymond Atkins's talents in Southern fiction: characters who move in with us, for better or worse; a plot that keeps the pages turning; and the stately, elegant prose of a born storyteller. Alternately hilarious, sad, and downright scary, this is Atkin's best novel yet. And the food! The man writes so well about a hot, buttered biscuit that you'll get fat just reading the words.
—Melanie Sumner, author of *The Ghost of Milagro Creek* and *The School of Beauty and Charm*

This book is a riot. Ray Atkins is richly talented and funny as you-know-what. Go ahead and get *Camp Redemption* right now. I guarantee that you'll delight in this read as I did.
—Lauretta Hannon, author of *The Cracker Queen:
A Memoir of a Jagged, Joyful Life* and named
"the funniest woman in Georgia" by *Southern Living*

At once smart and funny, Raymond Atkins's *Camp Redemption* is a gripping elegantly told tale that will keep you up reading long into the night. All hail a new master of Southern fiction!
—Jeffrey Stepakoff, bestselling author of *Fireworks over Toccoa*

In *Camp Redemption*, Ray Atkins twines the romance of Echota Lake's lore of valley enchantment with the colorful folkways of the Willinghams. Early Willingham (who can believe in the magic of the place when he smokes a little Panama Red) negotiates with considerable amusement a life with Ivey (half crackpot relation and half recipient of divine revelation) as their summer bible camp founders and then fills with a wealth of characters. Everything about *Camp Redemption* says the novel is a Janus, one head looking toward comedy and local color and the grittiness of daily life in a North Georgia realm of blessed backwardness, the other head peering— though not without comedy—into regions of the afterlife.
— Marly Youmans, *A Death at the White Camellia Orphanage*, inaugural winner of the Ferrol Sams Award for Fiction

Raymond Atkins's ability to capture the true cadence and beauty of the human voice is some of the best writing to be found anywhere. A beautiful, honest portrayal of faith and the gift of everlasting love.
—River Jordan, author of *Praying for Strangers*

MERCER
UNIVERSITY PRESS

Endowed by
TOM WATSON BROWN
and
THE WATSON-BROWN FOUNDATION, INC.

Camp Redemption

A Novel

Raymond L. Atkins

MERCER UNIVERSITY PRESS

MACON, GEORGIA

MUP H864

© 2013 Mercer University Press
1400 Coleman Avenue
Macon, Georgia 31207
All rights reserved

First Edition

Books published by Mercer University Press are printed on acid-free paper
that meets the requirements of the American National Standard for
Information Sciences—Permanence of Paper for Printed Library Materials.

Mercer University Press is a member of Green Press Initiative
(greenpressinitiative.org), a nonprofit organization working to help
publishers and printers increase their use of recycled paper and decrease
their use of fiber derived from endangered forests. This book is printed on
recycled paper.

ISBN   978-0-88146-426-9

Cataloging-in-Publication Data is available from the Library of Congress

For Marsha, as always, and for a fine armload of children, now grown. And for Charlie, the latest of the many lights of my life.

Acknowledgments

Thanks to Tony Grooms and the gang around the big table for helping launch *Camp Redemption*. Thanks to Anna Nichols and Jeanie Cassity for reading and advice. Thanks to everyone at Mercer University Press, and especially to my copy editor, Kelley Land. And finally, thanks to all who waited patiently for this one.

Camp Redemption

Prologue

The area that would eventually become the site of Camp Redemption arose in the aftermath of the serendipitous collision between the two land masses that would someday become North America and Africa. When the tectonic plates met, the oceans boiled, the heavens ripped, and the warring terrains buckled and heaved as they battled for ascendancy. Peaks and crags on both sides of the fault tumbled ever higher into the atmosphere, falling up as if the properties of physics had been suspended and the laws of gravity repealed. The two shelves of land never ceased to probe as each sought to subdue the other. Two times over the ensuing millennia, the mountains rose from the fault line; twice they climbed high and stood proud in their prime. And two times they were cast down, humbled and brought low by the passage of the endless seasons.

Eons upon eons later, the seismic violence casually drifted into a smoldering, one-eyed slumber. The land masses suspended their conflict and began to separate, as if they had each grown weary of the other's constant company. One journeyed east and south, but slowly, bare inches per century, while the other continued its westward exodus. When the waters finally receded and the sulfurous vapors dissipated, a long line of fallen mountains stood like tombstones that marked the boundary of the epic geologic clash. Most of the peaks remained where they had always been, give or take a double handful of miles, mutely posting guard along the verge of the conflict, but odd remnants of the mountain range had drifted as far away as Morocco and Scotland.

There were no human witnesses to the cataclysm, no spectators to the continental carnage. The events transpired long before the evolution of man or the invention of time. They occurred during an epoch when the adolescent sun rose and set at the random whim of the petulant, ivory moon, an age when the silent stars sparred with one another as they danced through the smoky velvet sky, each on its own long journey to the ends of one universe, and then on to the beginnings of another.

At the southern tip of the Appalachian range, a quiet valley calmly rested at the very spot where seas had once rolled and lava had fumed. The valley waited with infinite patience. Presently, company would come to call.

Chapter One

Early Willingham sat at the kitchen table with his sister, Ivey. They looked at one another silently, then cast their glances at the registration forms for Camp Redemption. The reservations lay scattered on the tabletop before them. It was mid-May, and the first of four summer camping sessions was scheduled for the beginning of June, just one day shy of three weeks away. The second session would commence in June as well, but toward the end of that month. Session three would begin in mid-July. And the fourth and final camp assembly took place during the second and third weeks of August, in the hot and humid dog days of Georgia summer.

Normally by the fifth month of the year, sixty or seventy deposits would have come in, and at the very least, the first camp session would be sold out or near to it. But so far this year, they had only received seven registrations. Of those seven, the check accompanying one had not managed to clear the bank, and another was a gratis enrollment, one of the several free bunks the Willinghams held each year for children in dire circumstances, youngsters who had the will but not the way. Further, the paltry number of campers in the queue wasn't just for the June assembly, which would have been a disaster all by itself. No, the seven reservations resting meekly on the kitchen table represented the total amount of business booked so far for the entire summer. It was an unacceptable situation, a financial catastrophe of the highest magnitude.

"Do you have any ideas?" Early asked Ivey.

She nodded her head and cleared her throat. "'Wait on Me, your Lord,'" she calmly replied. "'Be of good courage, and I shall strengthen your heart. Wait, I say, on Me.' Psalms 27:14."

Early was not surprised to hear her answer. He was fifty-four years of age, and he could remember the latter forty-five of them fairly clearly most of the time. In that entire span, his sister had encountered very few problems toward which she had not lobbed a Scripture or two, like sacred hand grenades. It was her way.

"Technically, that wasn't your idea," Early noted. "Besides, we *have* been waiting, and my heart is strong. But nothing much has been happening, and my bank account is weak."

Early and Ivey lived together in the Big House, as it had always been called, the family home place built over two hundred years ago by Seaborn, the initial Willingham in the area. Though the modern-day Willinghams had lost the facts of the story, that intrepid pioneer had acquired title to the valley in 1806 after first briefly and successfully negotiating with its former Chickasaw owner, Robert Corntassel, by striking him firmly between the shoulder blades with a mattock.

In his defense, Seaborn had been more than willing to pay for the property and had offered to do so, but Robert Corntassel had lived by the lake at the base of the cliff for all the long days of his life, and he did not wish to part with his home. He believed there was magic in the rainbows that the setting sun painted on the spray rising from the waterfall, the greens, lavenders, yellows, and reds floating skyward like colorful dreams on a mischievous breeze. And it was his intention to remain by the waters, catching brown trout, bass, and shellcrackers while contemplating the deeper meanings of existence—such as they were—until the time came for him to rejoin those who had gone on before him: his wife, his sons, and all of the many ancestors who now strolled the cold and quiet halls of the deceased.

Seaborn Willingham had been a sympathetic soul with the heart of a poet and the mind of a philosopher, and he would have taken *no* for an answer if he could have. But he had nine redheaded children and an understandably ailing wife down by the entrance to the valley, a ragged and tired family waiting in a broken wagon hitched to a sickly horse. Thus he was a motivated buyer not afforded the luxury of looking elsewhere for property. He was a man without options, so he regretfully hastened Robert Corntassel's reunion with his departed kin, and took the details of this journey with him to his own grave years later. Then he gave him a quick but decent Christian burial and planted his own family tree in the soil of the newly acquired and hastily named Willingham Valley. He began building the Big House the following year.

Early sat in the kitchen and reflected. He had known for some time that the economy was bad, but he hadn't realized until recently that it was appallingly so. Counting Ivey and himself, it took a staff of twenty to run the camp when it was in session, and even though most of these employees were high school and college students working summer jobs for pocket money, it still required a fair amount of currency to pay them. Additionally, Georgia Power wasn't giving away electricity, Webby Barrier at the Jottem Down Grocery wasn't handing free food out the back door, and Lucien Barkley over at the Roll Tide Insurance Agency wasn't automatically marking the monthly bill PAID. Early could weed out a few counselors, he supposed, or risk widespread high cholesterol by withholding a half cup of everyone's morning oatmeal, but even if he cut the payroll in half and only fed the campers hardtack and beans, the cash would still flow out of Willingham Valley like the Echota River.

He sighed and rubbed a hand through his closely cropped, jet-black hair. He was that rarest of all Willinghams, one who was not redheaded. Nor did he have bad eyes, a broad nose, buckteeth, a potbelly, or undersized legs. The genes for all these traits were dominant in the Willingham DNA, so much so that a trip through the family photo albums produced the eerie effect of looking at a series of pictures of the same few people taken at different times in history. But with his blue eyes, dark hair, and slim, tall frame, Early resembled none of them. He was not *homely as a Willingham*, as the local saying went, and he sometimes wondered if he had been bought from a roving band of gypsies or perhaps found crying in a basket on the doorstep.

He was also divorced, another anomaly within his line. As a general rule, Willinghams tended to enjoy lengthy and contented unions. But even the occasional unfortunate couple who made a bad match usually stuck it out until the absolute bitter end, whether they or their spouses liked it or not, a matrimonial version of life without parole. Early's plan when he had married Brandy Poteet on his twenty-eighth birthday had been to grow old with her. He proudly brought her home to the Big House, where he intended to cherish her as they raised a family and lived long and happy lives. It was a plan with potential. The year had been 1982, an optimistic time. The war in Vietnam was slowly but steadily becoming a dark memory. Ronald and Nancy Reagan were in the White House, the summer camp was flourishing, and Early and Brandy were as happy as two stray puppies playing in a Florsheim shoebox.

But trouble loomed in the mists of high Georgia. Brandy and her husband wanted to fill the Big House with children, but, due to a childhood case of the mumps that had gone irrevocably south, Early was unable to impregnate his wife. Finally, after four childless years, he suggested to his mate that they consider adopting some children. Unfortunately, Brandy was the do-it-yourself type and wanted to make her own offspring, so this idea held little appeal for her. After a long period of indecision, she left her husband for one Jesse Taylor, a dull but fertile textbook salesman from Opelika, Alabama.

That bleak day had been long ago, but there were moments when Early still missed her. He had dated a few women over the years since Brandy's departure, but he had never again married. Like the long line of Willinghams before him, he had been born to marry once, and he had done that. Brandy and the salesman from Opelika went on to produce five youngsters—each duller and more fertile than the last—and were now in the process of acquiring an assortment of dull, fertile grandchildren.

Back in the kitchen of the Big House, however, the size of Brandy and Jesse's extended family was not the issue at hand. Early repeated his original question to Ivey. "Do *you* have any ideas?"

"The Lord will provide," Ivey asserted as she, too, contemplated the short stack of correspondence on the table, scattering and restacking the pile as if that might make it larger. She spoke loudly and clearly so her words wouldn't peter out before they reached the heavenly plane. She wanted to give the hosts on high every opportunity to hear and act upon her expectation.

Ivey was the second rarest of all Willinghams, a woman. No one quite knew why, but throughout the long and colorful saga of the clan, Willingham fathers had tended to produce Willingham sons—red-haired, bowlegged, potbellied sons.

In addition to being the female miracle of the family tree, Ivey was also Early's business partner and his senior by eighteen years, a compact woman whose characteristic carrot top had mostly faded to a patchwork of white and gray. She was a devout member of the Washed in the Blood and the Fire Rapture Preparation Temple, the only female deacon in that earnest congregation. She was a loyal and dedicated parishioner who had never married. Sister Ivey, as she was known out at the church, claimed to have remained single so that she was more fully able to devote her life to Jesus. Her faith was strong, and she professed to having married her savior, at least in the metaphorical sense. Ivey was a pillar of her church, and none there doubted that her declaration of fealty was the absolute, gospel truth, although one or two of the congregation had unkindly noted that the fact that she was as homely as a typical Willingham may have also contributed to her spinsterhood.

"Camp is supposed to begin in three weeks," Early said, pointing out the obvious to his sister. "I know He likes to work in strange and mysterious ways, although I'll be damned if I have ever been able to figure out *why*." Early tended to meet the world head on, and he didn't think it was too much to ask that the Lord do business in a like manner, as a professional courtesy if for no other reason. "If He's going to provide, He needs to get on with it."

Unlike his sister, Early was not known for his unquestioning faith. He absolutely believed in God, most days, but he wasn't obsessive about it like Ivey was. He was of the opinion that the Almighty was not always one hundred percent on top of His game, that He sometimes let His vast attention drift, thus enabling the occasional sparrow to fall cold and unnoticed to the hard ground, or perhaps allowing the odd school bus to get itself plowed by a fast freight train. Along those same lines, Early believed that God surely didn't object to some well-meaning advice from time to time from one of His subordinates. He was certain that God could take a suggestion or two and might even welcome a little constructive input if it was warranted, provided the dissenting opinion was presented in a respectful manner and assuming it was preceded by the words *Dear* and *Lord*.

"Early Willingham, how many times do I have to tell you that you can't say things like that?" Ivey asked. "It's blasphemy to talk that way. 'Whom hast thou reproached and blasphemed? and against whom hast thou exalted thy voice, and

8

lifted up thine eyes on high? even against the Holy One of Israel.' Second Kings 19:22." As was always the case, his sister's encyclopedic knowledge of Scripture truly amazed Early. She had studied the sacred text for at least two hours on each and every day of his life and on most of the additional days of hers, and in that long time she had absorbed much that was both wise and profound.

"It wasn't blasphemy. Think of it more as honest doubt. And anyway, what's He going to do? Ruin the business we have spent our lives building? Run us stone-cold broke? Send us seven campers for a whole summer? It's too late for all that." Early clasped his hands behind his head and leaned back in his chair. He really didn't want to argue with his sister, but sometimes he just couldn't avoid it.

"He'll send you to hell, is what He'll do." Ivey shook her finger at Early as if he were an unruly child or a misbehaving pet.

"Well, there's that," he admitted. It was her ace in the hole, her trump card. "You know, it's not like we aren't on His side. I mean, you'd think since we run a *Bible* camp and all, He might be inclined to throw a little more business our way."

Early had spoken in a light tone, as if he were kidding, but truth be told, he was a bit peeved. After all, it wasn't as if they were running a sex camp or a summer retreat for Satanists. He and his sister were the good guys, the defenders of the faith. It was their job to spread the Word, and they had done so for a good long time. They deserved better than to go out with a whimper, to limp into the locker room with scraped knees, torn jerseys, and seven measly reservations.

Early wondered what they should do. He couldn't open the gates of the camp for so few children. It would bring down calamity of biblical proportions upon them. He shook his head. How did parents these days think they were going to get their youngsters into heaven if they didn't send them for religious instruction? Did they imagine that intimate knowledge of the divine word just happened on its own, that it was somehow innate? Salvation needed precise planning and flawless execution. It needed cabins, bunks, and Camp Redemption t-shirts to help it along. Early didn't know what the world was coming to, but he knew without question that he needed sixty campers per session to approach the break-even point. To make any money to speak of, he really needed eighty kids, and one hundred would be better still. He stood, stretched, and retrieved a can of Schlitz malt liquor from the refrigerator that was tucked up against the log wall of the kitchen. Then he turned to his sister.

"I'm going to go skip some stones at the lake and drink this can of malt liquor," he said solemnly. She nodded and patted his free hand.

"You go," she said, "and I'll pray for guidance while you're gone."

"That's a good idea. I think we could use a little guidance right now."

He walked out the kitchen door and down the gravel path past the dining hall. Then he turned right onto the trail that led to the lake.

Early had skipped stones at the lake at the base of the falls ever since he was a boy. The activity was a family tradition. Indeed, his first clear memory was of standing there next to the sturdy leg of his father while trying to perfect the sidearm throw necessary for a successful skip.

Robert Corntassel had once believed that there was magic in the spray that clung to the falls, and many members of the Willingham clan, from Seaborn on down through Early, were also of that opinion. Unlike his predecessors in philosophy, however, Early needed assistance to see the colors and images as they faded in and out between the cracks in the realities of the world. He required a leg up to the realm of mystery, a boost to the gentle land.

Thus he indulged another longstanding habit when he reached into the split bole of a dead fir tree that stood by the trail to the lake and retrieved a timeworn Dr. Grabow pipe and a plump plastic bag full of dreams. He removed a fat pinch from the bag and tamped his pipe. Then he carefully replaced his stash. He knew that one pipeful would be sufficient to his needs. He knew this because he was well acquainted with the quality of his dope. And he knew *that* because he had grown it himself, had nursed it from seed in the middle of a tall, thick stand of bamboo in a remote corner of the valley.

He grew three or four plants a year in his thicket, just enough for his own use. The tall plants blended in with the cane like chameleons, and even though there were several helicopter overflights per year by state law enforcement officials, his small but productive pot farm was invisible from above and had never been discovered. He had started years ago with a handful of Panama Red seeds and a strong desire to succeed, and he had refined that particular strain over a long period, had devoted much effort to the trial and error inherent in the experimental method, and had succeeded in producing a superior strain. He strolled on down to the lake, where he gathered a small pile of rocks suitable for skipping and sat on the stone bench he had built as a teenager. Then he popped the top on his malt liquor and lit his pipe.

He watched the water dance and the vapor swirl as he took slow, deep drags from his Dr. Grabow, followed by small sips from the tall boy. Presently, the troubles of the day eased, and Early began to hum absently. The breeze was cool with moisture, and a faint rainbow rose from the falls before disappearing into the air. The indigo, violet, yellow, and green tints danced in the sky like a miniature version of the Northern Lights.

Early had been skipping stones into these falls since he was old enough to throw, yet there always seemed to be one more flat rock that needed skimming across the surface of the lake. He had once asked his father about this unending supply of smooth, small stones, and Vester Willingham had solemnly replied that their valley was filled with enchantment both old and fine, and that at night, while Early slept, the little people rose silently from the depths of Lake Echota and skipped the stones back to shore. The story had troubled him at first because he wondered why little people lived in his lake. It had seemed an odd place to have a home. He had been just a boy at the time, and he hadn't quite known whether to believe his father or not, although the elder Willingham was known for his absolute honesty. It was commonly held that the man had never told a lie and would be hard pressed to do so if the need arose.

"Why do they live in the lake?" Early had asked.

"Because they always have," Vester Willingham had responded.

"What if they wanted to live somewhere else?"

"If they leave their home, they'll die."

Finally, Early had been forced to take it all on faith. He had slipped down to the lake many nights, but he had never seen the little people rise from the depths. As he grew older, he came to realize that this invisibility was part of the nature of the enchantment. Magic could not be seen or heard. It couldn't be controlled or harvested. It was because it was. So Early took the story as gospel—mostly because he wanted it to be true— and as for the veracity of the claim of the presence of magic in Willingham Valley, well, that was in the stones, the unending supply of stones.

Sadly, though, in the modern daylight world of recessions and failing camps, unpaid bills, and anemic bank accounts, there was no time or room for little people, water spirits, or

rainbows marking the paths on which the magical beings traveled. And there was scarce need in Ivey's cosmology of blood
and fire for the trappings of a mystic reality, a fragile, delicate
land where all things were possible. But in the evenings, by the
waters in the enchanted moments just before the sun stretched
and went to its nightly sleep, Early could take a puff from the
Dr. Grabow and a swallow from the can of Schlitz malt liquor,
and then he could see it all.

Chapter Two

Turning Willingham Valley into a Bible camp had originally been Ivey's idea. She had received a divine revelation on the subject one fine fall day in 1976. It had only been a week since their mother, Clairy, had rowed the wide gulf to heaven's shore, leaving the valley to Early and Ivey, brother and sister, descendants of Seaborn, the last of the long line of North Georgia Willinghams. Their father, Vester, had been a scholar, a historian, and an author. His *The Imaginative History of Willingham Valley* had been published in 1959 to scant acclaim. He had preceded his bride to the graveyard by ten years and a handful of days, helped along to his final reward by a broken tie-rod on his ancient Dodge pickup and by a deep pothole owned by the Georgia Department of Transportation, a yawning declivity that had been strategically located in a blind curve out on Highway 56.

Out of respect for both of their departed parents, Early had not yet discussed with his sister and co-landholder any of their possible courses of action as propertied orphans. He was not completely sure what they should do, anyway. His world had changed from one moment to the next, and he had yet to absorb the implications of his new situation. Sometimes, if asked, he would have proposed selling the valley on the spot to the highest bidder before sprinting down to the bank to be sure the check was negotiable. He was, after all, twenty-one years of age at the time, admittedly young and sometimes restless, and the wonders of the larger world occasionally whispered sweet promises to him. At those times, he craved a taste of the bright lights like a drunkard aching for a pint of rye, and he wanted to sample all the varied delights that an urban environment was reputed to offer.

But at other moments, Early was a confirmed country boy with roots sunk deep in the red clay. He had wandered the valley all his life and knew each cave and tree, every deer and hawk, and, of course, every remote stand of tall bamboo. Willingham Valley had been the backdrop of his existence. It had nurtured him, had raised him from a boy into a tall, strong man. It beckoned to him, and he could not imagine ever leaving.

His job as a mechanic at the Ford dealership over in Rome wasn't much of a consideration either way. He was mechanically inclined and good at his occupation—stoned or straight— and he made a decent living working on automobiles. He had started tinkering with small motors when he was twelve or so, and by the time he was sixteen, he had graduated to larger engines. He built his first car completely from odds and ends found in and around Duck Renfroe's junkyard, and Duck had said then that Early was the best natural mechanic he had ever seen. But as good as he was, the work held little interest for Early. He could take it or leave it, could walk away at any time without once looking back. Indeed, he had the habit of bringing his toolbox home with him every Friday. That way, if he decided to quit during the weekend, either because something better had come up or he simply decided that he'd had enough, then he wouldn't have to go back to the shop come Monday to retrieve his property.

"Mama came to see me in a dream last night," Ivey said to him on that day long past as they stood by the lake and skipped stones into the roaring waterfalls. They had walked over to the burial grounds on the far side of the valley to plant dwarf azaleas on both the fresh, raw mound that housed Clairy and the weathered green knoll that Vester had occupied for a decade and more. On the return leg of that cheerless trip, they had by mutual silent consent stopped at the water's edge.

Early could have used a Schlitz malt liquor and a pipeful of dope to help trim the ragged edge from the afternoon. Unfortunately, Ivey didn't approve of marijuana consumption, although her objections were of a nonspecific nature, since she wouldn't actually be able to identify the substance if a bale of it landed on her from out of the sky. And even though the Bible was specifically and conspicuously silent on the subject of cannabis, Early politely deferred to his sister's heightened sense of propriety on the matter and chewed a stick of gum instead.

The news of Ivey's midnight visitor did not surprise Early. His older sister had experienced flawed visions, weak signs, and semi-revelations ever since he could remember. She had once even claimed to have been blessed with stigmata, although the marks had sort of looked like shingles to Early, or perhaps a light case of poison oak. Another time, the raisins in her oatmeal had arranged themselves into what she took to be the likeness of Jesus. When Early snuck a peek while Ivey searched for the Polaroid camera so she could capture the moment for the multitudes, he was of the impression that the caricature was more reminiscent of Mickey Mouse with a beard and a halo. But whether it was Mickey or had in fact been Jesus with big, round ears and decidedly mouse-like whiskers, Ivey still thought it was a bowl full of miracle, and she had kept that cereal for several weeks until it started to develop a bad odor, at which time their mother had risked eternal damnation by throwing both the bowl and its contents out.

Ivey was of the firm belief that she had been touched by the hand of God, that she lived in a perpetual state of grace and was favored by the Almighty gaze. Early did not feel that it was his place to analyze these claims too closely or to confirm or dispute her convictions. The point was not about what he thought. Ivey believed with all her heart and soul, and her belief made her faith strong. Sometimes it seemed to Early that she was somehow in touch with the eternal realm, that she must actually be an imperfect but willing conduit for divine truth. And if this were the case, then perhaps her battery was just low or her antenna out of alignment. It could be that a simple adjustment to the vertical hold might make the messages come in with greater clarity. Maybe all she needed to be the next Joan of Arc was to relocate to the other side of the room and perhaps hold a piece of aluminum foil over her head or a straightened coat hanger clamped in her teeth.

Ivey was imbued with belief. She radiated with it, shone with it like the sun, and Early had felt since he was a boy that it would have been wrong to challenge her. She was happier than anyone else he knew, and what would be the point in spoiling that? So when he had doubts about her prophetic side, he kept them to himself or, when he became a little older, fired up the Dr. Grabow and analyzed his doubts with the broader spectrum of reflection they deserved. She was his sister, and she was a harmless and good-hearted soul, and an amazing cook on top of that. In Early's mind, there were plenty worse things to be guilty of than maybe being an instrument of God, or maybe being a little crazy, or maybe being a mystical, enchanted combination of both.

"What did Mama have on her mind?" he asked as he skipped a stone.

"She is an angel now."

"Well, that's no surprise. She was a good woman her entire life. If anyone ever deserved a pair of wings, it was Mama." Early slung an oval of granite out across the water and counted five skips before it disappeared into the mist. His best toss ever had produced an impressive nine hops, but as was the case with many of his skills, he could find no viable commercial outlet for the ability.

"Mama's fine," Ivey continued, "and she says hello." Early nodded. "She told me that Jesus sent her back down here to tell us to start a ministry here in the valley. A Bible camp for young people. Mama quoted Isaiah 50:4. She said, 'You, the Lord God, have given me the tongue of the learned, that I should know how to speak a word in season to him who is weary.'" The Book of Isaiah was Ivey's preferred portion of the Bible, with Psalms coming in a close second and Proverbs finishing a respectable third. Coincidentally, many of the messengers who spoke to her in dreams also dipped into those same divine texts to bolster their own arguments. Ivey could quote lengthy sections from all three at will and a goodly part of the rest of the Scriptures as well, and she often did just that.

"Mama always liked Isaiah," Early noted. Throughout her life, Clairy Willingham had read the Bible aloud to her husband and children. It was her daily ritual after supper, and even though she was now gone, he could still hear her soft voice as it wrapped itself around the sacred syllables, could see her rocking slowly in her old ladder-back rocker as she brought the holy words to life.

"It was one of her favorite chapters," Ivey agreed. "She spoke from it again right before she went back to heaven. Isaiah 54:13. 'And all thy children shall be taught of the Lord; and great shall be the peace of thy children.'"

"A Bible camp," Early said. He threw a stone. It skipped six times before sinking into the realm of the little people. As was often the case, he had only been half listening to her, but enough snippets of information had finally leapt across his distracted synapses to allow him to understand what she was saying. The news seemed to be that his mother and Jesus wanted them to go into the Bible camp business, and that Ivey thought it was a peach of an idea. This was an unexpected development.

"That's what she said," Ivey replied. "I've been giving it some thought this morning, and I think it would be a good idea to name it Camp Redemption. I've always liked that name."

"Camp Redemption? Isn't that—?"

"Uh huh. That's the same name that Munroe Willingham gave his army encampment back during the Civil War." Munroe had been Seaborn Willingham's youngest son, the first of several Willingham men to eventually get himself shot for no particularly good reason. He had built his training camp across the lake, and the remnants of it were still there. Early had read the story in his father's book.

Not long after the cannons snarled and the fires licked the antebellum skies over Charleston harbor, Munroe had attempted to volunteer his services to Captain John Brown Gordon of the First Alabama Regiment, which was forming just over the state line at Fort Payne. At that time, Munroe was one of the few remaining occupants of the valley. He had lost his wife and both of his small children to the bullneck diphtheria epidemic of 1849, and the sorrow of his loss had cast him adrift. He spent a fair portion of the following years sitting on a stool in the burial grounds in Willingham Valley, drinking whiskey and talking to his family as they slept the long sleep. What he needed was a cause, a reason to get up from his perch and engage with life once more. So even though he had never owned a slave or even met anyone from farther north than Bluefield, Kentucky, he decided that shooting at a few Yankees might be just the tonic he needed.

Unfortunately, Munroe Willingham's heart was in the right place, but it was arguably the only part of his body that was, and his enlistment was regretfully declined. This refusal was due to the combination of hunched back, weak chest, bad eyes, crooked fingers, and clubbed foot he possessed.

The Willinghams were a stubborn lot, however, a family prone to have it their own way, and Munroe subsequently determined to raise his own troop, one in which he would be allowed to serve. So he spent the first two years of the war constructing a training facility up in Willingham Valley and staffing it with other rejects and misfits from the various armies of the Confederacy, men like him who had been denied the privilege of service to the cause. He named this facility Camp Redemption, and it was there that he and his ragged recruits lived, planned, and trained before marching forth to confront the enemy and redeem their honor.

The camp was rustic and utilitarian. It sat on one side of the lake at the base of the falls, opposite the Willingham family compound two hundred yards distant on the other shore. It consisted of rough cabins, a selection of tents, an administration building and storehouse, a few privies dug downstream as per army regulations, and a large drill field. The minimum requirements for enlistment were relatively few, but even so, Munroe was not the only patriot who had been excluded, and his force soon outgrew these humble facilities. As time and history passed, many of the excess erstwhile soldiers found themselves billeted in the caverns in the stone edifices of the valley, some of which were deep, large, and dry.

As was the case with the camp, the campers weren't much to look at, either. Although none of the men were as profoundly impaired as Munroe, there were twisted feet, hunched backs, and crossed eyes enough to share. But the soldiers were an earnest group for the most part in spite of their many physical difficulties, a collection of volunteers who wanted to do their part for the cause of states' rights, and the few malingerers who managed to make their way up into the valley were soon weeded out. Munroe had a humble nature and had taken the rank of sergeant, although by rights he could have claimed officer status since he had raised and funded the regiment. He was as hard as cast iron when it came to his volunteer force, however, and those who did not share his dream did not remain in the valley long. He was a stern taskmaster who drilled his troop relentlessly. He worked them hard because he intended to fight them hard. He had sworn that he was going to make a difference in the war, and he wanted his troop to be ready when the bugles sounded and the shot flew.

The group's first and last battle occurred early in May of 1864, when they tramped out of Willingham Valley and engaged with a body of Northern skirmishers. These Yankees were members of the Army of the Cumberland led by General William Tecumseh Sherman, whose malevolent gaze had drifted south and east, toward Atlanta, Macon, and the ancient, sounding sea. The Georgia Irregulars, as Munroe called his fighting force, met the enemy at sundown just outside the little village of Resaca, Georgia, about thirty miles north of Willingham Valley. The ensuing battle was fierce, and in that fray, the Irregulars were killed quickly and to the last man. None of the opposing force suffered any wounds.

Come sunrise, the Union soldiers ventured out from behind the hastily erected breastworks to view their handi-work. They were abashed at the physical condition of the men they had dispatched in the darkness, even though they had not known in the heat of the fight that their opponents were maimed, halt, and infirm. The Yankees were ashamed and confused, somehow, as if they had committed an unintentional mortal sin, a transgression that would stain their souls and limit their prospects in the land of promise to come. As for the Irregulars, they died with their boots on, or at least, those who had feet did, and they mercifully went to their various rewards without the knowledge that their deaths had no impact whatsoever on the outcome of the war, or even on Sherman's march to the sea, and that for all the good their ultimate sacrifices had brought, they might just as well have stayed on the porch, sipped good corn whiskey, and talked about the weather or the price of hogs.

But all of that was ancient history. Back at the falls, Early looked at Ivey. It was normal protocol whenever his sister had one of her revelations for a departed loved one to do the revealing, so it was no surprise that Clairy Willingham had floated over from the cemetery for a chat with her daughter. In addition to deceased Willinghams, the odd biblical VIP—an archangel, perhaps, or a minor prophet—would sometimes pack a box lunch and make the long trip from heaven to speak with Ivey. But this was the first time Early could recall Jesus becoming involved in the process, even if it had been in a second-hand, as-told-to capacity. His sister was hauling out the heavy artillery for this particular vision, the heavenly A-list. In light of the old family story about Munroe and his Irregulars, he ventured to raise a point.

"Are you sure about naming it Camp Redemption?" he asked. "Munroe got his ass shot off. All of his men got theirs shot off, too." Actually, family records, although sketchy, had indicated that Munroe's backside was one of the few places on his spindly frame that had *not* taken fire, but Early had forgotten that fact, and he was just trying to make a point, anyway.

"Early Willingham, you can't say that word! It's blasphemy!" She closed her eyes for the briefest of moments and sent a quick prayer skyward on behalf of her brother.

"*Ass* is not blasphemy," he replied. "*Mary* rode an ass into Bethlehem."

"Well, it's still ugly, the way you say it."

"Maybe it is a little ugly. Sorry. Let's get back to your dream. What else did Mama say?"

"She told us to fix up the family compound for the girls, and to rebuild Munroe's old Civil War camp across the lake for the boys." A thought seemed to cross her mind. "We'll have to put the bridge back up, so they can walk back and forth." The plank bridge built over a century ago had been washed out by a flood sometime during the thirties and was never replaced. The temporary expedient of using a rowboat to cross had become a permanent solution due to habit and inertia. The next closest span across the river was the state highway bridge several miles downstream, completely outside of the valley.

"And all of this came from Jesus, by way of Mama's angel?" Early was impressed. It was an audacious plan, a layered scheme that had traveled a tremendous distance along mystic channels before arriving in the tawdry world of men. He wasn't particularly enthusiastic about the idea, but there was no getting around the fact that the scope of the project was grand.

"Every word of it! It's a miracle! The youngsters will come here in the summers. They'll breathe the fresh air, fish, and swim. They'll have decent fun while we teach them the word of the Lord." Ivey was so excited that she couldn't catch her breath. Early couldn't recall ever seeing her quite this joyful before.

Early was not nearly as ecstatic. He had honestly never considered running any kind of camp. He had toyed with the possibility of opening his own garage a time or two, but when it came down to cases, he just wasn't that enthusiastic about the idea of operating a business, period. He was simply not driven that way. He liked to go home at night and leave work behind, and the few business owners he knew did not seem to have that luxury. The worry of the enterprise was always on their minds. Thus, now that his sister had presented her vision, he wasn't surprised that his first impression was that he wanted to run a camp about as much as he wanted to dive from Echota Falls into the rocky pool below. On the long list of life experiences he hoped to have, rebuilding and then operating Camp Redemption was nowhere near the top. But he wanted to be fair and hear his sister out.

"How are we supposed to pay for all of this? We'll have to do a lot of work if we're going to try to turn this place into a summer camp. It'll take a lot of money. All the cabins need repair, especially the ones at the old Civil War camp. Some of them may even need to be torn down and replaced.

Early was a practical person, and he assumed that a camp was not just going to appear in a bright flash, and equally certain that a pile of money was not going to drift down from on high That would be too easy. That wasn't the way things were done. Christian texts were packed full of poor souls who had been forced to perform their divine assignments the hard way, and he was willing to bet that the current endeavor would be no different. In the long and varied history of the world, the good Lord had shown a decided preference for seeing the faithful sweat. He had demonstrated a predilection toward arranging for the expression of fealty to be as unpleasant an experience as possible, and Early didn't figure that establishing this camp would somehow escape that apparently central requirement.

"Mama told us to go to the bank and borrow the money," Ivey continued. "We can use the valley for security." The statement made Early a bit squeamish. As was usually the case during the early stages of a revelation, he wasn't quite sure whether he was dealing with a crazy sister or divine will, although he was leaning marginally toward the former on this occasion. But either way, regardless of the nature of the revelation, his parents had instilled in him a Southerner's instinctive fear of banks and, by association, bankers, and he hated to rely on either unless there was no other way.

"You want us to borrow the money?"

"It's not *my* idea," she said as she held up her hands, making it abundantly clear that she wasn't that wild about banks, either. The burden was on Clairy Willingham and Jesus.

"Excuse me. Jesus wants us to borrow the money? I didn't realize He gave financial advice."

"You hush. That's enough blasphemy for one day."

"Ivey, I don't know if I want to run a camp. I do know that even if I wanted to, I don't have the first clue about how to do it, and neither do you. Being a high school librarian doesn't exactly qualify you. And even if I wanted to run a camp and knew how to do it, I'm sure I don't want to go down to the bank and borrow the money to do it with."

"But we have to."

"Why?"

"*Jesus* told us."

"Well, to get right down to it, Mama told us. I don't know why He needs us anyway. He could run His own camp. He wouldn't even have to buy any Bibles. He already knows all the stories. He was *there.*" Early quickly held up his hands to ward off the inevitable accusation of blasphemy.

They went back and forth for several days on the subject of turning Willingham Valley into Camp Redemption. Actually, Early did most of the talking during this debate, since Ivey simply rested her entire case on their divine mandate and met each point that her brother raised with a serene and secure *Because Jesus told us to.*

Early had no real philosophical issues with the idea of building a Bible camp, although it sounded like it was going to involve a goodly amount of money and sweat, especially during that bridge-building phase of the project. He didn't want to go into debt, and, for that matter, he wasn't so sure that he wanted to commit to running the finished product, but he had to admit that Ivey was a natural fit for the role. As far as his own participation was concerned, he liked kids all right, and he had to admit that Willingham Valley would be an ideal setting for a summer camp. And even when it came down to the Bible part of the equation, he believed there were several good precepts in the sacred texts, along with a passing few that surely must have been typos. But he had never before considered the possibility of combining all of these separate strands into a career.

He and his sister each owned fifty percent of Willingham Valley, so neither was the majority shareholder, in a manner of speaking. After Vester and Clairy Willingham passed into eternity, Early had inherited the southern half of the valley, the portion that contained the Big House and the burial plot, and Ivey had received the northern half, which included Munroe's old camp as well as Early's marijuana patch. The river and lake separated the holdings, and the little people belonged to no one. The Willinghams had been land poor since the day that Seaborn planted his feet in the soil of the valley and his mattock in Robert Corntassel. The family owned property that was worth a good deal of money, but they had no cash. As a result, neither Early nor Ivey had the means to buy the other out. Since the plan for the resurrection of Camp Redemption included both sides of the river, both Early and Ivey would have to agree on it.

And there was another consideration. Ivey may have been a bit of a nut, to put the matter kindly, but she was a nut who believed that the one and only, actual Son of God had sent word to her to build a summer camp. Ivey had received many revelations during her lifetime, and some of these had sprung from sources other than dead relatives. But she had *never* had contact with anyone this high up the sacred food chain, and Early knew she wasn't going to change her mind. Jesus said it, she believed it, and that settled it. The vision was set in her mind and heart like rebar in concrete, and people who believe in celestial disclosure don't generally think that compliance is optional. She was going to start a Bible camp. Of that, Early was certain.

Ivey was Early's only sister, and with that genetic link had come a ponderous responsibility that Early had not sought. For as she had lain during her final moments among the living, Clairy Willingham had extracted from Early the promise that he would nurture his older sibling, that he would help her steer clear of the rocks and shoals of the wide world.

"Early," she had said, her voice a bare whisper.

"Yes, Mama," he had replied.

"I'm going to see Daddy now. You have to promise..." She drifted off for so long that he thought she had passed, that she was again in the arms of her beloved Vester. Then she breathed and opened her eyes. They were watery and unfocused.

"Promise what, Mama?" he asked.

"Promise me you'll watch out for Ivey. She's one of God's special children."

"I promise."

"She's different, Early."

"I know, Mama. I promise I'll take care of her." Clairy Willingham sighed as she completed her last bit of mothering. Then she cast loose the bowline and drifted effortlessly to the far shore.

And that had been that. He was trapped. In the complicated hierarchy of promises, a deathbed promise to a mother is the most sacred, and Early knew it. Most days he didn't believe in a literal hell, but he figured he'd end up there anyway if he reneged on his final promise to his mother. He was necessary to the successful implementation of the plan. Ivey wasn't capable of managing the day-to-day affairs of an enterprise as complex as the one she was proposing. She had the spiritual vision but not the business sense. Her mind did not work that way. Her faith could not make payroll, and her belief could not repay a bank loan. If he didn't help her, she would ultimately fail. If he decided to pack his bag and put the wind at his back, he would be committing the basest of sins.

So in the end, Early agreed to help Ivey with her enterprise. He realized that due to her habit of hearing prophecy, a case could probably be made for having her declared incompetent, or maybe even crazy. But he would not do that, not now or ever, unless perhaps she started getting messages from beyond the pale instructing her to axe-murder the unfaithful or to toss them from high places. And even then, his actions might be ameliorated somewhat under the right circumstances, such as if he happened to agree with the names on the sacred hit list.

Mostly he agreed to the idea because he knew his sister was going ahead with or without him. He still wasn't completely sure that he wanted to go into the camp business, at least not forever, but they would give it a go and see what they saw. And he had to admit that another reason he stayed was because he couldn't come up with a better plan. He had reached adulthood without a burning need to pursue any particular dream, so for the time being, he supposed it wouldn't kill him to share Ivey's. He was already tired of being a mechanic, even though he had only been doing that for a couple of years, and he had no interest in college. What he really liked to do was nothing much. He liked to smoke his Dr. Grabow, drink an occasional Schlitz malt liquor, skip a few stones, and watch the water flow slowly by. If that work paid a little better, he would make it his career, his life's labor.

"I'll help you get the thing up and going," he told her. "But if something comes along I like better, we might have to take another look."

"Didn't you tell me there wasn't anything else you were just dying to go do?" she asked.

"I did say that." He had to admit it.

"Well, don't you see?" Ivey said. "It's as clear to me as a summer day. God has chosen you for this!"

Early didn't know how he felt about being chosen for camp construction followed by camp operation, and he sort of wished he had been consulted on the matter. But he stayed. He told himself it was only for a while, that Ivey would lose interest eventually, or receive new orders, and then he would be free to pursue another course if he wished. And who knew? He might like being half owner of a Bible camp. He might indeed be the chosen one. Ivey's project might be what he was born to do. He would see. It could have been worse, he supposed. At least their mother had not told Ivey to build an ark or to part the lake so they could walk across before drowning a selection of unruly Egyptians—or perhaps Alabamians—in hot but fruitless pursuit. Building a camp was doable, so they moved forward with their assignment.

Early quit his job at the Ford dealership, and Ivey quit hers over at the high school. Using the deed to the valley as their security, they went down to the Farmers and Merchants Bank, and even though they were neither farmers nor merchants, they borrowed some money.

"Don't mention Jesus or Mama when we ask for the money," Early told Ivey before they entered the bank.

"Why not?" she asked.

"Trust me."

They got the loan, and much like their ancestor, Munroe, for two years they worked and built, fixed and planned. Camp Redemption slowly took shape until it came to resemble the blueprint in Ivey's mind, and even though Early had begun the labor as a somewhat grudging participant, he became proud of the camp that grew beneath his hands.

They began their project on the south side of the lake at the ancestral Willingham compound, the site of the Big House. It was Early's plan to work from best to worst, and the structures at the family compound were in much better condition than their counterparts across the lake. Although older, they were better built to begin with, and the years had not lain as heavily upon them. The six original cabins were repaired and modernized. Each was roofed, plumbed, and rewired. Doors were hung and windows glazed and caulked. Floors were sanded and varnished. Screens were replaced and ceiling fans installed. Whenever they lost their way, Ivey received a handy visitation from some angelic messenger and the answer to their quandary was revealed. Once the work on the family cabins was completed, these became the girls' residences. They were named Peter, Andrew, James, John, Philip, and Bartholomew, after six of the Apostles of Jesus. In addition, a new kitchen and dining hall, a bathhouse, a laundry, an infirmary, and a chapel were constructed on the site.

Across the clear green pool that was Lake Echota, over on the north side of the valley, the cabins in Munroe Willingham's old Civil War encampment were renovated to house the male campers. These buildings were in much worse shape than the others, and it took Early and a crew of three men hired from town nearly a year to make them habitable. Termites had apparently been dining on two of the structures for quite some time, and the men had to raze and replace them. The rest of the buildings were salvageable. As the days passed, the cabins slowly came into their own under Early's watchful gaze, and once they were completed, they, too, were named for the followers of Christ, becoming Matthew, Thomas, Thaddeus, Simon, Nathanael, and Matthias. A separate bathhouse, an outbuilding which later became a stable, and a small recreation building were added, and the bridge was rebuilt across the Echota River on the pilings of the original article.

"When you named the cabins," Early commented, "you forgot one of the Jameses, and you didn't name one after Judas, either."

Personally, he had wanted to use selected Bible books as cabin names, favorites such as Genesis, Corinthians, Ephesians, and Ecclesiastes, and perhaps one named Lamentations to put the bad kids into, or maybe even Revelation, a nice, quiet cabin where youthful miscreants could sit and think about their short, bleak futures in this world and reflect on the larger idea of a long eternity full of torment if they didn't straighten up. They could perform penance while they viewed a lurid mural of the Four Horsemen sauntering across the wall. Clip, clop, clip, clop. White, red, black, and pale. Pestilence, War, Famine, and Death. Early felt his idea held much promise for modifying the behaviors of misbehaving children, but Ivey dug in like a blind mule by the water's edge at the suggestion, so they compromised as they usually did and had done it her way.

"I know very well there were two Jameses. I'm the one who taught *you* that before you were even old enough to read. But I think having boys' and girls' cabins both named James can only lead to trouble. Sure as the world, someone is bound to walk into the wrong place at the wrong time, and we can't be having that." The very thought of it—like a chill wind from the second circle of hell—made her shudder. Boxer shorts might be glimpsed, or panties and brassieres, and then who knew what all might happen?

"What about a Judas cabin?" Early asked.

"I don't intend to name anything after Mr. Iscariot."

"You do realize that he was just doing what he was told to do, that *somebody* had to betray Jesus for the whole thing to work."

"You hush." She placed her hand over his lips. He removed it and took it in his, and he smiled a fond smile at her.

"Maybe we could dedicate the septic tank in his honor. I know, I know. Septic tanks are blasphemy."

To Early's great surprise, but not to Ivey's, once they opened the front gate and hung out the welcome sign, the camp quickly became a commercial success. It lost a little money the first year, but it managed to break even the second. After that, it made a fair profit every year except 1992, when a big ice storm hit North Georgia and the camp sustained damage in excess of $100,000.

"I personally know of two beer joints that survived the storm without a scratch," Early told his sister the day after the storm. They sat in the yellow glow of a kerosene lamp at the table in the kitchen of the Big House. He made the remarks upon returning from a trip to Sequoyah to arrange for a generator and to hire contractors to begin the removal of fallen trees from the tops of his broken cabins. He had become aware of the beer joints' good fortune while stopping at each, briefly, as he made his way back to camp. "I mean to say that they never even lost their electricity. One of them still has cable. Yet the only Bible camp in the northern half of the entire state of Georgia just got pretty much wiped out by an act of God. I'm confused. Does Mama have anything she needs to tell us?"

"The Lord works in mysterious ways."

"That's a country fact," he said as he shouldered into his flannel coat, grabbed a malt liquor, and headed toward the lake. He had never skipped stones on ice before and was looking forward to the experience.

Still, with the exception of that one six-figure hiccup, that one dropped stitch in the divine tapestry, running the camp had been relatively trouble free. Ivey took care of the spiritual end of the business. Her religious agenda for the campers was low-keyed and reasonable, and once she got the hang of ministering to a younger crowd, she almost never scared the children with visions or revelations anymore. Early's strengths lay more in the direction of the practicalities of business, so he spent his days managing the camp facilities and its employees.

During the nine-month off-season, Ivey prepared herself spiritually for the coming year as well as for eternity, and she quilted in her spare time. Early made repairs, skipped stones, smoked a little weed from time to time, and took an occasional trip to places with concrete sidewalks instead of dirt paths and streetlights in place of trees. It wasn't a bad life, all things considered, and time passed, as time inevitably will.

Chapter Three

Before they knew it, it was 2010, and Ivey and Early were facing their worst camp season ever. Three more reservations came in for Camp Redemption during the next week, bringing the total to an anemic ten, one of which still had an unfunded check stapled to it, like a flag of surrender. Early had held out hope until the last minute that the overall outlook would improve, but with only two weeks to go until the first session was set to begin, he knew that there was no further point in wishing for a miracle. Those were his sister's specialty, anyway, and if anyone could drum one up, it was Ivey Willingham. But she hadn't so far, and barring a successful intercession by the Almighty, their business prospects were bleak.

He called her to the weathered plank table that served as their office. The kitchen table was twelve feet long and six feet wide, a handmade affair constructed of quarter-sawn chestnut planks worked smooth with drawknives and jack planes. It could sit thirty or more with ease. It was well over 150 years old, and many generations of Willinghams had arranged themselves around it during its long tenure, as if it were the anchor that held them to the valley and to one another. It had no finish other than the dull patina of age and wear that had been buffed into the flat timbers by a century and a half of constant use. Early sat his sister down, held her hands in his, and began to speak.

"I don't know how to say this gently, so I'm just going to come right out with it. We're not going to be able to run the camp this year. There's just not enough business. I'm sorry, but I've looked at it from all sides, and I can't see any way to avoid canceling the entire summer season. We'll lose a lot less money by just shutting down. We need to do it right away—cancel camp, I mean—so the few parents who were planning on sending their kids might have time to make other arrangements."

Ivey's reaction was immediate, negative, and not unexpected.

"We can't cancel the camp! This is our ministry. We have to do it. Jesus *told* us to do it!" She looked over her shoulders, first one and then the other, as if she expected Jesus to be sitting there with His attorney, concern and mild disapproval etched on His sacred features as he tapped His finger at the pertinent clause in the contract, drawing their attention to the cogent phrases buried in the fine print.

"I understand all that, Ivey, and I'm truly sorry. All I can say is, it's a tough year. People are having a hard time and can't afford to send their children to summer camp, or else they have the money, but they're afraid to spend it. And you can't really blame them. I don't know what all the reasons are, but it doesn't matter much, because for us the end result is no campers. I don't know what else to do but cancel. I guess I've known it for a while, but I just hated to admit it. Maybe the economy will improve by next year. I hope so." Early said this in an attempt to console his sister, but he silently doubted the camp business would ever recover, at least in its present incarnation.

Camp Redemption's attendance numbers had been on a slow but steady decline for the last several years, a trend that had culminated in the current disaster. When Early discussed his worries with the other camp owners he knew—tennis, equestrian, swimming, gymnastics, and even one of the nudist variety—they all reported similar woes. Only his colleagues at the computer camp seemed to be doing brisk business, but Early was a card-carrying member of the generation who understood computers only a little and liked them even less, so he didn't see a technology revolution in Camp Redemption's future.

"We could run at a loss this year," Ivey said, "and then we could make it up next year."

"I thought about that, so I ran some figures, and I think it would be a big mistake. We would lose a lot of money."

"How much?"

"Fifty thousand or more. And that's money we don't have. So we would have to borrow it. If we're careful, if one of us doesn't get sick or break a leg, and if we don't have some other kind of emergency, we might have enough money saved to get us through to next year. And that's just a maybe. We might have to borrow a little just to get by, anyway. I could go back to working for someone else, I suppose, but all I know how to do is run a camp and fix cars, and it's been a long time since I fixed cars for a living. I don't know how well I'd do at it now."

"Money isn't everything, you know," Ivey said. "'It is easier for a camel to go through the eye of a needle than for a rich man to enter into the kingdom of God.' Matthew 19:24."

"That's what I hear. If you've ever had concerns about squeezing through the eye of that needle, set your mind to rest. We can walk through it side by side and never touch metal. We could probably drive through it in the truck. So, like I said, if we try to run the camp this year, we'd have to borrow the money to do it with."

"And you think fifty thousand dollars would do it?"

"I think it would. This year. But we've got to think about what will happen if we don't get any business again next year. To be honest with you, I'm about half convinced that next year will be as bad as this year. Maybe worse, if that's possible. I think it's going to take a long time for the economy to recover, and summer camps are luxuries that people can do without. People have to eat, and they have to heat their homes. They have to go to the doctor when they're sick. They don't have to send their kids off to camp, and if I'm right, if next year is bad, too, then we'd have to borrow even more money. The problem with borrowing money is that it has to be paid back." Early looked at his sister as he asked her a question. "What would Vester Willingham have said about borrowing money to run the camp?"

"Daddy would have called it *throwing good money after bad*." She looked sheepish, but they both knew it was the truth.

"And he would have been right."

Over the years, Ivey had consistently refused even to consider the economic side of their enterprise. It was almost as if she felt that doing so would lessen the holiness of their mission, would somehow cheapen the nobility of the act and diminish the sanctity of the calling. But Early felt it was time for her to hear some fiscal truth, even if it did cause her inner light to dim a bit.

"You're seventy-two, and I'm fifty-four. We're both too old to be going to the bank on a fool's errand. If we run the camp at a loss this summer—and we will if we try to do it with ten campers, that's a guaranteed fact—then we'll be deep in the hole come fall. I don't want to be in any holes at my age, deep or otherwise. I want to be winding down toward my golden years. I want to go fishing. I want to smell the roses. Smoke my pipe. Skip some stones. Write my memoirs. That kind of stuff." Early was already smoking the pipe on a regular basis, but what Ivey didn't know wouldn't hurt either of them.

He paused for a moment, because a new thought had occurred to him during the course of his chat with his sister. His mind often worked that way, concocting novel remedies for problems, positing interesting takes on issues, and con-juring unique solutions to dilemmas while he was presenting the facts of the case to others. He decided to share his new thoughts with his business partner.

"While we're talking, let's talk about all of it. What if we have to shut down for good? Two bad years would probably wipe us out—three will for sure—and we're already having our first one." He shrugged, not because he didn't care but because he was helpless in the face of the reality. "It could be that the heyday of summer camps is coming to an end. I don't know if that's true or not, and I would hate it, but nothing lasts forever."

"Shut down Camp Redemption?" Ivey looked stricken. "Close the camp? What would we do then?"

"I don't know, Ivey. I don't have a clue. It has just now occurred to me that we might have to." They had never really talked about what would come *after*, because Ivey had made it clear that she intended to run the camp until she died, after which he was free to do whatever he wished. Now it looked like they would have to discuss the subject whether she wanted to or not. "We're just talking here, okay?" he said. "Maybe we wouldn't do anything. Maybe we'd retire. You're certainly entitled to some rest, and as for me, it wouldn't make me too mad to lay down my burdens."

"We still wouldn't have any money," she observed.

"We have land," he said. "We're getting older, and neither one of us has anyone but the other to leave it to when we die. When we get ready to retire, we'll be able to finance our retirement by selling our land."

"Sell the valley?"

"Sell some of it, anyway. People do it all the time. It's called cashing in your equity. It's like having money in the bank, only you have it in the land instead." He paused, then continued. "One of the many things you don't know about the worldly side of the camp business is that we have a standing offer from Gilla Newman for everything north of the river, for your side of the valley." Gilla Newman, a local entrepreneur, was the richest man in the county, just as his father before him had once been, and just as his son would one day be if someone didn't shoot him in the meantime. Gilla's Christian name was Stanley, but everyone around Sequoyah called him Gilla—short for Magilla—in recognition of his remarkable resemblance to the bungling cartoon gorilla of the same name.

"I haven't mentioned it to you before," Early said, "because I never thought we would take him up on his offer. Now, I don't know what might happen. Times are changing." He shrugged again. It was a hard conversation.

"Early, you know we can't sell the valley. I'm leaving my half to the church when I die. It's in my will. We talked about that, and you told me you didn't care!"

"I *don't* care. It's your half and you can do what you want with it. Mama and Daddy left it to you. But we have to be practical. If we get into tight times, maybe we could sell your half to Gilla so we'd have money to live on, and then leave the church my half instead. There are a lot of different ways to do things. Anyway, Gilla's proposal is for about two hundred acres. He wants to build a housing development when the real estate market comes back. So if we decide it's time to close the camp, and if we sell that half of the valley, at least we'd have enough money to live on and we'd still have the Big House plus this side of the valley to live in. Think of it like cashing in our retirement savings."

"If we did that, what would happen when I died?"

"The church would get this half, and I would move."

"I don't like it one bit," she said. She sat there, shaking her head slowly. Early realized that she was absorbing a lot of new information. He had expected her to accuse him of blasphemy when he mentioned closing the camp and perhaps selling part of the valley, but the look of betrayal on her face was worse. He felt guilty for bringing the whole business up, as if he were engaged in an illicit activity, like running arms or slipping down Mexico way to rustle a few unsuspecting steers.

"I'm not saying we should or we shouldn't," he said. "I'm just passing along information I have that I thought you'd like to know. Just get acquainted with the idea, and give it some thought. You never know what might happen. I didn't want to hit you with it cold, later on. Think on it, and pray on it. One of your good, long prayers couldn't hurt us in the least. We'll talk about it again tomorrow." It was important to him that Ivey agreed and he didn't want to upset his sister. But he also didn't want to lose fifty or sixty thousand dollars over the next three months because the economy was in the trough and the Almighty had neglected to update His business plan.

"I'm going to go ahead and refund the deposits that have already come in," he continued. "Whatever else we decide to do, at least we know for sure that we can't operate this year with just ten kids."

Ivey didn't answer, which Early took as grudging acquiescence. She stood slowly and shuffled quietly from the kitchen. She looked old and broken, like a vintage doll with the stuffing ripped out.

Early felt like a heel, but the hard reality of a bad economy had beset them, and the wolves were howling across the valley. He had made up his mind years ago that he would stand by Ivey at the helm—occasionally high, perhaps, but with feet planted firmly nonetheless—as she steered their little enterprise through the troubled spiritual waters of modern times, right up until that sad but triumphant day when she was called home. But a camp needed campers, and the current supply was regrettably scant.

Early placed the old rotary-dial telephone on the table in front of him and viewed the first application. He had bad news to share and funds to return, and he found both tasks dismal. Still, the money wouldn't refund itself, and he was the type who liked to get unpleasant duties behind him. So he picked up the receiver, took a deep breath, and began dialing numbers. By the end of the day he had managed to make contact with all ten of his former patrons, including an odd and terse conversation with a seemingly unpleasant and decidedly sleepy man named Mr. Jimenez.

Early made the call to the Jimenez household last, but that was because the application was on the bottom of the stack and not because the boy in question was their gratis camper. Someone answered on the ninth ring.

"Hello?" The loud, accented voice coming from the earpiece had a slight edge to it, like a dull, nicked chisel.

"Is this Mr. Jimenez?"

"Yes. My name is Jimenez. What do you want?"

"Mr. Jimenez, this is Early Willingham, calling from Camp Redemption in Sequoyah, Georgia. I'm afraid I have some bad news. We're going to have to cancel camp this year."

"*Who* is this?"

"Early Willingham. From Camp Redemption. In Sequoyah, Georgia." Early spoke slowly and carefully.

"You must have the wrong number. I have never heard of you, and I don't know about any camps in Georgia."

"Maybe your wife made the arrangements?"

"She doesn't know about any camps, either. I work nights and sleep days. I need to get some sleep. Don't call back."

And then he hung up. Early was annoyed by the man's demeanor, and it was probably just as well that the call was short. After all, he had been willing to let Mr. Jimenez's boy come to camp for free. He didn't expect thanks for that, but neither did he wish to be treated like a redheaded Willingham just because the plan hadn't worked out. Early looked at the application and saw that the mother, Isobel Jimenez, had filled out the paperwork and made the request. He supposed it was possible that the father didn't know about the camp. It wouldn't be the first time in the history of marriage that a man and his wife didn't talk much. If Early were married to Mr.

41

Jimenez, he wouldn't talk to him much, either, and he damn sure wouldn't cook for him, or tickle the ivories with him on a Saturday night.

A letter from Isobel Jimenez had accompanied her son's application. In it, she stated that the boy had gotten into a bit of trouble—apparently he and some companions had broken out several windshields and scratched a few paint jobs at a car lot—and she believed that she needed to get him away from his tough friends, the bad girls and worse boys who had led her son down the rocky, rutted road to crime. She went on to note that she had recently lost her job as a stitcher of socks, and her husband's overtime at the paper mill had been cut out. Thus the family was on hard times and she couldn't afford to pay for camp, but she knew in her heart that she needed to arrange a change of scenery for her oldest boy. The priest at her church had confirmed the story with a letter of his own, and both Ivey and Early had agreed that Isobel's son should come to camp. They both believed that two weeks in the mountains, away from bad influences and car windshields, would be good for the mildly wayward boy.

Sighing, Early gathered up the papers scattered on the tabletop and placed them in the record box he had optimistically labeled *2010*. The small stack of documents seemed forlorn in the bottom of the cardboard container.

Breakfast was a quiet affair the next morning, but what it lacked in conversation was more than made up for in courses. Ivey had outdone herself, and Early enjoyed hearty portions of fried eggs, spicy homemade sausage, fragrant cheese grits, crispy hash browns, and steaming buttermilk biscuits spread with real butter—all smothered with two large spoonfuls of cream gravy. After he ate all he could hold plus one biscuit more, he sat back contentedly and worked a toothpick.

"That may have been the best breakfast I've ever had," he said to his sister. Given Ivey's high level of cooking skill, this was quite a compliment. "If you've decided to do me in by feeding me to death, I appreciate the consideration. It beats stabbing or shooting."

"I'm glad you liked it," she quietly replied. There was a tone in her voice that Early recognized, one that told him there were still matters to discuss and issues to resolve. It didn't surprise him. He had known they weren't finished yesterday, that the eye of the storm was merely passing overhead and the second half of the hurricane had yet to arrive. He stirred sugar into his coffee.

"Well, let's get this over with," he said as he took a sip. "Did you think about what I said yesterday?"

"I thought about it, and I prayed about it, too. I worried with it most of the night, right up until I drifted off early this morning. Then, while I was sleeping, I had a vision." Early had been hoping for this development. One of the many traits he admired in Ivey was her ability to have a divine visitation when she needed one. It was like she had the heavenly hosts on speed dial. Sometimes he could almost see them sitting around a golden telephone, maybe playing a couple hands of gin and drinking coffee while waiting for her call.

"How's Mama doing?" he asked. Clairy Willingham was a regular visitor to her daughter, a frequent flyer from the timeless kingdom. Indeed, their mother was much chattier now than she had ever been while alive. And she certainly got around more.

"It wasn't Mama," Ivey replied.

Early was surprised. "Daddy?" he inquired. Vester Willingham hadn't been to see his daughter in quite a while, although in his defense, he had been a sick old man when he had died, and it was a long trip to see the kids.

"No, it wasn't Daddy, either. It was an Indian man, a Chickasaw named Robert Corntassel." She poured herself a cup of coffee and joined him at the table. She added canned milk and two spoons of sugar. Then she splashed a portion of the brew into a deep saucer to cool.

"That doesn't sound like a Chickasaw name to me. At least, not the Robert part. How did you know he was a Chickasaw?"

"He *told* me he was one. How else would I know? Then he told me that it was our task to help the needy, and that Jesus would tell us when to begin, and who to begin with. He said 'Trust in Me, your Lord, and do good, so you shall dwell in the land, and truly you shall be fed.' That's from Psalms."

"Robert didn't mention our cash flow problem, did he?" Early was confused; he couldn't quite catch the drift of the revelation.

"No, he didn't talk about money at all."

"Did he say anything else?"

"He said that his back hurt, and that it was good to see the waterfalls again, and that all of our ancestors and some of his will haunt you until the end of time and beyond if you decide to sell either half of the valley to Gilla Newman. After that, he just sort of drifted away like a puff of smoke." Early wasn't sure he liked smoky, dire warnings from beyond the pale. Being haunted until the end of time—and then some— sounded unpleasant and permanent, like losing a limb.

"Robert told you that his back hurt, and that I shouldn't sell half the valley to Gilla?"

"That's what he said." Ivey took a sip of coffee from her saucer and began to butter a biscuit.

"And he mentioned Gilla Newman by name?"

"He did.

Early sighed. "Ivey, I'm sure Robert is a well-meaning spirit, but it doesn't sound like his visit was a whole lot of help to us in our present situation. I was sort of hoping that if you received guidance, it would be something along the lines of Jesus understanding that we're in the middle of a recession,

44

and that no good can come of us going broke trying to run in the red, and maybe even that you shouldn't be mad at me for suggesting that we take a year off."

"Well, he didn't," she said, sounding defensive. She was just the receiver, after all, the cosmic radio, and she couldn't be held responsible for the contents of the broadcast. "But he didn't need to. I am a grown woman, and I understood every word you told me yesterday."

This was another unexpected surprise. Early thought he might be making progress, at least on the subject of canceling camp for the year. They could get back to Gilla Newman's offer later if the need arose.

"So you're good with us taking this year off, at least?"

"No, I am not good with it at all. I think it's a terrible thing to have to do, but there's no way around it that I can see. When you're right, you're right. And this time, you're right. We have to do it. If we were to have two or three bad years in a row, we might end up losing the valley, and the valley is our home. I will certainly miss the children this year. But I understand why it is necessary. Besides, the good Lord helps those who help themselves. Isn't that what you always say?"

Ivey was being reasonable and practical. Early didn't know what to say, and he almost teared up with the emotion of the moment.

"Okay, then," he stammered. "We'll just take it easy this summer. Maybe we can even go on a little trip for a change. To someplace cheap. We haven't been anywhere during the summer in a long, long time. You know what? We could go to Panama City."

"Oh, no, we can't go on a trip."

"Why not?"

"Robert told us we have to help the needy."

"Sure we do. Later today we'll gather up some sacks of clothes and run them down to the Goodwill."

45

"I think Robert had more in mind than a drive to the Goodwill."

Early wasn't sure he liked the sound of this. For a total stranger, and a dead one, to boot, Robert seemed to have firm opinions on a large number of subjects, including some that were clearly none of his affair.

"What else do you think we need to do?"

"I'm not exactly sure, but I know that the Lord wouldn't waste a perfectly good vision just to tell us to donate some old clothes. It wouldn't make sense, since we already do that, anyway. No, I think we're going to have to wait for a sign. We'll know it when we see it, and my heart tells me it won't be very long. Remember what Robert said. He told us that Jesus will tell us when it's time to begin."

Early sighed yet again. For years he had followed the divinely inspired advice of a selection of dead relatives, so he supposed he shouldn't have any issues with a deceased Chickasaw with a bad back telling him what to do.

"What kind of a sign?" he asked. "You mean like a burning bush, or manna falling from the sky? Something like the Echota turning blood red?"

"It doesn't necessarily have to be one of those," Ivey said. "Sometimes signs are subtle."

"Subtle signs must be in a part of the Bible I didn't read," he noted.

"Early Willingham, may the good Lord forgive you for the words that come out of your mouth! I've prayed for you every day of your life, from your birthing day right on down until this morning. And I believe in my heart that my effort has kept you out of serious trouble so far. But I'm an old woman, and I'll be gone one of these days. I don't know who is going to pray for you then!" The warning was clear. Once she was gone, he would be on his own, and the chips would then fall where they might. "As for the sign, you have to be patient. We'll know it when we see it." So they settled in to wait by going about their business as usual, and as Ivey had predicted, it wasn't long until their sign appeared.

Later that day, as Early prepared to nail down a few loose shingles on Nathanael, he noticed a broken pane in one of the windows. A shattered glass was a common occurrence, although it was a bit odd to encounter one when camp was out. But he had replaced so many windowpanes over the years that he didn't give this one much thought. Plus, he had stopped at the falls before beginning his afternoon chores and had enjoyed a pipeful, so he was quite mellow.

He removed the tape measure from his tool belt and stepped up close to the window to take the measurements for a new piece of glass. As he worked, he glanced into the cabin. An unexpected sight greeted him, and he did a double take. There before him—reclined on one of the bottom bunks with his hands behind his head—was the sleeping form of a fully clothed, road-worn boy. He was snoring softly. Early was intrigued. In thirty years of camp upkeep, he had never once found a spare boy in a cabin during the off-season. It was a novelty of the highest order. He abandoned his tools in favor of his key ring. He quietly unlocked the door and opened it. Then he slowly stepped over to the snoring intruder, tiptoeing carefully so as not to disturb him. He carefully placed a straight-backed chair beside the bunk and silently sat.

"It looks like someone has been sleeping in my bed!" he said. The boy's eyes flew wide open. He startled, jumped up, hit his head on the slats of the top bunk, and fell back onto his bare mattress. Then he did the exact same thing a second time. Finally, he grabbed the top of his head, grimaced, and stayed put.

"That hurt," the boy said.

"It looked like it did," Early agreed. "Especially the second time." The trespasser appeared to be fourteen or maybe fifteen, slight of stature with handsome features and black hair cut short. His coal-black eyes held defiance when they met Early's, defiance, confidence, and maybe a touch of fear. But only just. Early had frightened him, but he was recovering fast.

"You scared me!" It was more of an accusation than a statement of fact, as if Early should feel remorse for his actions and perhaps apologize.

"You broke into my cabin. From where I sit, that means you're in a lot more trouble than I am."

The boy looked over at the broken pane, then back at Early. After a moment, he lowered his eyes. "You gonna call the Five-O?"

"Who?"

"The po po. The 'lice. The police."

Early shook his head. "Po po?" he asked. "Whatever happened to *cops*? I ought to call them just because you *said* po po." He looked around the room. "It doesn't look like you stole anything. It sort of looks like you just needed a place to lie down. I don't normally send people to jail for taking a nap, but that mostly applies to folks I know, local people who don't vandalize my cabins. Since you're not one of those, I might have to make an exception and give Austell Poe a call. He's the law around these parts, a serious kind of guy. Not much of a kidder at all. He believes in making examples. You know the type. He likes to find some kid who breaks the law and land on him like a meteor. Once the dust settles, there's not much left of the lawbreaker, but all of his buddies tend to behave themselves. Anyway, I really hate to have that kind of business on my conscience unless it's absolutely necessary. So you're going to have to help me make the decision. It's the least you can do, considering the spot you've put me in. Are you a desperate criminal? Do we need to make an example out of you? Should I call the law?"

"I wish you wouldn't," the boy said quietly. He sounded contrite, and although Early knew this to be an ability that most teens could turn on at will when the need arose, the contrition did seem genuine. Early looked at the young man closely. He had met thousands of young people as they came through the camp. He had learned over time to spot the *problem* gene, the rung on the DNA ladder that spelled trouble, and he just didn't see that genetic trait in the teen before him.

"Fair enough," he said. "Instead of turning you in to— what was it, the po po?— I'll teach you how to replace a windowpane, since you broke one of mine. It's a good skill to know, especially if you ever plan on having kids or if you want to own a summer camp." Early stood and offered his hand. "My name is Early Willingham. What's yours?"

"My name is Jesús," he said. "Jesús Jimenez."

Early shook hands briefly, then lowered his arm and sat back down in his chair. It was more of a plop than a sit, actually, as if he had been gently and playfully jabbed by a huge finger. Jesús Jimenez. He now recognized his visitor from the picture that was attached to his camp application. Jesús Jimenez was the wayward young man who liked to break windshields and scratch paint jobs. He stood there before Early, still apparently breaking windows. Ivey would have a fit. Early knew that he was about to be knee-deep in halleluiahs, because the boy was definitely needy, and he certainly looked like he could use a little help. And, of course, there was the name. Jesús *was* the sign. The prophecy was fulfilled.

Chapter Four

"It's a miracle!" Ivey said as she sat at the kitchen table and watched Jesús eat another plate of food.

"The true miracle is how much that boy can eat," replied Early. Their guest was on his third helping of pinto beans and corn bread, and he hadn't slowed down appreciably. His application indicated that Jesús Jimenez was fifteen years of age. He was the oldest of the three children, all boys, belonging to Roberto and Isobel Jimenez of Apalachicola, Florida.

According to Jesús, he had left home three weeks ago and had walked and hitchhiked via a serendipitous route right to their front door. He had arrived at Camp Redemption with nothing but the dirty clothes on his back and the worn tennis shoes on his feet. Early needed to call the boy's parents and share the news that their son was safe, but he was holding off out of a nagging sense of uneasiness. Several aspects of Mr. Jimenez had not set well with Early. For one thing, he had not mentioned his missing child when they talked, which Early now found odd, considering that, according to Jesús, he had been absent for twenty-one days. Additionally, Mr. Jimenez had denied knowing anything about Camp Redemption, which didn't sound right, either. And finally, Early simply had not liked the man. He had been rude and abrupt, and Early was a big believer in good first impressions.

Thus he wanted to chat with the boy a little more before he made the call, both to scratch that little itch between his shoulder blades and as a means of deferring what could be an unpleasant task, depending on who picked up the phone on the other end. Jesús sopped up the last of his beans with his final bite of corn bread. Then he took a long drink of cold buttermilk, a substance he had apparently not encountered in the wilds of Apalachicola that he seemed to like a great deal. He sat back and sighed with contentment.

"Are you full?" Early asked. "There's more, if you want it." Jesús shook his head and slumped back in his chair.

"I'm done. I'm sorry I ate so much, but the last time I had anything to eat was yesterday. A whole day is a long time to go without food."

"I like to see a boy eat," Ivey interjected. She patted Jesús's hand. She had never actually had a sign from God sit at her table and smack his lips while asking for thirds, so this was a new experience for her. She was elated. The apple pie she had thrown together was bubbling and browning in the oven.

"Well, Jesús, if you're through eating, I guess we need to talk."

The runaway's voice was tinged with dread and resignation. "Here it comes," he said.

"Here it comes," Early agreed. "Why are you here?"

"I came to camp. My mom signed me up." He looked away as he spoke. Early liked it that Jesús appeared to be a poor liar. The fact that he could not look his inquisitor in the eye indicated that he was perhaps a novice at deception, and Early took this as a sign of good character.

"That's true," Early agreed. "She did sign you up. Right here's your application." He held it up. "But you're two weeks early. Come to think of it, you're a year and two weeks early, because we canceled camp this season." Jesús looked surprised at this news. The interrogation was not going his way. "Our out-of-state campers generally arrive in some type of vehicle, like a bus or their parents' car. Sometimes their grandparents bring them. We frown on youngsters hitchhiking to camp. It's actually an unwritten rule right now, sort of a guideline, but we're thinking about putting it into the brochure next year as a requirement. It sets a bad tone, gives the place the wrong feel."

He paused, and the silence grew long. Early could sense that Ivey was a little uncomfortable with Jesús. Her reticence was understandable. Robert Corntassel had been ambiguous about the nature of the sign, which is often the way it is with revelations, so perhaps Ivey had expected someone taller, a somber, dark-haired man wearing flowing robes and leather sandals, an angelic brown-eyed traveler with a long, knobby walking stick who would utter the occasional *thee* or *thou*. Finally, Early spoke again.

"You told me you left home three weeks ago. When I talked to your father, he didn't mention that you were missing, and he claimed that he didn't know anything about this camp. He also said your mother didn't know anything about it. So, either I shouldn't put too much stock into what *he* said, or else I shouldn't pay too much attention to *your* story. Which is it? Who should I believe?"

"You talked to my old man?" Jesús grimaced as if he had stepped on glass, and Ivey looked distressed. She bustled up out of her chair and began clearing the table. She stacked all the empty dishes and serving bowls in the sink. Then she wrung the dishcloth and wiped the crumbs from the table and countertops into her free hand. After completing these chores, she stepped over to check the pie. When she opened the oven, the odor of apples and cinnamon filled the room.

"I talked to him," Early confirmed. "Don't worry, though, I didn't tell him about you. Not yet, anyway. I called him before I even knew you were here to tell him that we weren't going to have camp this year. That's when he told me he didn't know anything about your coming here. But I need to know what's happening. Why didn't he tell me that you were missing? He should have told me to be on the lookout for you. Any father would. And why didn't he know you were coming to camp? I need some answers, Jesús. Why are you here?"

Jesús was silent for a moment. Then he began to tell his tale. "My father's a liar. He *didn't* know about the camp until three weeks ago, when Mama told him. After she let him know, he went nuts because she hadn't gotten his permission for me to come. He started hitting her. He told her that he was the man of the house, and that nothing happened without his say-so. And it really made him mad when he found out that Mama had talked to the priest down at the church and got it fixed up for me to come here for free. He said he wasn't about to take charity from a bunch of white people in Georgia. Then he took off his belt and really tore into her. I tried to pull him off, but I couldn't do much with him. He's a lot stronger than I am." He lapsed into silence.

"What happened then?" Early asked. Their guest remained quiet. He had a pained expression on his features, and Early supposed he was reliving the moment, maybe deciding what to include in the story and what to leave out.

Jesús spoke again, but slowly and with scant affect, as if he were in a trance. "Finally he just threw down the belt and started using his fists on her. He jabbed at her a couple of times, and then he caught her under the chin and knocked her out. I thought for a minute he had killed her, but then I saw her chest moving, so I knew she was breathing. I ran to grab the phone. I was going to call 911. He knocked it out of my hand, and then he started whaling away on me with the belt. He beat me a while, and when he asked me if I'd had enough, I told him to go screw himself. I guess I was mad. But it was a mistake, even if it did feel pretty good at the time. He got his second wind and beat on me until I passed out." He paused, as if to collect his thoughts. "He's beaten my mother before, but nothing like this time. And he's never beat on me before. I mean, *really* beat on me. He's always hollered and backhanded and slapped, but it's like he went crazy this time. I really think he was trying to kill me, or maybe he didn't even care whether he did or not.

"When I came to, I was in the woods about twenty miles north of town. I recognized where I was—a place called Tate's Hell forest. I think he must've thought I was dead, or near about it, and he was dumping the body. Tate's Hell is mostly swamps, mosquitoes, moccasins, scrub pine, and alligators. There are bears and panthers out there, too, and coyotes. If I had been dead, it would've been a good place to lose the evidence, because something would've eaten me in a day or two. Anyway, I figured I needed a change of scenery, and twenty miles was a good head start, so I walked out of the woods to the road and just kept on heading up that highway." Jesús stood and pulled up his shirt. His torso, front and back, was crisscrossed with red welts that morphed into purple, black, and blue. It was obvious that he had been severely whipped.

Ivey gasped, and her hand strayed up to her mouth. "Sweet Lord Jesus," she said. There were tears in her eyes. It was a horrid sight, a reminder that there would always be a sufficiency of evil.

"You should have gotten yourself to a phone and called the police," Early said. He, too, was shocked by the scars. It was beyond him how anyone could do that to a child, or to any other living creature for that matter.

"Mama's afraid of the police, so I couldn't call them. She's illegal, and she's always been scared that if she went to the police about my father, she'd end up getting shipped to Mexico, and she'd never see us again. Me and my brothers were born here, but she never got her citizenship. Neither did my father. She wanted to, but my father wouldn't let her. It's something he has over her. Like not letting her learn to drive. And Mama's really afraid of what will happen to all of us if she ever gets sent back."

He lowered his shirt and reclaimed his chair. "My father's a big man at the church. He goes every day. They can't open the door without him running in there and hitting his knees. But it's all show. He's put my mother in the hospital twice. The first time he did, he told everyone it was a car wreck. The next time, he said she fell down the stairs." He appeared to gather his thoughts, and his eyes flashed. "If I ever see him again, there won't be any fair fight to it. I'll stab him in the back before he even knows I'm there. If I catch him asleep, I'll cut his throat. If I have a gun, I'll shoot him. I don't even care if I go to jail."

Early grimaced. This was hard talk of cold steel and hot lead, but he had seen the look in the boy's eyes when he spoke. Jesús was afraid of his father's violence, but he meant what he said. If they ever met again, his old man had best not turn his back or drop his guard.

"Anyway," the boy said, "none of that matters anymore, because I'm not going back to Apalachicola. Ever. I'd be crazy to. He almost killed me this time, and if he finds me there and I don't get him first, there won't be any almost to it next time."

"Do you have any other family?" Early asked. "Somewhere you could go?"

"Not in this country. My father came here way before I was born. I heard two men whispering about him at the church one time, and they said he killed someone in Mexico, and he had to leave the country. I didn't believe it then, but I do now. I think all of his people are dead. My mother snuck in the country a couple of years after he did. She came in on a shrimp boat, worked her way across the Gulf, heading shrimp. She has some sisters down in Mexico somewhere, but I don't know who they are or where they live. I don't even know if they know that they have nephews up here." He paused for a sip of buttermilk. Then he continued. "Mama followed my father all the way to Apalachicola, but if I was her, I wouldn't have followed him across the street. My mama is a pretty woman. She's funny and nice, and there are men who would marry her right now if she'd just get rid of *him*. But she says divorce is a sin, and he'd probably kill her if she tried. She says that he didn't used to be like he is now, that he used to be a decent man. But I think she's lying about that. I think he's been evil since the day he was born."

Ivey blanched.

"Jesús, why did you come *here*?" Early asked.

"Well, it's kind of a long story."

"Take your time."

"I thought the whole idea of coming to camp was pretty lame, but it was going to get me away from my father for two weeks, so I was willing to give it a shot. But after he left me out in Tate's Hell, your camp started looking a whole lot better to me. And I couldn't live out there in the woods. I had to go somewhere. Since going home didn't seem like such a hot idea, the first thing I did was go to a friend's house. He let me stay a while, to kind of heal up and get some rest. But I couldn't stay there long. I laid up two weeks, and then I borrowed some money from him and started heading this way. I did a lot of walking, and I took some rides from truck drivers, who are kind of cool and will buy you a burger if you're hungry.

"Whenever someone picked me up, I just went wherever they were going, as long as they were going north, or east, or west. It didn't matter to me as long as it was away from Apalachicola. I had to backtrack a couple of times, but it wasn't like I needed to be in any kind of hurry. I figured I'd get here when I got here. Anyway, after a while I didn't even know where I was until my last ride dropped me off in that little town down the road called Sequoyah. Man! You guys have got to be kidding with that place! But I remembered the name from the brochure you sent to my house. I remembered that it was near your camp. So I walked here. I was trying to lay low in that cabin when you found me, at least until camp started. After that, I thought maybe I might be able to blend in with the rest of the kids for a while."

Early whistled softly. It was quite a story, topped off by a fifteen-mile hike from Sequoyah on an empty stomach. He had to admit that Jesús had a pretty good head on his shoulders. He had come up with a reasonable, workable plan.

Early didn't quite know what to do next, but the boy's narrative had the ring of truth, and it seemed that sending him back home might be a hasty move, sort of like giving a steer a hot shower and a meal before herding him on through the packing house door. He looked at Ivey and saw that she was staring back at him with intent. She mouthed the word *Jesus* and nodded at the boy. It came as no surprise to Early that she had homed in on the name. He reached a decision.

"Jesús," he said, "why don't you rest up here a while before you make any big moves? How would that be? I want to help you make a good choice about what to do next, and right now I have no idea what that is. We need to think about all of this for a day or two."

"You won't call my father?"

"I won't do anything without talking to you first."

"How do I know I can trust you?"

"Well, I'm half owner of a Bible camp." Early smiled. "If I tell a lie, the state will take away my license, and then I'll have to go work in the sawmill, which is something I really don't want to do. I didn't call the police when I found you, and I didn't shoot you for breaking into my cabin, so you should give me the benefit of the doubt. It was my favorite cabin, too. That ought to count for something. Besides, I didn't really hit it off with your father, and I don't feel like talking to him right now."

Jesús considered the offer of respite. Then he nodded to himself and stuck out his hand to seal the deal. "Okay. You seem like a good dude. Your mother seems pretty cool, too. I'll stay a little while."

"Good," Early said, glancing at Ivey. "She's not my mother, by the way. She's my sister. Her name is Ivey."

Jesús and Early shook on the deal. Then the boy took Ivey's hand as well.

"Welcome to Camp Redemption," she said.

Later, after another meal, Jesús slept an exhausted sleep in one of the upstairs bedrooms. Over the years, the Willinghams had acquired a fair selection of clothing, cast-offs misplaced by a long succession of forgotten campers that Ivey had held on to for emergencies. So Jesús was wearing clean underwear and mismatched pajamas, and he had a change of clothes to don when he awoke. While he rested, Early and Ivey sat at the kitchen table and discussed his future.

"What the hell are we going to do with him?" Early began.

"Hush. That word is blasphemy. You know how I feel about blasphemy."

"No, what I *feel* like saying is blasphemy. What I actually said is just bad manners. I'll ask again. What do you think we should do with Jesús?"

"He needs shoes. We should buy him some shoes."

"You know what I mean," Early said.

"There's no doubt about what we should do! His coming was foretold. We are duty-bound to help him. It's our sacred obligation, like following the Ten Commandments."

"We are helping him. We're taking care of him and letting him stay for a few days. We'll even buy him some shoes. I'm talking about after that. We ought to call his mother, I guess, but it sounds like the poor woman can't protect him. It sounds like she's in worse trouble than he is. I don't know what we should do next."

Ivey's next statement caught him on his blind side.

"I think we should keep him right here with us."

"What? You mean permanently? We can't just keep him. He's not a runaway dog. He's a runaway boy, and he's not up for grabs."

"I know it sounds crazy, but my heart tells me that we should keep him! We sure can't send him back home! There's no telling what might happen to him. And we'd be responsible, because we could have prevented it. I couldn't live with that."

Early hated to admit it, but she might have a point. Normally he believed that a youngster belonged with his parents, but in the case of Jesús, that might not be the best course.

Ivey took his silence as an opportunity to quote from Psalms: "'You deliver me from my enemies. Yes, You lift me up above those who rise up against me. You have delivered me from the violent man.'"

"You got anything from Isaiah for me?" Early asked. "You haven't been dipping into your favorite prophet much lately. Have you two fallen out?"

"'They make haste to shed innocent blood.' Isaiah 59:7. Now hush."

"I'll admit that going home might not be the best thing for him," Early said. "But there must be other choices. Maybe we can help him find some relatives. Maybe we can get him into a foster home. I'm not sure what options are available, but I don't think it will be a good idea for him to just hang around camp indefinitely. I'm sure there are laws about this kind of thing, and I guarantee that letting him stay here from now on is illegal. I probably broke the law when I didn't call his parents as soon as I realized who he was, but we need to get this sorted out before I make that call."

Early's take on the law was somewhat similar to his relationship with the Bible. He respected both, but he wasn't obsessive about absolute adherence to either, especially those portions he considered wrong, mean-spirited, or downright stupid. Still, he felt it prudent to remain at least on nodding terms with the intent of both the Gospels and the secular statutes when possible.

"Early, I don't like to have disagreements with you," his sister said. "It upsets me to no end. But we don't have a choice. This is prophecy at work. We can't ignore the will of the Lord, no more than Moses could have told Him that he didn't feel much like climbing Mount Sinai to get those stone tablets." Early pinched the bridge of his nose while he thought, and what he thought, mostly, was that he was willing to lay good odds against even money that Moses had at least muttered a bit on the way up. Early was certain that each stubbed toe and scratched shin had produced at least a grunt and a sigh.

"Let's compromise," he said. "We'll look after him for the rest of the week. He's pretty scrawny anyway, and he seems to enjoy your cooking, so maybe you can fatten him up a little. In the meantime, I'll try to find out what options there are besides just sending him back home to Apalachicola." He planned to discuss the subject with Charnell Jackson, his friend and occasional attorney. Maybe he would have some ideas about what to do for the boy, his mother, and his siblings.

"'You are my hiding place; You will preserve me from trouble; You will surround me with songs of deliverance.' Psalms 32:7." Ivey beamed as she spoke, clearly grateful for the reprieve.

"Boy, howdy," came Early's noncommittal reply.

Chapter Five

Early sat across from Charnell Jackson and stirred his mug of coffee. The two had met in the Jesus is Going out of Business Diner, the name for Sequoyah's only restaurant. The eatery actually possessed no official name and never had, but it did have history, which is sometimes better, and which was how it had earned its unofficial name. The previous owner of the restaurant was an old Navy cook named Wilson Crab, who, for reasons known only to himself and to his maker, preferred to be called Hoghead. He was a pious but mostly illiterate man who liked to tape religious slogans written on pieces of cardboard to the front window of his diner. He advertised his weekly specials in that same glass pane, and often the close proximity and unintended overlap of the two would produce unique sentiments and unlikely turns of phrase.

Some of these serendipitous slogans included The Road to Hell Is Paved with Country Fried Steak, Jesus is the Reason for the Catfish Fingers, and the never-to-be-forgotten Christ Died for the Best Fried Chicken in the County. When, after many years of creative advertising and culinary service to the community, Hoghead decided that it was time to sell his restaurant and retire to the Old Sailor's Home, he taped up one last message to notify passersby of his professional intentions, and the Jesus is Going out of Business Diner was born.

Charnell Jackson was Sequoyah's sole lawyer, a designation he had held since about the time that Richard Nixon had refused on general principle to give back Checkers the dog. Thus Charnell was venerable and closing in fast on ancient. Physically he was a train wreck, but when it came to mental acuity, he was as sharp as a box of new razor blades.

He wore scratched and bent rimless reading glasses balanced on the tip of his nose and a white Vandyke beard on top of a graying three-day stubble. He always sported a loud bowtie. Early noted that today's was yellow. He had also taken to wearing a greasy gray fedora sometime during his sixtieth year, and the passing of the seasons had done nothing to improve its appearance.

"I need to ask you a few questions," Early began. "Hypothetical questions."

Charnell grunted as he dunked a piece of dry wheat toast into his coffee prior to taking a tentative bite. "Hypothetical questions my aching, tired old ass," he grumbled around his food. "Ever since I became a lawyer, it seems like every damn conversation I've had has been hypothetical. Either that, or it's about someone's *brother*, or about *a guy I know*. Speak up, Early. I'm not getting any younger, and I'm damn sure not getting any prettier. What kind of trouble have you gotten yourself into?"

As time had sauntered by, Charnell had evolved from a plainspoken young individual into an exceptionally blunt old coot. He had once been a large man, tall and broad-shouldered, but the years had tugged him this way and pulled him that, and he had grown smaller and less distinct even as he grew more cantankerous. He had caved in upon himself like a weathered outbuilding. His ears were the notable exception. They seemed to be particularly sensitive to the effects of gravity and had become long and unwieldy, with the tops leaning away from his skull like pink flower petals and the lobes stretching to the hinge of his jaw like misplaced wattles.

"No, it's nothing like that," Early said. "This is just something I've been wondering about. Something I read about in a book."

Charnell sighed, took out a small note pad, flipped it open, and began to write. "You're a terrible liar," he said.

"Ivey likes it that way."

"She doesn't necessarily have to always get what she likes."

"You tell her."

"Give me a dollar," Charnell said brusquely.

Early removed the billfold from his jeans pocket and complied with the request by sliding a bill across the Formica tabletop. Charnell ripped the note from the pad and passed it to his companion. "Okay. That's your receipt. Now, I am on retainer. You are officially paying me for legal advice. That means that whatever you say is in confidence. It's against the law for me to rat you out. Well, mostly, anyway. If it comes down to your ass or mine, it's been good to know you. But other than that, you're safe. So, shoot. And don't spare any of the juicy details. I haven't heard a good story in months." He leaned forward and clasped his hands around his coffee cup, eager to hear of the sins of man. It was the part of the job he liked the best, the part he would've done for free.

Early took a sip of his coffee, composed his thoughts, and waded in. "Okay. A kid ran away from home and showed up at Camp Redemption. He was actually signed up to be a camper this summer, anyway, but he sort of decided to come on a little early after his father beat him unconscious and left him to die in a deserted patch of woods. The kid has the scars to prove that the story is probably true, and I believe him. So does Ivey, but she's not that tough an audience. Anyway, *somebody* laid into this boy with a belt or a strap, and it looks like they didn't stop until they got tired. Now he's here, beat all to pieces and slowly healing up, and he says that he will not go back home. Not now. Not ever. Not for any reason, not for anybody. On top of that, he says he'll kill his old man if he ever gets the chance, and from the look in his eyes when he said it, I believe him. What can I do to help this kid without breaking the law?" Early took another sip of his coffee as he waited for Charnell to respond.

"How old is he?"

"He's fifteen. But he seems older, sometimes, the way that kids who have had a rough time do."

"Is he from around here?"

"He's from Florida. Apalachicola."

"And his father is the only one abusing him?"

"According to the kid, he's slapped the entire family around some, but this is the first time he's laid in like this. He *has* put the mother into the hospital twice. I don't know how he got away with that."

"Does the boy have any relatives he can turn to? Somewhere he can go live? A grandmother or an aunt? Maybe an older sibling?"

"No relatives in this country, and he's the oldest child. He's got two brothers. Oh, and the reason he doesn't want to call the police is because his parents are here illegally from Mexico, and he's afraid if he goes to the authorities, they'll end up deported."

"That's a wrinkle. And he's probably right. Illegal aliens are a real hot topic these days. Is there anything else I need to know?"

"I wouldn't doubt it, but that's all I've gotten from him so far."

Charnell stroked his little beard for a moment, a habit he had when mulling the facts and when looking at the backsides of women. Then he looked Early in the eye. "My professional advice is that you need to call the police and hand the whole mess over to them. The *state* police. Stay away from Austell Poe on this. The sooner you make the call, the better." Charnell slid his cell phone across the table. "Here. Use mine. The battery is freshly charged."

Early did not reach for the device. "In your opinion," he asked, "what chain of events will I set in motion if I turn this kid in? Will he end up back home at the mercy of the father? Will the mother get deported? I don't want to cause him or his family any more trouble than they already have. I'd rather let him just keep on running than to have him go back to what he came from. The man left him in the *woods*, Charnell. I can't get that out of my head. He left him in the woods to die."

"Well, I'd have to brush up on my Florida case law, but most likely, if the abuse is apparent like you say, the boy and his siblings would end up in foster homes in Florida, which could be good or bad, depending on the luck of the draw. Some foster parents do it because it's the right thing to do. They tend to be decent folks, mostly. Others do it for the money, and they, unfortunately, aren't always the best choice for a child. Whichever type of foster parent they get, it's almost a certainty that they would be split apart and placed in separate homes. Very few foster parents are able to take more than one child. Once the kids get picked up, the mother might very well end up taking that slow bus ride back to Mexico. The old man would probably spend some time at the graybar motel, which is where the son of a bitch should have been all along if he likes to hit women and children."

Charnell sipped his coffee and frowned. "That's unless the judge who conducts the hearing is asleep, drunk, incompetent, mean, just plain ignorant, hates Mexicans, hates women, hates children, or all of the above, which is the case more often than you might think. In that event, the boy could land right back where he started from, only this time his old man would really have a hard-on for him. If that happened, he and maybe the rest of his family could end up hurt or dead, because once abusers get away with it a time or two, they start developing notions of imperviousness. They start thinking they have the right to do it, that they're untouchable. And the sad part is, sometimes they do get away with it and keep on doing so." Charnell dipped a corner of his toast in the coffee and had a bite.

"How can you stand to eat toast dipped in coffee?" Early asked. Charnell had been thorough in his explanations, and this was the only question that Early had.

"My teeth aren't what they used to be. Most of them are chipped or loose, and they hurt all the time. But as bad as eating toast dipped in coffee is, it's not as bad as going to the dentist or starving to death. I hate going to the dentist more than I hate anything else in the world, and that's a long list. Did you know that as a group, dentists are even more despised than lawyers?"

"I didn't know that."

"It's true. They have a high suicide rate, too."

"What a great fact," Early said, though his tone suggested that he thought the opposite. "Maybe I need to find a better lawyer, or at least one with better teeth. I can't believe I paid a dollar to hear you tell me that there's nothing I can do for my runaway. I mostly knew that before I hired you, and I didn't even go to law school. What I need is an angle."

"I'm the best lawyer in town."

"You're the only lawyer in town."

"Therefore, I'm the best. Look, I hate it that the kid's prospects are not good, but that's the way it is. He has a lousy set of alternatives, but I can't help that and neither can you. There are seldom any winners in these cases. You lose a little or you lose a lot, but you lose all the same. The lawyers get paid regardless of how it comes out, the judge moves on to the next no-win case, and everyone else goes home and cries about what a cold, hard world it is. And they're absolutely right. It is a tough world for a kid like this. He has no rights to speak of, and he could end up living under an overpass if he's lucky or dead if he's not."

"He deserves better choices."

"He does for a fact, and so do about a million more just like him. But you can't help who your parents are. The real problem is that you don't have to pass any kind of screening test before you get to have kids. All you have to have are two people who are mutually agreeable to the idea of sexual intercourse, and you would be amazed at how unselective some women are."

"What about men's selectivity?"

"Are you kidding me? As a general rule, men do not have the ability to say *no*. They'll crawl into bed with anything, anytime. Your average male would screw a downed telephone pole if it had breasts and a vagina. No, it's the women who have to be in charge. It's their duty to regulate the activity. And when they neglect their obligation to the race and sleep with mean, stupid men, bad things happen. That's why there are so many mean, stupid people running around. It's a genetic condition. They came from mean, stupid fathers, who came from mean, stupid fathers, who came from mean, stupid fathers. All the way back to the first mean, stupid caveman, who was really mean and exceptionally stupid. If only his wife had just said *oh hell no*, it would be a better world today."

"If only."

"And that's why smart young people who want to get rich go to law school. Sooner or later, mean, stupid people always do mean, stupid things. They can't help it. They're mean and stupid, so what else are they going to do? Feed the widows and orphans? Nope. They're going to screw up, and when they do, they need lawyers to keep them out of jail."

"You're a real ray of sunshine this morning."

"No, I'm not. I'm a grouchy old son of a bitch, but I know what I'm talking about, and I only lie in court, when I'm getting paid to." He lit a slim cigarillo before continuing, and sweet smoke with a hint of blueberry filled their corner of the

67

diner. "You've known me all your life, so you know I'm not much on Chinese folks ever since the bastards tried to kill me three damn times back during the Korean War."

Early nodded. He had heard the stories on many occasions, and it did appear as if Charnell was not ever going to forgive or forget. Even though the Chinese boys had been shooting at almost everyone south of the thirty-eighth parallel at the time, Charnell had taken the entire matter personally and had held his grudge for better than fifty years thus far.

"But they do have the right idea when it comes to having kids," Charnell continued. "One child per couple is all you're allowed to have. Period. It's a good system, because if you happen to be a woman who screwed up and married a mean and stupid man—which is kind of likely even if you're *not* Chinese—it limits the amount of damage you can do."

"I'll keep all that in mind. But getting back to my particular kid in Georgia, what if someone came forward who would be willing to look after him for a while? A good Samaritan type. Someone not terribly mean or excessively stupid."

"Like you?"

"Theoretically."

"Hmm. In theory, I would have to say that it would be nearly impossible for you to legally end up with custody of the kid."

"How about illegally?" Early asked. He figured that if he was going to explore the topic, he might as well take a complete look.

Charnell groaned loudly and puffed his cigarillo until the tip glowed red, like a beacon in the night. "I should have charged you two dollars. Illegally speaking, you would be safer trying to kiss a mad rattlesnake's ass in a burlap sack than to try something like keeping an abused, out-of-state, runaway minor. Right off, I can only think of six laws you'd be bending or breaking, some of them federal, but if you give me a couple of days, I know I can come up with a few more." He looked at Early over the tops of his glasses.

Early had not supposed that the news would be good, so the information imparted by Charnell did not give him great pause. He had known before asking that it would be a bad idea, and that he couldn't expect to just keep a runaway kid without encountering some difficulties. But he also knew that he couldn't live with himself if he turned his back on Jesús and something unfortunate happened to him. Life was too short to end up feeling guilty for the rest of it because he had declined to take a stand.

Early sighed and caught Charnell's eye. "Thanks for the advice. Looks like I've got some considering to do." He knew in general what the plan would probably be, but the specifics were far away.

"Can I ask *you* a question now?"

"First you have to give me a dollar."

"It doesn't work in reverse like that."

"That figures. Ask away."

"What is he to you? This world is a rotten old place, and there are probably more children in trouble than not. We can't save them all. Hell, we can't even save most of them. Why do you feel the need to rescue this particular one?"

"That's a fair question, and it deserves a good answer. But I don't have a good answer for you. There's just something about him that speaks to me."

"What are you going to do?"

"I guess I'm going to let him stay a little while, at least until he heals up. Maybe an idea about what to do with him on a permanent basis will come to me in the meantime." Early cleared his throat. "Anyway, Ivey is firmly convinced we should keep him, and I don't want to have a big argument with her right now. She believes he is a sign from God. She thinks he was sent to us from above. I'm afraid his name doesn't help matters."

"What's his name? Gabriel? Abraham? Peter?"

"Jesús."

"Yeah, I can see where that would get her all stirred up." Charnell chuckled as he signaled for a coffee refill. Their waitress, Candace Shellnut, topped off both of their cups.

Candace was half owner of the Jesus is Going out of Business Diner. She was an aging beauty—still awfully easy to look at—and she had the rare ability of making almost every man who came into the diner think that she had eyes only for him, that she was *this* close to tossing her apron and caution to the wind and having a fling with the lucky patron. Thus her tips generally runneth over, so much so that she had been able to retire the mortgage on the diner in a mere nine years. Her husband and business partner, Anderson, was in the back working the grill. He was aware of his wife's sales strategies, and his only comment on them was made on the day she garnered over one hundred dollars in gratuities. At that time, after they had counted the money twice, he had looked the mother of his children straight in the eye and suggested that perhaps she should begin to work the tables topless. Maybe not the breakfast and lunch trade, due to the family nature of the establishment, but the supper crowd, for sure. Anderson loved Candace, but money was money and business was business.

Charnell took an appreciative sip from his freshly topped cup as he watched their waitress make her way across the diner. "Candace is looking mighty fine this morning," he said. He had already placed a five-dollar tip on the table. His check for coffee and toast would come to around two dollars, including tax.

"I think she really likes you," Early replied. "And I hear she has plenty of money, too." Early was not completely immune to Candace's charms, but he was a practical man who understood that she probably wouldn't leave her successful business, loving husband, and three children for him just because he left an extra dollar, or even two, tucked under the napkin dispenser. "But we were talking about Jesús. If I let him stay at the camp a while, what kind of trouble will I be in if I get caught?"

"You could be looking at the jail kind of trouble, or at least, you might be if I weren't your attorney."

"Well, then."

"By the way, as your lawyer I feel I would be remiss if I did not remind you that, unlike most of your kinfolks, you're a *pretty* Willingham. And as such, you don't want to be taking showers down at Reidsville prison for the next fifteen years." Charnell had accused Early of prettiness ever since Early was just a young sprout, and Early had denied the dreaded affliction for just about as long.

"I am not pretty, and I don't appreciate that kind of talk."

"You're prettier than Ivey."

"That's *your* opinion."

Early did not leap to his sister's defense for two reasons. First, Charnell was right. Ivey wasn't hideous by any stretch, but Early was definitely the better looking of the pair in the classical sense. And second, Charnell had been stepping out with Ivey for well over fifty years, although perhaps dating wasn't the appropriate word to describe their association. They went shopping together, had supper from time to time, and even went for the occasional drive, but Early had never witnessed any romance between the two. When he thought about the nature of the relationship, which he didn't do often, he assumed that they were either the most discrete couple in the history of the world, or that they were lifelong friends who happened to be of opposite sexes. And he leaned toward the latter. But whatever was going on, Early figured that after that much time in tandem, both of them had the right to say just about whatever they wanted, either to or about the other. Seniority has its privileges.

"Anyway, we're both prettier than you," Early said.

"That's true," Charnell admitted.

"And just because you're an old pud doesn't mean I won't turn Ivey loose on you. If I tell her about that five-dollar tip there on the table, you're in for a hard road." Early could just hear her calling Charnell an *old fool*.

"You'd let her hit a defenseless man?"

"No, I don't believe in standing idly by while innocent people get hurt, which has absolutely nothing to do with her giving *you* a couple of smacks." They both took another sip of coffee. Then Charnell spoke. "How long has Jesús been up at the camp?"

"He showed up yesterday. He's a real smart kid. Kind of polite, like maybe his mama tried to raise him right."

"Well, my advice to you stands," Charnell said. "If you try to keep him, you could wind up in a bind, and the kid will probably end up back in Apalachicola, regardless of what you do. If you won't call the police, at least contact the Florida Department of Family and Children's Services—or whatever it is they call it down there—and drop a dime on the father. I think you can even do that anonymously. I know you can here. They'll come out and investigate, and if there are signs of family abuse, the state will step in. Unfortunately, when you do, you might be causing problems for the mother. But she's a grown woman, and if I were her, I'd much rather get sent back to Mexico if it meant that my kids were safe. I'm not trying to minimize the woman's problems, but I don't know how she can put up with it, anyway. I don't know if I could, no matter how afraid I was." Charnell knocked wood, or, in this case, Formica.

Raymond L. Atkins

"I don't know what I'd do," Early said. "I'd like to think I'd do what was best for my children, but she's living with a guy who has already put her in the hospital twice. Hell, he took one of the kids for a ride and didn't come back with him. This is a scary guy. I guess you never know how you would behave in that situation until you've been there."

A thought occurred to Charnell, and he slapped the tabletop with his palm. "Of course, since she hasn't already done something about all of this, you can't rule out the possibility that she might actually be complicit. So you need to watch out. Families are complicated, and family law is a snake pit. No one ever tells the whole truth, and you never know who is out-and-out lying and who is only fibbing. If you try to call her to let her know Jesús is okay and it turns out she's involved in his abuse, you're a dead duck and Jesús is on the way back to the Sunshine State. There are several different scenarios that could be in play. Jesús might not know the whole story. Or he might be lying, trying to protect his mother by selling out his father. Sometimes kids do that. You just can't tell, and it wouldn't be the first time that things didn't turn out to be like they seemed."

"If it all goes sour, I know a pretty good lawyer. He once got a guy off on a murder charge by basing his entire defense on the fact that the victim needed killing. And if my attorney lets me down, my sister has some serious spiritual connections."

"It was my finest hour," Charnell said, fondly remembering what may have indeed been the pinnacle of a long and occasionally distinguished career. "The son of a bitch really *did* need killing, and yours truly convinced the jury to agree. By the time I got through with them, most of the jurors wished they'd shot him themselves. The problem with me being your lawyer, though, is that Old Charnell may not always be around

73

to get you out of trouble. And your sister has a serious case of snakes in her head."

"That's true, but at least they're Christian snakes," Early said, "and you're too mean to ever die."

"I expect I will pass along someday, but I'm in no hurry. Unlike you, I haven't been storing up rewards in heaven. As a general rule, lawyers go straight to hell. It's actually a law in this state, and I think it might be in the code book over in Alabama, too." He signaled for the check. "What are you going to do with Jesús once the campers start showing up?"

"That won't be a problem. We're canceling camp this year. No business."

"Say what?"

"We only have ten bunks sold for the entire summer. We'll lose too much money if we try to run with just ten kids."

"I hate to hear that. You and Ivey have been in business for how long, now?"

"Thirty years, but I have a funny feeling that this might be it. I think this is the beginning of the end, that maybe we're winding down."

"It's just one bad year. You'll recover. The campers will be back." Charnell leaned over and patted Early's arm in reassurance.

"I hope you're right. At least for Ivey's sake. She won't know what to do with herself if we close down for good. She loves the camp and always has. But you know how sometimes you can sense a change? Like something's going to happen, but you don't know what? I've been having that feeling all spring. It's almost like I can smell it. Change is in the wind."

"What if you're right and the days of Camp Redemption are numbered? What will you do then?"

"I really don't know."

"Do you have the money to retire?"

"No."

"So what will you do for a payday if you close the camp?"

"Again, I don't really know. Gilla Newman wants to buy the far side of the valley, Ivey's side, everything north of the water, to build a housing development. If we sold it to him, I could sit over on my half, smoke my pipe, skip stones, and watch the rich people make house payments. But Ivey's set on giving her part of the valley to the church. That leaves me with the option of selling my side." Early shrugged. "To tell you the truth, I'd hate to sell *any* of it. It's been in our family a long time. But if the money situation gets tight, we might have to."

"What'd Ivey think about the idea of selling out?"

"Not much. I mentioned in passing the possibility of selling half the valley. That night, she had a vision on the subject. A deceased Chickasaw Indian with a hurt back came to her and told her that we are now under a divine mandate to use the camp and the valley to help the needy. And if we have read the signs correctly, we'll be starting that project by lending aid and comfort to our runaway, Jesús. Plus, the Chickasaw informed Ivey that if I sell any part of the valley to Gilla Newman, I'll be joining you for a long roast in hell."

"Well, I can't say I'd mind the company. Did the Chickasaw say how he hurt his back?"

"He didn't mention."

"If he got injured in the valley, you could be liable."

"I'll refer anything I get on that right along to you."

"Good. Now, since you have me on retainer, let me give you my professional legal opinion. Gilla Newman is a piece of shit, just like his daddy was before him."

"Thanks."

"And his boy Stanley didn't fall too far from the shit tree, either. My advice is to stay away from any Newman wanting to transact any business deal. All of them, including the dead one, would climb a tree to screw you rather than stand flat-footed on the ground and give you a fair shake."

"Tell me something I don't know."

Charnell had been the attorney of record for Mr. Frank Newman—Gilla's father—for many years leading up to that old man's sudden death and subsequent departure to significantly warmer climates. He had once been Gilla's attorney as well, until Gilla fired him in favor of a shave-tailed barrister from Atlanta, a youngster who, in Charnell's opinion, couldn't even litigate himself out of an *implied* contract. Charnell was a bad man to cross, a formidable opponent with a long memory, a questionable attitude, and a mean streak, and even though he had not cared one whit about the loss of Gilla's business and had actually been considering dropping *him*, the termination had rankled on the basis of principle.

"I'm curious," Charnell said. "How much did Gilla offer?"

Early told him the figure they had discussed.

"Shit. That's no money at all. That half of the valley is easily worth twice that amount. Maybe even more. Your old buddy Gilla is trying to shaft you."

"He's not my old buddy, and I know it's low. It doesn't really matter what the land is worth. It only matters what I can get if we have to sell it. And right now, his offer is the only one on the table. It's a buyer's market. But like I said, it's all a moot point, anyway. Ivey wants to leave that land to Brother Rickey Lee and the Rapture Preparation Temple. She's set on it. She had a vision."

"Maybe you can sell him your half and move over to hers."

"I actually mentioned that to Gilla. He doesn't want my side, and I guess I really don't want him to have it. We both feel the way we do for the same reason. The cemetery's on my side. Like I said, he wants to put in a housing development for rich folks, and if he bought my side, he'd have to move the cemetery, because apparently it's hard to sell a $500,000 home if it has a view of the graveyard. Go figure. Anyway, I don't

76

want him digging up the relatives. I think letting him in there with a backhoe might get me to hell even quicker than selling Ivey's half of the valley. Even if I would consider relocating the cemetery, Gilla wouldn't. It would cost him a pile of money, and you know what a tight-fisted bastard he is."

"I could buy your side," Charnell said casually. "I'll give you one dollar more than Gilla offered."

"Huh? Why would you want to do that?"

"To own half of a Bible camp."

"Okay. I'll bite. Why do you want to do that?"

"I'm getting tired of living in town. I might just enjoy being a country boy for a while. And if anyone ever needed to go to Bible camp, it's me."

"That's for sure. But there's more, right?"

"Well, it would seriously piss Gilla Newman off if I slipped in behind him on his land deal. And with the exceptions of sex, bourbon, pork rinds, and cigars, seriously pissing off Gilla Newman is just about my favorite thing in the whole world."

Early grinned as he stood. "I'll keep your offer in mind," he said as he started for the door.

"And give that damn boy back," Charnell said quietly to his client's retreating back.

Chapter Six

Several days had passed since his chat with Charnell, and still Early had not decided on the best overall solution for Jesús. He did not intend to send the boy back to an abusive father, but the craggy lawyer's advice about the legalities of the matter had remained with him, and he was still uncertain about his alternative courses of action. He had talked to his sister about their visitor on three separate instances, and she had been no help whatsoever. Each conversation had been a frustrating and inconclusive carbon copy of the last.

"I still don't know what we are going to do about Jesús," he had said to her only yesterday, on the occasion of their most recent and, in his opinion, final chat on the subject.

"Why do you keep bringing this up?" Ivey was exasperated. There was no question in her mind as to what was to be done, or at whose instruction. It couldn't be any clearer if it were chiseled into a pair of stone tablets. "We're already doing what we have to do. We're taking care of him. It's the Lord's command."

"But Charnell said…"

"God outranks Charnell Jackson. Charnell may not believe it, but I do, and you'd better. 'Trust in Me, your Lord, with all your heart, and lean not on your own understanding. In your ways, acknowledge Me, and I will direct your paths.' Proverbs. Verse three. Chapter five."

"Right. You can't beat Proverbs. But when the time comes for someone to go to prison for stealing a kid, I'm thinking that it will be me and not the Lord who ends up wearing state issue and picking up trash out on the right of way."

The Bible was chock full of regular folks who had found themselves dangling in the eternal breeze due to divine whim, and Early did not want to be among that august company. He was not averse to the concept of performing good works on the earthly plane in anticipation of reaping a big reward in heaven. It sounded like a sweet deal, and reaping was good work if it could be obtained. But none of that meant he needed to go out of his way to seek excessive grief while he was here.

"You shouldn't talk that way," his sister said. "It's blasphemy. Anyway, He won't let you get arrested."

"Are you kidding me? He loves letting people get arrested! I think it's His hobby! How many examples do you want?"

"Shush." She put her finger to her lips as she sneaked a quick look skyward.

"I'm just saying."

"If it comes down to it, what makes you think that they'll take you to jail instead of me?"

It actually wasn't a bad question, and since Ivey had posed relatively few of those in her time, he wasn't prepared for this one. So since he didn't have an answer handy, he just made one up. "They usually take the man, that's all." Particularly if the man appears to be exponentially less insane than the woman.

In point of fact, he had the feeling that in the long annals of mankind, this particular situation—the divinely mandated harboring of an abused runaway child in violation of Florida, Georgia, and federal statutes—had never before presented itself, and he was fairly sure there were no precedents set nor any laws on the books dealing with who, specifically, could expect to take the rap. Maybe it *would* be Ivey. Who knew?

"We'll just see about that," she said. "If they arrest one of us, we'll tell them they have to take both of us." Ivey had long been a proponent of the maxim that misery loves company. It was one of the cornerstones of her faith. In contrast, Early believed that misery was miserable and should be avoided whenever possible. It was a key area in which their philosophies differed. In his view, a miserable person plus a miserable companion equaled twice as much misery for the rest of humanity to steer clear of at all costs, lest they become miserable as well. It was a simple equation.

"I don't think you get to tell them anything. I think they pretty much like you to stand there and keep your mouth shut. Besides, if you're in jail too, who'll bring me cigarettes and candy bars? Who'll come see me on Sundays and holidays?" Early supposed that Charnell Jackson might do the honors, at least to begin with, because if Early found himself in jail, the fact would loom large that his lawyer had failed to keep him *out*, and perhaps he would feel guilty about that. So even though the aging barrister tended to avoid places of incarceration whenever possible—he said they made him nervous—he might make an exception in this case.

"Early, you don't smoke," Ivey was saying, "and you don't like sweets very much, either." Despite the fact that her favorite book was mounded over with metaphor, Ivey was a very literal person at heart.

"Trust me. If this deal goes bad and I end up in the slam, I'll be up to a couple of packs a day in no time. And I'll need the candy for trade."

Early didn't know a great deal about jail. He had only been incarcerated once—at the tender age of seventeen for public drunkenness and underage drinking—and then only for about eight hours until he had slept off his excess. The incident had taken place over in Sand Valley, Alabama, and the policeman of that town in those days, Wendell Blackmon, had released the boy once he regained sobriety, because it appeared he was already suffering sufficiently for his crimes.

"The only reason I haven't called your folks is because I know your mama, and this would break her heart," Wendell had said at the open door of the cell. "So go on home. But if I catch you doing this again, I'll be putting you in the back of the cruiser and driving over to Willingham Valley to have a talk with Vester and Clairy."

So Early was relatively unskilled in the art of being imprisoned. If it came down to it, he supposed that holding a low profile and blending in were important components of being a successful jailbird. He suspected he ought to look into the possibility of acquiring tattoos. Maybe L-O-V-E on the fingers of his right hand and H-A-T-E on the fingers of his left. And he figured he might ought to consider conversion to the Muslim faith, which he had heard was a popular religion inside the penitentiary walls, although if he did trade his Bible for a Koran, he would need to do it on the sly so that Ivey would not find out about his defection and get her fundamentalist drawers into a twist.

Their conversation concerning the fate of Jesús had lagged then, and the only outcome to the chat was Early's resolution to refrain from ever bringing up the subject with Ivey again. He was firm on that point. Any subsequent decisions on the matter would be unilateral. A man could only take so much.

As for their houseguest, Jesús didn't do much during his first days with the Willinghams besides sleep, eat, and languish. His three weeks of life on the road had taken their toll, and he had arrived at Camp Redemption as worn as an old tire. He needed the time to recover both physically and mentally, so he slept twelve hours to the stretch, ate like a lumberjack when he was awake, and wandered about the valley in his spare time. He had been a Florida boy his entire life, but his short time in the Georgia countryside seemed to be agreeing with him.

Early accompanied him on most of his explorations throughout Willingham Valley, both as a guard and as a tour guide. He wanted Jesús to enjoy his stay, but at the same time he didn't want to have to explain what had happened should his charge tumble from a cliff or get hopelessly lost in a cave. Nor did he want to have to explain the contents of his little garden patch. So they walked the trails together and talked of many things under the sun, and in this manner, they got to know one another.

The boy seemed to appreciate the historical essence of the valley and the fact that people of one stamp or another had roamed the land for years uncounted. He liked the charcoal murals decorating the rugged walls of the cool, damp caverns that burrowed into the mountain rocks, black and gray renderings of ancient huntsmen bringing down deer, bear, and elk—hunters frozen in time and carbon—ensuring for eternity that their families would have meat. And he liked the more recent renderings, silent testimonials carved in the soft stone or scribed with pencil or charred sticks by members of Munroe Willingham's troop, sentiments such as *Dam I Hate Beans, E.B. Crowe-1863*, and *Tomorrow we go I hope I make it, Charlie Otwell*.

Jesús was also fascinated by the simple carvings above the waterfalls, furtive petroglyphs engraved into the supple stone: birds, fish, bison, women, men, the sun, the moon, and the whimsical, capricious gods. From around the valley, Jesús collected a flint arrowhead, a stone scraper, and a slag of oxidized iron that may have once been a dagger, all silent witnesses to the unending saga of the many peoples who had bonded with the land. Early showed him the dugout canoe he had found as a boy, the once-sturdy vessel carved from a single chestnut log, its gunwales now paper-thin but still holding their shape. But of all the wonders the valley held for Jesús, the boneyard with its collection of earthen mounds and gravestones was his favorite spot.

"Those mounds were here when my ancestors arrived," Early said on their first trip together to the hallowed grounds. "My father told me that this valley belonged to the Indians long before my people ever came over from Europe. They were here before Columbus and even the Vikings. This was their home. And they all rest here now, so I guess you could say they never left. The first Willingham in these parts was a man named Seaborn, and he bought the valley from the last Indian to ever live here." Early gestured toward the mounds. "I don't know where he is, but my father told the story that he died of a broken heart soon after he sold the land, and that he's buried here somewhere. That was over two hundred years ago, and my family has been in the valley ever since."

They stood at the northern end of the plot, looking across the headstones and markers to the mounds behind and to the mountains beyond that. Above them, white clouds hovered in layers, filling the blue sky with an impressionistic image of the resting place below. The azaleas and mountain laurels had begun to bloom, and the colors of spring were scattered in disarray across the valley and up the ridgelines. They were the colors of renewal. It was a peaceful scene but a somber one.

The mounds were impressive, both because of their size and because of the primitive technology that had been available to the builders, who had raised them by hand, one basketful of soil at a time. There were five mounds, two quite large. The two outsized mounds each measured ninety-seven feet square at the base and forty-four feet square at the summit. Early had no idea what the measurements represented, but he knew they must have some significance. He had measured both knolls, and they were exactly the same. One of these structures was at the southwest corner of the valley tucked in close to the base of the mountain. The other was about two hundred yards due east of its twin, and each mound formed a corner of a triangle. The remaining three mounds were a little over one hundred yards north of the others and together formed the third corner of the same imaginary triangle. These three mounds were funerary in nature and much smaller than their two cousins. Inside the triangle formed by the five mounds lay the Willingham family cemetery.

It was late in what had been a gentle day. A line of shadow crept through the calm afternoon and meandered across the monuments like a sundial marking eternity. In addition to the deceased Native American population in that corner of the valley, over two hundred Willinghams lay in repose in the family plot. There was also a fair scattering of non-family occupants who had for one reason or another found themselves in need of a final place to stay, including many of Munroe Willingham's Georgia Irregulars, who had been gathered up by a sad delegation of wives and families and brought home to rest. Many of the older markers were carved of wood and were worn nearly smooth by wind and time, and a few of the stone monuments had crumbled or tilted as the seasons danced upon them.

The cemetery was well kept by Early, and he sometimes wondered what would become of the burial ground once he and his sister had passed. Ivey frankly hoped for bodily ascension to a spot in the general vicinity of the heavenly throne when her time came, but Early had a nice place picked out for her in the cemetery, anyway, just in case she was forced to travel to heaven along more traditional paths. And his own final instructions included the request that he be quietly tucked into the corner of the top of the easternmost mound, which was one of the two larger, ceremonial knolls. He wanted to be buried facing east, up high where he could catch the morning sun as it crept over the rim of the world and brought the day. He knew that it wouldn't matter, really, because whether he was in heaven, or elsewhere, or nowhere at all, he wouldn't actually feel that sunshine as it warmed the sod, then the ground, and then, finally, his sad old bones. But he liked the idea of it anyway. Barring accident or illness, he felt that he would outlive Ivey, but his turn would come. And then there would be none. The last of the Georgia Willinghams would be planted with the first, and with all the many souls in between. Early supposed that the place would then fade to dust and ruin, as all things eventually must.

"My ancestors were mostly Indians," Jesús said. He squatted by one of the older Willingham markers, feeling the worn, pitted stone with his hand. "My mama told me."

"I read somewhere that they think all the natives in North and South America came from the same ancestors. The article said that these first Americans walked here across a land bridge from Siberia. If that's true, then some of the people under these mounds are your great-great-great-great-kinfolks."

"You don't think you have any Indian blood?"

"There's probably a little in there somewhere. Most people have some. But my forebears came from England."

"Why are those two mounds in the back bigger than the three over here?" Jesús asked.

"My father said that the two in the back were ceremonial places, like churches. The ones in front have people in them. He thought they buried their dead on top of each other until the mound got up to a certain height, and then they started another one. You see how the three funeral mounds are different shapes and sizes? They're not built evenly like the other two. My father figured that they were just about to start on another mound when the white people began showing up. Once that happened, it wasn't too long before the Indians were all gone. My father used to say that we fell on them like a tree. He said we just crushed them into the ground."

"Why did he think they were going to start on another mound?"

"I never really asked him. I just figured he knew what he was talking about and took it as a fact. He was a professor at Shorter College over in Rome. He loved history. Especially the history of this valley." At that moment, Early was reminded of the many talks he and Vester had shared at this spot. He reached over and patted Jesús lightly on the shoulder.

"I feel bad for them," Jesús said, gesturing toward the smaller mounds.

"I do too, Jesús. I always have. The world changed, and they couldn't change with it. Or else they wouldn't change. Either way, they're gone from here, except for these piles of dirt and the bones under them."

"But I think it's kind of cool that your ancestors put their cemetery out here with them."

"You're right," Early agreed. "It is kind of cool."

Occasionally, late in the evening after the toils of the day were past, Early liked to walk to the boneyard and sit quietly. He would tamp the Dr. Grabow full of his special blend, and, after a puff or two, he sometimes thought he caught a glimpse of one or another of the many spirits that wandered the valley at night: Munroe Willingham and his luckless followers, Robert Corntassel, Seaborn Willingham, and a multitude of others—Spanish, French, English, Cherokee, Creek, Chickasaw—and one ragged shade of a woman from Romania who had found herself a long way from home when her time had come to walk the bridge to forever. The dead far outnumbered the living in Willingham Valley, and their whispery voices and shuffling steps could be heard every time the breeze sighed through the branches and scattered the brittle leaves. The land possessed them now, held them like a mother holds her firstborn, and it was loath to loosen its grasp and let them drift free.

Early and Jesús sat on the bench that faced the plots of Seaborn Willingham, the patriarch of the clan, and his wife, Geneva. Seaborn had been an ironworker by trade and everything else by necessity, and the black iron angel that guarded the plot was impressive. She stood close to ten feet tall from sandal to wing tip, and her flowing robes were so lifelike that Early often expected them to ripple in the breeze. She stood on a granite base on which quiet words were chiseled: *Surely goodness and mercy shall follow me all the days of my life, and I will dwell in the House of the Lord forever.* It was Early's favorite verse. Man and boy quietly contemplated the epitaph. Across the clearing, a doe slowly made her way up the side of one of the mounds as she browsed the tender grass of spring.

"I like that," Jesús said, pointing at the monument.

"The angel or the words?"

"Both."

"My father told me that Seaborn Willingham made the angel himself. I showed you his blast furnace and coke ovens down by the river. You see that mountain over there? That's where he dug his coal. If you go up there now, you can still see the tunnels where they just shoveled the coal right out of the mountainside. The ones that haven't caved in, anyway. And if you go one valley over, down that way, you can look at the pit where he dug his iron ore. My father said it took Seaborn almost two years to get the monument like he wanted it, that he cast and recast until he had it just so. He used sand and clay to make his molds. Look here. When you get up close, you can see that it was made in several pieces. Then he riveted it together. He also quarried and polished the base, and chiseled the inscription. You can see that the letters are all just a bit different from each other."

Jesús stepped to the monument and ran his fingers over the carvings in the stone. "I like it here," he said.

"It is a pretty spot," Early acknowledged.

"No, I mean I like it *here*. In the valley. At the camp. With you and Miss Ivey." He made a broad gesture. "With all of this."

"We like you being here, too." It was true. Early had taken a big shine to the boy in a short span of time. He was generally only as sociable as he had to be, and it was unusual for him to warm to a stranger so quickly.

"I don't know what I'm going to do," Jesús said, "but right now I feel safe. I haven't felt safe in a long time."

"Safe is good," Early said. "Safe is about the best thing there is." They sat quietly then, until the sun was gone, the air turned cool, and the stars winked on, one then another like fireflies. The pale moon rose like a phantom, and the angel became a shadow among the shades of darkness.

One week to the day after his arrival, Jesús came to the breakfast table like a man with a purpose. He wore new clothing that Ivey had bought for him, and he carried one of the Camp Redemption travel bags that were usually given to campers as a souvenir before they packed for home. He looked clean, rested, well fed, and apparently ready to continue his journey.

"Good morning, Jesús," Ivey said. She was making blueberry pancakes and bacon for breakfast. A tall stack of the fragrant, golden cakes already stood on a platter, and another three flapjacks bubbled on her ancient cast-iron griddle.

"Morning, Miss Ivey," Jesús said. He sat down, poured a glass of orange juice, and grabbed a piece of the crisp bacon. "Morning, Early," he continued as he took a bite and began to crunch.

Early looked up from his paper and saw the travel bag. He folded the paper, set it aside, and nodded at the valise. "Are you going somewhere?" he asked.

"Yeah, I think it's time I got out of here. I've stayed long enough. I need to be moving on." He reached out with his fork, speared five blueberry pancakes, and put them on his plate. Then he picked up the top cake as if it were a piece of toast and patiently began to butter it.

Upon this revelation, Ivey dropped her spatula and made a noise that sounded like a stifled sob. She clenched her apron tails into a wad and looked at Early. She nodded at her brother, then at Jesús. Early held up his palms to placate her, to assure her that he had the situation covered.

"Jesús, you haven't been a bit of trouble, and we don't want you to go," he said. "We haven't even known you were here most of the time. I don't think getting right back out on the highway is a good idea. You told me just the other day that you liked it here and that you felt safe, so what's your hurry?"

Early was still waiting for a solution to The Jesús Problem, and he had hoped for more time. He had skipped many a stone while considering the issue, but still he was perplexed.

"If I get caught here, you're screwed. I heard you and Miss Ivey talking about it the other day when you thought I was asleep. You guys have been good to me, and I don't want to be the one to get you into trouble. So I'm heading back out." He folded his buttered pancake over like a taco and ate it in two quick bites.

"Do you even know where you're going?" Early asked. Maybe Jesús had at last remembered the existence of a kindhearted aunt or a gentle and loving grandfather. If so, Early would be more than happy to give him a lift.

"I don't know," Jesús said, as he completely ignored the bottle of syrup that was right in front of him and began to butter another blueberry pancake. All Early could figure was that this was the way they ate them in Apalachicola. He began to speak.

"Why don't you just slow down a minute while we think this through?" Early said, keeping his tone as even as possible. "First off, hitchhiking is dangerous. You never know what kind of person is going to pick you up. You hear about hitchhikers getting robbed or killed all the time. You also hear about kids who just go missing and are never seen again. Like those kids on the milk cartons or on the posters at Walmart. You've got to wonder how many of them took a ride from the wrong person. You got away with hitchhiking while you were on the way here, but don't let that give you a false sense of security. You were fortunate. You might not be so lucky the second time."

"It's true," Ivey said from her vantage point at the stove. She had regained her spatula and her composure, but she was paying more attention to the conversation than to the breakfast, and the flapjacks were scorching on the griddle as a result. She turned off the burner, set the griddle aside, and came to the table.

"Listen to her," Early said, nodding at his sister.

"We had a man speak at the church," she said. "There are some really bad people out there who just want to hurt children. They're predators, like wolves or tigers. The man said these people are sick, but I thought a better word for what they are is *evil*. And a lot of the time they get their victims by just picking them up."

Early remembered the day Ivey had come home after hearing that speaker. She had been appalled that such meanness existed, although she still believed that good would eventually triumph over all. Early had consoled her while harboring the unspoken thought that good eventually triumphing over evil wouldn't help someone who needed the triumph to happen sooner rather than later. He had always been confused about the purpose of evil, anyway. He wondered why God didn't simply dispense with it altogether. For the life of him, Early couldn't understand why He didn't just chalk it off as an idea that hadn't worked out. In his opinion, a world without wickedness would be intrinsically better than one with it.

"I'll be careful," Jesús said with the optimism and immortality of youth.

Early sighed with frustration. "These people don't run around wearing t-shirts that say Bad Person," he pointed out. "They actually try to hide what they're up to. They go to a lot of trouble to not tip you off. They pretend they're nice folks until they get you onto a deserted stretch of highway. And then it's too late to be sorry. But here's another thought. In addition to hitchhiking being dangerous, it's also illegal. Where do you think your next stop will be if the police pick you up for hitchhiking?"

Jesús paused to give that one some thought, and when a frown flitted across his features, Early knew that he had arrived at the correct answer.

"Home, I guess," the boy said quietly.

"Apalachicola would be my guess, too," Early agreed. "And that's a place you need to avoid. So, since you have nowhere to go and no way to get there anyway—not to mention the fact that you don't have any money—maybe you ought to take a little more time and come up with a better plan. What will you eat? Where will you sleep? How will you avoid the police? When you came here, at least you had a destination in mind. But you can't count on finding another camp that will take you in. And you can't count on another Ivey and Early Willingham willing to help you. We're nice people. We almost never do away with children. What if you run up on something like the Charles Manson Family Summer Camp next time?"

Jesús crunched a strip of bacon and seemed to consider the idea.

After a moment, Early spoke again. During his conversation with Jesús, he had finally decided what he needed to do. "If you want to go, I guess I can't stop you. Not without calling the police, anyway, which I said I wouldn't do. You'll be making a mistake if you leave right now, but the good Lord looks after fools and children, so maybe you'll be all right. Maybe. But it's too bad, really, because I was about to offer you a job here at the camp. Even though we're not having sessions this year, there is still plenty of work to do, and I'm getting too old to take care of all of it by myself. I was going to offer you a hundred dollars a week, cash, plus room and board, to help me keep the place up. You know, mowing and tending the cemetery, feeding the horses, some cabin repair, that kind of stuff."

Jesús listened to these words in silence. Then he was quiet for a longer time, as if he were holding them to the light and inspecting them for flaws and imperfections. Finally, he spoke.

"Thanks, Early," he said. "I appreciate the offer of a job, but I don't want any more charity. And for sure I don't want to be the cause of you getting sent to jail. I've got enough to feel bad about."

"It won't be charity," Early replied. "I really was going to hire someone anyway, so it might as well be you. I've been talking to Ivey about it all spring. Isn't that right, Ivey?" He crossed his fingers as he turned to his sister for backup.

"That's right," she replied without hesitation, telling the first lie to cross her lips in many long days. She looked both sheepish and proud, as if she had done the wrong thing but for the right reason. Early was proud of her as well, but he knew there would have to be some extra prayers tonight.

"And you don't need to worry about anyone going to jail, either," Early continued. "I've talked to a lawyer I know, and he says not to fret. We might be bending the law a little bit by not telling your folks where you are. But it's just a little, and we'll have to let it bend for now. I don't want you to get hurt again. I couldn't live with myself if you went back home and something bad happened to you."

Jesús appeared to consider his options as he selected another piece of bacon.

"There's not much bacon out on the open road," Early observed. "Or blueberry pancakes, for that matter." He nudged the platter toward Jesús.

"I'll stay," Jesús said. "For a little while, anyway."

Early didn't know if it had been his talk that had done the trick or if the bacon had turned the tide. "That's good," he said. He stood and clapped Jesús on the back.

"Praise the Lord!" Ivey shouted. She came up behind Jesús and hugged the boy until his air ran low.

So it was decided. They offered to make his accommodations in the Big House a permanent arrangement, but he asked if he could stay in one of the empty cabins instead. The Willinghams agreed. Jesús chose Philip, because it had a nice view, and they moved him in. He selected the bunk in the center of the large room as his own. Early dragged one of the rockers from the porch while Ivey stowed Jesús' meager possessions in the footlocker by the bed.

"I wish he had decided to stay in the Big House," Ivey said later that evening back in the Big House. Her maternal instincts were having their way with her.

"He's a kid. He doesn't want to spend every minute of the day with two old people. He'll be fine out there. You'll see him at least three times every day. I guarantee it."

"Maybe you're right," she said, but she sounded unconvinced.

"What are you thinking?" Early asked.

"I think he'll get lonesome."

"He's not living in a cave on the other side of the valley, Ivey. He's right over there." Early was pointing at the cabin, at humble Philip, plainly visible from the kitchen window.

Chapter Seven

The next day was Sunday, and Ivey conjured a breakfast of
fried country ham, buttermilk biscuits, and her world-famous
home fries, which may or may not have actually been world
famous, but which were pretty popular in Willingham Valley.
Early and Ivey were early risers, so the sun had barely cleared
the horizon when they finished their meal. Early took his
coffee cup to the porch and sipped as he watched the
awakening of the day. The sky was clear, and a few stars still
twinkled, although most had already fled the coming of the
sun. On the horizon, he could see the crescent moon clearly in
the early morning sky. Inside, Ivey was clattering and banging
as she cleared the table and stacked the dishes. The windows
in Philip were dark, and Early supposed that Jesús was still in
his bunk.

The Willinghams had two distinctly different Sunday
rituals, depending on the time of year. When they were hosting
campers, they arose before the sun and fed the multitudes
before marching them all into the little chapel in the valley for
a long morning of prayer and reflection, the dual keystones of
Bible camping. Occasionally a visiting pastor would come to
preach, but most weeks it was Ivey banging the pulpit. She
was a good preacher with a talent for discourse, and she could
sermonize at least until the lunch bell rang and usually a good
bit longer. Indeed, she often became engrossed in her selected
topic and ran over her allotted time, causing the campers to
fidget and fret as their eyes glazed over. On those days, Early
had to stand just inside the door of the sanctuary and make the
cut motion under his chin, like a director on a movie set.

Early did not actually attend these weekly camp services. He had nothing against them and in fact enjoyed hearing his sister preach, finding Ivey's combination of religious fervor and simple sincerity refreshing. But over the years, Early and Ivey had discovered that if any of their flock were going to stray, it would be during the unsupervised block of time while chapel was in session. So instead of coming to meeting, Early roamed the camp, searching the nooks and crannies for stragglers and sluggards, whom he then herded into the back pews of the chapel before they got themselves into trouble, spiritually or otherwise. Usually the backsliders were counselors. They meant no real harm but were of the age when hormones plus opportunity could evolve into momentary lapses of religious zeal, which could in turn lead to forays into worldly pleasures.

During the nine-month off-season, the Sunday ritual was quite different. Then, Ivey attended services at the Washed in the Blood and the Fire Rapture Preparation Temple. Worship at the temple was a daylong affair presided over by Brother Rickey Lee, a chubby little man on whom the spirit lay like a warm velvet cloak. Sunday service was a series of events that included Sunday school, first preaching, a covered-dish dinner on the grounds at noon, second preaching, and altar call. Early always drove his sister to church because, even though she was an excellent driver, she had never bothered to acquire a driver's license, so she only drove outside the valley in cases of extreme emergency.

Early normally dropped her off at the church by nine o'clock, and once she and her Bible, devilled eggs, and macaroni and cheese had entered the house of worship, he would shift the pickup into gear and drive five miles to his next destination, Hugh Don Monfort's beer joint out on the Alabama highway. Once there, he and Hugh Don would explore religious and philosophical issues while slowly sipping tall cans of Schlitz malt liquor in Early's case and short cans of Pabst Blue Ribbon in Hugh Don's.

Hugh Don and Early would while away the remainder of the morning and the shank of the afternoon as they pondered questions such as, *Why didn't God have someone run over Hitler with a meat truck prior to 1930? What intrinsic value do streets of gold and pearly gates have for dead people in heaven?* and, their perennial favorite, *Is God really going to send over a billion Chinese people to hell just because they have never heard of Him?*

Hugh Don and Early were equal-opportunity philosophers, thus their inquiries into the questions of the ages were not limited to Christian themes. They explored other hard issues as well, including *What point is there to coming back as something else in the next life if you don't even know that you have come back at all? If a female Muslim dies in the name of the faith, are there an armload of virgins waiting for her in heaven, and if there are, what sex are they, and, depending on the answer to that question, what does all of that mean?* And *Who in the hell was Jain and what in the hell is Jainism?*

When two o'clock rolled around, Early would drain his final Schlitz malt liquor and begin to sip strong black coffee instead. At around four o'clock, he would bid Hugh Don adieu and head back to pick up his sister. The journey home was usually silent as each reviewed the cogent truths, both the sacred and the profane, that had been revealed during the course of the day.

So, since camp had been cancelled this year, Ivey and Early were up with the sun making ready for their respective trips to worship. Ivey had cooked chicken and dumplings the night before and planned on carrying the leftovers—about two gallons of them—to the potluck dinner on the grounds out at the church. When the nourishment of the spirit was an all-day affair, the nourishment of the body had to be given due consideration.

"It seems kind of sacrilegious to carry leftovers to the house of the Lord," Early said. The real sacrilege to him was in taking the perfectly tasty dumplings he had hoped to eat later that day and feeding them to a covey of hungry parishioners. It just didn't seem right.

"Hush," Ivey replied. "Brother Rickey has a taste for my dumplings."

"Brother Rickey looks like he has a taste for almost everything."

"Don't you worry about Brother Rickey. Anyway, I left some dumplings for you in the fridge. Now, go wake Jesús up. He needs to get ready for church."

Early was gratified to hear that his dumpling needs had been allowed for, but the request to awaken Jesús took him by surprise.

"Ivey, I don't think he ought to go to your church."

"Well, he certainly can't go to Hugh Don Monfort's beer joint with you, now, can he?"

She had a small point, but Early felt that she was missing the larger issue completely. "I'm not so sure he needs to be going anywhere," Early replied. "I think maybe he needs to stay put, right here at the camp, out of sight. If we start flashing him around, folks might begin to wonder who he is, where he came from, and why he's here. Then there'll be trouble."

She pondered his words. She was an honest and decent woman, thus the concept of deceit was coming to her slowly, like a turtle crossing the state highway on a cool morning.

"I guess that makes sense, but young people need to go to church," she said firmly. "It says so in the Bible. 'And Abraham said unto his young men, Abide ye here with the ass; and I and the lad will go yonder and worship, and come again to you.' Genesis 22:5."

"I told you *ass* wasn't blasphemy, and I've got nothing against him going to church. I just think we ought to keep him away from other people until we figure out how we're going to explain him." He snapped his fingers. "I tell you what we can do. Why don't we have chapel here this morning, and *you* preach to him? He and I will both come. I haven't gotten to listen to you lead a service in a long time."

Ivey thought this suggestion over for a moment before grudgingly acquiescing. "I guess that'll have to do."

So Ivey prepared for services while Early went to rouse Jesús. After a quick breakfast for the boy, the two sat side by side in the chapel while Ivey presented a discourse on God's prescription for the many ills of the wicked world.

She had a lengthy catalog of the shortcomings of humanity, and it was alphabetized and annotated for the convenience and edification of the listener. Early had heard his sister speak from this list of the weaknesses of mankind on many occasions—indeed, the topic was one of her favorites—and he agreed with most of her points. In her sermon, the cure for all the sins of the wicked race of men was pretty much the same, and Early had to concede that her proposed remedy would no doubt lower the incidence of tomfoolery around the camp, perhaps dramatically, although he wasn't sure how well that flaming sword in the mighty right hand of God was going to go over in town.

Jesús took his religion silently, for the most part, although he did lean over at one point to share a whisper with his pew mate. "I'm Catholic," he murmured.

"Don't tell Ivey," Early whispered back. Jesús nodded, as if he could sense the problems that this admission might bring. "You're an honorary Washed in the Blood and the Fire Rapture Preparationist this morning. And when she asks us to give her an *amen*, raise both of your hands and give her one."

"Got it."

Later, after a full morning of church followed by a brunch of chicken and dumplings, Early found himself with a half day of leisure to spend. So he decided to take a drive over to Hugh Don Monfort's place for some stimulating conversation and a can or two of malt liquor. He shared this plan with his sister, who asked for a ride as far as the church.

"I'd like to go hear Brother Rickey preach a bit this afternoon," she said. "Do you think Jesús will be all right if we leave him for a while?"

"I think he'll be fine, but I'll go check."

Early found Jesús prone on his bunk reading through a stack of leftover comic books. The boy indicated that he would be happy with that pastime for the remainder of the evening. Early and Ivey rode in silence as far as the church, where Early let his sister out just in time for the second preaching. Then he pulled back onto the road and made his way to the beer joint.

After a short drive, he turned off the Alabama highway onto the well-traveled gravel road that led to a small clearing in the piney woods. This little dale contained Hugh Don Monfort's old white frame house. Sometimes it was called The Mansion on the Hill, even though the structure was far from a mansion and there was no hill in sight. But it was more commonly known as the beer joint. It was a diminutive domicile, but even a small house can hold a lot of beer, and Hugh Don saw to it that his beer joint was always stocked with a sufficiency of cold beverages, cheap cigars, and playing cards.

Early parked to the side of the drive-through, got out of the truck, and slowly walked up to the door. Once there, he knocked loudly. Then he stepped to the edge of the porch to await permission to enter. Hugh Don was a gentleman bootlegger and a paragon of Christian virtue, a veritable saint among the sinners of the new South, but it was still a bad idea to burst into his place of business unannounced. He had prayed over everyone he had ever shot, but he had shot them just the same, and Early had no desire to be prayed over that afternoon by anyone other than Ivey, and he could even do without that. He heard a chair squeak on a plank floor, then deliberate footsteps as they made their way toward him, followed by an almost imperceptible click. The flap over the peephole in the door slid aside, and Early found himself looking at a single blue eye. Then the flap dropped back into place, the latch clicked, and the door opened. Hugh Don stood there smiling. He slowly lowered the hammer before holstering his .45-caliber revolver.

"Come in! Come in!" he hollered, as if his guest were hard of hearing or standing far away. "I didn't think I was going to see you today. Figured maybe camp had already started. Thought Miss Ivey was preaching and you were sneaking around in the bushes trying to flush out scamps. It's been kind of quiet around here today. All the heavy drinkers are sleeping off last night, and everyone else is sittin' down to Sunday dinner."

Hugh Don Monfort was a shockingly thin individual, like a refugee from the gulag. He was ropy and tall, with sunken pale-blue eyes and a permanently creased forehead. Winter and summer, he wore a long-sleeved flannel shirt buttoned at the neck and sleeves, and an old ball cap was always perched jauntily atop his head, like a family heirloom. He was completely bald, he always needed a shave, and his nose looked one size too small for his head. He was a kind-hearted man who had decided early on that selling beer and liquor in a dry county was a more satisfying career path than any other, although, to be completely honest, he had not acquainted himself with many alternatives before making his choice.

It was true that his chosen occupation was technically illegal, but aside from that, Hugh Don was an honest bootlegger who charged a fair price for a necessary service. He would not sell to minors unless they had proven they could hold their liquor, would not sell to people he did not know unless they could produce the name of someone he *was* acquainted with, and would not allow anyone who became inebriated to leave his establishment behind the wheel of a vehicle until they had eaten a couple of hard-boiled eggs and sipped a few cups of scalding black coffee.

Hugh Don slapped Early on the back. Then he retrieved a can of Schlitz malt liquor from one of the many refrigerators that lined two entire walls of the big room, wiped it with a cotton cloth, and handed it to his friend. He stepped to another cooler and retrieved a can of Pabst Blue Ribbon for himself. Early looked at the widescreen TV that occupied the prominent spot on the third wall and noted that his fellow philosophe was watching a soccer match broadcast in a foreign language, a contest snatched from the ether by the big satellite dish outside. The rest of the room's furnishings included a round oak table surrounded by eight leather-upholstered chairs that had once been whiskey barrels at the Jack Daniels Distillery, a greasy blue velvet recliner for Hugh Don to relax in, an old porch rocker that Early liked, a few straight chairs staged here and there, and an electric stove. A pan of brown-shelled eggs was simmering on one of the stove burners. Hugh Don liked hard-boiled eggs with salt and pepper. He rarely ate anything else.

"I didn't know you liked to watch soccer," Early said, nodding at the television. He popped the top of his malt liquor and took an appreciative sip. Everyone who knew Hugh Don knew that his favorite sports were professional wrestling, football, stock car racing, and more professional wrestling.

He had, in his younger years, attempted to break into the pro wrestling circuit, tussling for two years under the *nom d'étape* of The Redneck Ranger. Unfortunately, his career had been cut short one bleak night in the high school gymnasium in Lafayette, Georgia. During that sad interlude, a local grandmother by the name of Adilee Fontain beat him unconscious with a folding chair after he had roughed up her hero, The Masked Butcher. The Butcher's given name was Ottis Spivey, and he was actually a bona fide butcher down at the Piggly Wiggly when he wasn't rolling around with other rowdy men inside the squared circle. Hugh Don's public humiliation at the hands of a bifocaled little old lady was a setback of the highest order, and he had retired from the sport shortly thereafter.

"I hate the shit. It's the stupidest damn thing I've ever seen, and I'm an old man who has seen a lot. I can't even understand what the damn game is about. A bunch of foreign boys in short pants running around kicking a ball. What the hell is that? They aren't even allowed to catch the ball. What good is there in having a ball if you can't catch it?" He took a drink of Pabst, belched loudly, and continued. "When I was a boy, they didn't have soccer. At least, they didn't have it here. They played it over in Europe, I guess, but who gave a shit about that? They can do whatever they want to over there, as long as they keep it over there. *Here*, we had football in the fall, basketball in the winter, and baseball in the spring and summer. And everything was fine. But now, right down the road in Sequoyah, and even over in Sand Valley, Georgia kids and Alabama kids are playing soccer in school. Boys and girls playing together! Charnell Jackson was here the other night, and do you know what he told me?"

"What'd he tell you, Hugh Don?"

"I'll tell you what he told me. He said that soccer is the most popular game in the world. Not baseball. Not even football, for Christ's sake. A bunch of foreigners with hairy legs and names you can't even say are beating out good old American football." He shook his head, like he couldn't believe his own words. "I don't know what the world is coming to. It's

Sodom and Gomorrah all over again. This could be the
beginning of the end times. I'm telling you, Early, I don't know
how long the Lord is going to let it continue."

Early didn't know either, but he thought it was a fairly
safe bet that the brimstone would rain down on illegal beer
joints before it singed the soccer field in town, hairy legs or not.

"If you don't like soccer, then why are you watching it?"
Early sat in his chair and began to rock slowly. It seemed an
eminently reasonable question.

"I was hoping to catch a glimpse of Burton Turner. He
ended up over in Spain playing soccer for one of their teams."
Hugh Don pointed at the widescreen. "I think he plays for
those boys right there, the ones in the striped shirts."

"How do you know that?"

"His mama told me. She was by here the other day picking
up her bottle of sherry. First she swore me to secrecy, because
they're still looking for him. Then she told me where he was."

Most of Hugh Don's customers preferred beer, and there
wasn't much call for sherry among his patrons, but he kept a
bottle or two around for the high-class trade. Plus, he was kind
of sweet on Maxine Turner, and he swore that if he ever got
enough sherry into her, she might just realize what a catch he
was.

Maxine's son, Burton, was a bad boy gone worse, a local
sports hero who had been too lazy to succeed and too stupid to
steal. During his high school years, he had been the star of
every team that the Sequoyah Indians fielded, and upon his
graduation he accepted a football scholarship from the
University of Georgia. But even though he was an exceptional
football player, the life of the gridiron idol was not to be his
destiny. He was placed on academic probation at the end of his
first semester after earning four D's and one F, which was an
amazing feat even for a sports-scholarship student from
Sequoyah, considering the classes he had attempted. He

reversed this trend during his second semester by earning four F's and a D. The D was an honest mark, and he was sort of proud of it, but the F's were all the result of being caught cheating in a variety of courses. The crime of dishonesty was discouraged at the college and was punishable by banishment from between the hedges, so Burton was expelled, and he slunk home in disgrace.

He went to work in his Uncle Earl's upholstery shop, and over the ensuing months, he developed an aversion to working for his money, to his Uncle Earl, and to twill, a robust material that rubbed all the skin from his knuckles. Finally, after toiling for an entire week on a particularly shoddy and stubborn Victorian camel-back sofa that had spent the last one hundred years moldering in a shed behind Frog Scott's mama's house, Burton had withstood all of the good, honest labor he could take. Although he badly needed it to, the job wasn't helping him build any of the character that Uncle Earl had promised. So he snapped, and in his desperation, he robbed Jackson's Bait Emporium on the east side of Sequoyah. Unfortunately, Burton was not much better at robbery than he was at academics or upholstery, and the heist was less than successful.

As Jackson Dillon later told the story, he looked up from the minnow tank on that fateful day, and there before him stood a large man with one leg of an intact pair of panty hose stretched over his head. This masked man pointed a weapon that bore great resemblance to a staple gun. The thief also wore a blue work shirt, one that had the words *Earl's Upholstery* stitched over the left pocket and the name *Burton Turner* stitched over the right.

"I thought my time had come," Jackson said after the ordeal. "I thought he was going to staple my ass any minute."

The mystery bandit got away with nearly twenty dollars in singles and change, plus some night crawlers and two cans of Vienna sausages. After a brief investigation during which the phrase *No one could be that damn stupid* was repeated several times, the Sequoyah policeman, Austell Poe, was forced to conclude that apparently someone could indeed be that stupid, and he went to arrest Burton Turner for the crime of armed robbery. But it was too late. Burton wasn't smart enough for much, but he was smart enough to know that it was time to run. So he kissed his mama, gave her back her panty hose, changed his shirt, shoved two boxes of Little Debbies plus the Vienna sausages into a sack, and fled into the darkness, just another fugitive on the lam from the world of the honest and the law-abiding. Luckily, twenty dollars and a bag of snacks go a long way, because the next time Burton surfaced, it was as a Spanish soccer player who went by the name of El Chico.

Back at the beer joint, Early Willingham and Hugh Don Monfort watched the soccer game in silence for a few minutes, but no matter how hard they looked, they couldn't spot Burton.

"Why don't you turn the sound up?" Early asked, thinking that the words *El Chico* might drift in over the airwaves. Then at least they'd know they were on the right track, that one of the hairy-legged boys on the screen was Burton.

"It wouldn't do a damn bit of good. I don't know what language they're speaking, but it ain't American, that's for sure."

"Maybe it's Spanish," Early noted.

"Maybe," Hugh Don said dubiously.

"His name would still be the same, though. Try it."

Hugh Don shrugged and turned up the volume. They listened for a few somber moments, but the combination of syllables they sought was not offered by the either of the two presumably Spanish announcers, and Hugh Don finally sighed as he hit the mute button on the remote.

"Maybe we can't spot him because he's wearing a pair of panty hose on his head," he noted philosophically.

"Yeah, that worked pretty well for him the last time he did it," Early replied.

"At least he let his mama take 'em off before he drug 'em over his head," Hugh Don observed.

"That's something."

"I'll tell you one thing. I'd damn sure like to help Maxine slide out of her panty hose." Hugh Don sounded morose. His unrequited love was heavy on him, like a rusty anchor on the sea floor.

"I know you would, Hugh Don," Early said. Every beer drinker in town knew how Hugh Don Monfort felt about Maxine Turner. It was one of his favorite topics of conversation, especially after he got himself around a few Pabst Blue Ribbons. "Why don't you just tell her how you feel?"

"She's a nice woman. She wouldn't want anything to do with an old bootlegger like me."

Especially if she knew that he liked to speculate about her panty hose at the beer joint, Early thought.

"You'll never know if you don't try," he said. "And she might not be as picky as you think. I mean, her son is wanted for armed robbery with a staple gun, after all. And he's a soccer player, to boot. That ought to have lowered her standards some."

The mention of Burton Turner snapped Hugh Don from his funk. "No one could be that damn stupid," he said, shaking his head. Even two years after the crime had been committed, people still reiterated the phrase with fair frequency.

"Kind of makes you feel bad for the whole human race, doesn't it?" Early noted. "Makes you wonder how we ever came out on top."

Hugh Don shook his head and shrugged, as if to say that it beat the holy hell out of him. "Well, I don't see him, and I can't watch this shit anymore," he said as he switched off the game.

"Maxine must have gotten the name of the team wrong. He must be playing for someone else."

"Maybe he tried to rob another bait shop, and now he's on the run again." Burton wasn't necessarily the type of individual who would learn from his mistakes. " I bet he went in there with a pair of Spanish panty hose on his head. He was wearing his team jersey. It had El Chico stitched across his back, and his phone number under that. He probably got around twenty pesos, plus some Vienna sausages."

Both men chuckled as they imagined the latest escapade of Burton Turner, international bait-store thief.

"You think they have Vienna sausages over there?" Hugh Don asked. He pointed at the blank television screen like it was a map of Spain.

"I don't know."

"They must have. What else would they eat with saltine crackers? What would they take with them when they went fishing?"

"I guess you've got a point."

"Reckon what they call them?"

"I don't know. The Vienna part would be the same. That's the name of a city. I don't know the word for sausage."

"On some Spanish words, you just say *el* before them and add an *o* at the end. Like *el sausage-o*."

"I don't think this is one of those words," Early said.

"You reckon Burton knows that *El Chico* means *the boy*?" Hugh Don asked. Early looked at him in surprise.

"How did you know that?" The bootlegger's cultural diversity initiative was in its infancy, but at least he was making the effort. So far it had only extended to stocking a few bottles of Corona beer for the many Latinos now living in the area and to adding el- and -o to the occasional noun, but Rome wasn't built in a day.

"One of the Mexicans told me. You might know him. Juan Guiterrez. He's a real good boy. Likes Budweiser." Hugh Don had learned his letters back in the days of phonetic pronunciation, thus leaving Early to believe that a Budweiser-drinking Mexican boy named Jew-anne Guitar-ez had done this bit of translation.

"Just thinking about it, I bet Burton *doesn't* know what it means," Early said. "He doesn't even speak English all that well. I think he should have taken the name *El Dumb-Ass*."

Early had never cared much for Burton, but even so, he thought it was unfortunate that the young man would most likely be on the run for the rest of his life—or in prison, if he couldn't keep running—because he had robbed a bait shop with a staple gun. The general consensus around Sequoyah notwithstanding, Burton *was* that damn stupid, and if he ever got caught, Early hoped that the judge would show him mercy on those grounds. He had been a fugitive for two years, so he had already paid pretty dearly for a box of night crawlers, some potted meat, and twenty dollars in singles and change.

"Well, I'll just tell his mama I saw him, anyway," Hugh Don said. "She doesn't have a satellite dish, so she can't get the Spanish soccer channel. The poor thing has never seen him play, and she misses him. I'll tell her I saw him score a point. That'll make her happy."

"You're one of the good ones, Hugh Don." Early held up his Schlitz malt liquor in salute. He liked it that his bootlegger took the time to observe the niceties, that he had enough class to lie to a grieving mother about her ne'er-do-well baby boy. And the fact that Hugh Don wanted to get into her panty hose only marginally detracted from the nobility of his gesture.

"I wish you'd tell that to some of the boys," Hugh Don said, changing subjects as he made reference to his clientele. "I raised my prices last week just a little. I went up fifty cents for a six-pack of beer and a dollar for a bottle of liquor, and you'd think I'd been caught with everyone's wives or something! Hell, I haven't bumped my prices in five years! It's like they don't understand that I have to drive forty miles each way to buy the stuff."

"They just want to fuss," Early said.

"Well, they can get over it. Gasoline is higher. Beer is higher. Liquor is going straight out the damn roof. And payoffs? Don't even talk to me about that! They're more than ever. Every time the law comes in the door, it's at least a hundred bucks. Sometimes it's more, if one of 'em is keeping up a girlfriend or has a house payment coming due." He shook his head in disgust. "Plus, there's wear and tear on my car and upkeep on the building."

From the looks of the beer joint's exterior, Early assumed that the outlay for upkeep probably wasn't that significant, but he didn't want to interrupt his friend while he was on such an eloquent roll. Perhaps the bootlegger had been forced to make significant cuts in the landscaping budget due to financial considerations. Hugh Don continued his diatribe. "I tell you, if some of 'em think I'm making so damn much money, I'll just go get me a day job, and *they* can give bootlegging a try."

Hugh Don drained his Pabst and retrieved a fresh can. It wasn't the economics of the matter that had his mainspring wound so tight. He had forgotten where he had buried more money than most people would ever have. It was the principle of the situation that had him fired up. He was being maligned, and he didn't care for it. "You want another one?" he asked. Early nodded and received a fresh can of malt liquor.

"I'll tell you something else," Hugh Don continued. "The ones that holler the loudest are the ones that never pay their bills in the first damn place! Rascal Thompson is the worst. That cheap bastard told me that he just might have to go and take his business somewhere else. I told him *please* and offered him ten dollars to pay for his gas."

Rascal Thompson had not earned his nickname performing charitable works. Early had never cared for *him* much, either, but Rascal didn't seem to mind.

"That reminds me. I need to pay my bill."

"I ain't worried about *your* bill," Hugh Don said.

"Well, did he take his business and go somewhere else?" Early asked. This was mostly a rhetorical question, since Hugh Don Monfort also owned the only other beer joint in the county. He was the sole bootlegger in an otherwise dry county. Over the years, others had tried to follow in his footsteps, but these hopefuls had not been able to compete with Hugh Don's commitment to quality, dedication to service, or fair price. Nor had they been able to rise above his tendency to buy out the competition, or, barring that, to burn them out on moonless nights. Hugh Don had not attended the Harvard School of Business, and he had not read the works of either John Maynard Keynes or Adam Smith. But he had a strong grasp of the principles of economics, nonetheless, and he knew the value inherent in a monopoly.

"Shit. What do you think he did?"

"Rascal is a forgiving man. He believes in second chances."

"He believes in free beer. If he wasn't married to my daughter, I'd cut him off without another can." Hugh Don also knew the value of peace in the family.

"Maybe *she'll* cut him off," Early said.

"Maybe. I wish she'd cut him *loose*. I told her not to marry him in the first place, but she went ahead just to spite me. That girl has always been willful, just like her mama. Anyway, what were we talking about?"

"Your niceness."

"Right! Like I said, I am just too damn nice for my own good."

"It's a sickness with you," Early agreed.

"No, really." It seemed important to Hugh Don that Early understand the gravity of this affliction, the heroism inherent in living with the condition on a daily basis. "I'll prove it to you. Do you know Millie Donovan?"

"Sure. Everybody knows Millie."

"Just yesterday, I gave that poor girl five hundred dollars. Now, is *that* nice, or am I just full of shit?"

"That definitely qualifies as nice," Early agreed, choosing not to sully the moment or the gesture by mentioning that the two choices posited by Hugh Don were not mutually exclusive. "Is she in some kind of a bind?"

"She's in bad trouble. She's broke, and behind on the rent, and her and them kids are about to get themselves thrown out."

"Doesn't she rent from Stanley Newman? I thought he was sweet on her. Throwing her out is not the best way to get in her good graces."

"Naw, she used to rent from him. But he put the moves on her, and she told him to go screw himself, so he sold the house."

As Millie had recounted the tale to Hugh Don, she had remained Stanley's tenant for a little over four years. During that time, his unrequited love for her would ebb and flow depending on whether or not he had a girlfriend or several during those rocky periods when he and his wife weren't reading from the same page, or even from the same book. But Millie had always held him off, sometimes barely and once with a butcher knife. Then, finally, matters had come to a head, as matters have a tendency to do.

Stanley's wife, JoEllen Newman, acquired her fill of her husband's roving eye on the very evening that his paramour at the time, Nadine Montgomery, showed up at the Newman home inquiring as to the whereabouts of her loving man. The poor girl was barely nineteen, broke, six months pregnant, and quite surprised to learn that her boyfriend was married. JoEllen fronted the distraught woman bus fare back to her mama's house in Waycross plus some pocket money for the trip. Then she gave her husband the boot in the figurative sense as well as in the literal. He landed at Millie's house about two hours later—around midnight or so—drunk, remorseful at having been caught, and ready for one more run at the tenant of his dreams.

"Hey, Sweet Thing," he said. Millie had the safety chain latched and was viewing him through a two-inch field.

"Go home," she said sternly. "You smell like you've been drinking, the rent's not due for ten days, and I don't need you waking the kids up." She had spent a long day and was in no mood for Stanley Newman.

"I've left my wife for you," he confessed.

"That wasn't the smartest thing you've ever done, Stanley. Go somewhere and sleep it off. Then take a shower, shave, and go back home and apologize. Get down on your knees and ask her for another chance. The way I see it, that's your only hope." She started to close the door, but he pushed back until the chain caught.

"I want *you*."

"Wanting something and getting it are two different things. I want a nice house, a fine car, and some money in the bank. That ain't happening, either."

"I can make it happen."

"Like you did for JoEllen?"

"I love you, Millie. Let me in." He tried to reach in through the opening. She leaned on the door and pinned his wayward arm at the wrist. His hand flapped like a crippled bird.

"Stanley, if you don't leave now right now, I'll call the police." She let her weight off the door and he snatched his hand back out.

"This is my door," he said.

"Wrong. It's my door until the end of the month. I mean it about calling the police."

"Shit. Austell Poe won't do nothin' to me. I own him. I'm a big man in this town."

"Please. Just go home."

"This is your last chance. You better think about it! Once I step off this porch, you'll never hear from me again."

"Stanley, it's late and we're both tired. Everything will look brighter to you in the morning."

"I mean it! Once I'm gone, I'm gone."

"I believe you, Stanley. I just really don't care. Goodnight."

"Last call!" he said. She closed the door.

Stanley was as good as his word, and those words were the last he ever spoke to her. He sold the house the following week to a group of investors from Chattanooga who had no interest in Millie, her family, or her past problems with men. The fledgling real estate moguls decided to raise Millie's rent by two hundred dollars per month. This increase placed a huge strain on her budget. She couldn't pay, and three months later, she and her children were about to be evicted.

Early was angry on Millie Donovan's behalf. "You mean to tell me that Stanley Newman sold the house out from under her because she wouldn't sleep with him?" This was scurrilous behavior, even for a Newman.

"He did for a fact."

"Stanley Newman is one sorry excuse for a man," Early said.

"He makes his own daddy look like the Pope."

"What's Millie going to do?"

"She says she's gonna kill Stanley the next time she sees him. Says she's goin' to cut his pecker off and feed it to him, first. I would pay good money to see that and loan her my Buck knife, besides. But other than that, she don't really know. Austell Poe should have already put her and those kids out in

113

the front yard, but he can't bring himself to do it, so he has gone and lost the eviction papers. Again. The judge told him if he loses those papers one more time, that's not all he'll lose." Hugh Don shook his head. "I just hate it when Austell goes and does something decent. It messes up my entire world view."

Early nodded. He knew what Hugh Don meant. "I wonder if she even has a car," he said.

"Not one that runs. When I gave her the money, I told her I'd help her move once she found a place. But how's she going to find a house if she doesn't have a way to go? And how's she going to find one that she can afford? "

"I think I'll swing by and see her on the way home," Early said. "Maybe I'll bring her some groceries and offer her the use of the truck." He felt like he ought to do something.

"Her house is not on your way home," Hugh Don pointed out.

"I guess I'll take the scenic route," came Early's reply.

Chapter Eight

Millie Donovan was a local girl who had come up rough and fast under the indifferent care of Patsy and Stu Fields, a lackluster pair who were smart enough to figure out the mechanics of copulation but clueless as to what to do with the inevitable result of the exercise. They were not mean people, although they were a touch stupid. In point of fact, Patsy and Stu regarded their daughter with something akin to interest whenever they noticed her—which admittedly wasn't often— and they had no objection to feeding her when they remembered to. They merely held an extremely low standard for themselves, one that they managed to live up to most days. Patsy and Stu liked to arise late, smoke marijuana, copulate, eat food that did not require heat to prepare, and then smoke more marijuana before finishing off the day with more vigorous copulation. Millie had been an accidental by-product of this process, an unlucky roll of the dice.

Millie survived her childhood and adolescence through a combination of luck and the kindness of others, although she did receive a timely assist from on high just before her fourteenth birthday when a gnarled hackberry tree riddled with carpenter ants fell on top of the Ford Pinto her parents were copulating in at the time. Everyone knew that Pintos tended to blow up when hit from behind, but it turned out that they also exploded quite readily when struck by hackberry trees from above. Thus the Lord called Patsy and Stu home in a roar of red and orange flame, and Millie was mercifully left on her own.

She spent the remainder of her young years with Patsy's older sister, Aunt Jess. Aunt Jess worked at a bookstore because she loved books and the worlds they opened, and she worked at a bookstore in Memphis because that was as far as she had been able to travel from Sequoyah before her money ran out. Aunt Jess wasn't a natural surrogate parent, but she had a good heart, and that counted for a great deal. She had never wanted children and had not the first clue about raising one, but what she lacked in ability she made up for in effort, and luckily Patsy and Stu had only set the bar about ankle high to begin with.

In Millie's studied and expert opinion, her aunt was a large improvement over her departed parents in all areas of child-rearing: she removed the food from the cans and warmed it prior to mealtime, she paid the bills before strangers came to the front door to make inquiries, she did not smoke marijuana in front of her niece, and if she had to have sex—which Millie never actually verified—she apparently performed the act somewhere besides the living-room floor, which had been one of Patsy and Stu's favorite spots.

Time passed, and eventually Millie turned eighteen. She considered her options before deciding that she wanted to get a job, move out on her own, and have a little fun.

"You should go on to college," Aunt Jess said in her blunt manner. "Let me help you." They were having their conversation while sitting on a rusty bench in Tom Lee Park on the eastern bank of the Mississippi River. The pair liked to take lunch to that spot on a Sunday afternoon and watch as the barges and other river traffic made way against the clutching eddies. It wasn't the safest spot in Memphis for two women alone, but it was among the prettiest.

"I don't want to go to college right now," Millie replied. "I've been going to school for twelve years. I want to do something else for a while." A tug horn spoke in the foreground and echoed from the buildings behind them.

"You should go now, while you're young," Aunt Jess said. "It'll never be this easy again."

"I'll go back in a year or two. I promise."

"I was always going to go back to school, but I never made it. Something will come up. Then something else will. Before you know it, you'll be forty-five like me, and you'll still be intending to go back. You should do it now."

"Maybe I'll get married. Then my husband can send me to school."

"Now, there's a great idea. You saw what getting married did for your mother." Aunt Jess was better with books than she was with people, and when it came to people, she was better with women than she was with men. Still, she was nothing if not thorough, and she was not prone to taking much on faith. She had found herself a man once, and she had deliberately set out to discover what all the fuss and bother was about. And when all was said and done, she hadn't been much impressed.

His name was Mackey Wallach, and Aunt Jess had given him a good, solid six-month whirl before declaring the trial an abject failure and moving his belongings, his temperament, and his fragile ego onto the landing outside her apartment door. Simply put, it was her contention that the one thing he *had* been good for could be accomplished quicker, better, and with much less mess and bother without him. Her sister's subsequent marriage to Stu Fields had done nothing to soften her view that the vast majority of males were simply more trouble than they were worth.

"I'll think about going to college," Millie said to end the conversation. But she didn't think about it long. She wasn't willful so much as she was merely eighteen, and she was going to have to discover her own path and make her own mistakes. Her mind was made up about college, though, and when she finally grew weary of listening to her aunt's arguments, she moved out so she wouldn't have to listen any longer. She lived on her own in Memphis for a short time, but in truth she had never cared much for the big city, so she drifted back to Sequoyah, back to the small house that Patsy and Stu had left behind when they traveled the sacred road. She set up housekeeping, took a job at a fast food place over in Rome, and began to work hard at having fun.

She soon encountered a prime specimen of a man. He was older than her by a decade or so and went by the name of Switch Donovan. He was slim and wiry with a full head of blond, curly hair, handsome in the manner of a '50s matinee star. They first met at the takeout window of the restaurant where she worked. She handed out his sackful of Combo #5, their hands touched as he passed his ten-dollar bill to her, and she felt a small tingle at the contact. Then he asked for extra ketchup, and she noted with approval his use of *please* and *thank you.* Later that night when her shift ended, Switch was waiting for her in the parking lot. He had romance on his mind and onion rings on his breath, but the rituals of love do not always allow for proper dental hygiene. He swept Millie off her feet with his smooth talk and worldly ways, and a whirlwind courtship followed. Three months shy of her nineteenth birthday, Millie found herself cast in the role of happily married woman.

Switch Donavon was an itinerant brakeman—a boomer— on the Norfolk and Southern, although whether his name was because of the job or whether the job was because of the name, no one actually knew. But whichever it was, he was gone most of the time, ostensibly building freight trains car by car and riding them from one rail yard to another. The sporadic nature of his visits home came as a surprise to Millie, although perhaps they shouldn't have, given the nature of his work. He had told her that he was a railroad man before they married, and she should have inferred from this that there would be a certain amount of fluidity to his work schedule. It was true that she had only seen him once every three or four days during their short courtship, but she had assumed that he would be home every night once they were man and wife, and she was disappointed when this turned out not to be the case. Still, when he did come home, they made the most of their time together. Switch was an amorous man, and Millie was a willing young wife, or at least she was for starters.

He managed to impregnate her three times in five years, an impressive tally by anyone's yardstick. Millie was relatively content with her marriage at first, which was to say that most days she managed to hush the nagging voices in the back of her head, the ones that whispered in the quiet hours before the dawn that Aunt Jess had not been too far off the mark with her advice. Every time Switch left for another turn on the road, Little Aunt Jess—as Millie had come to call the subconscious critic of her lifestyle—murmured that she had settled for a pittance, that she had sold her future far too cheaply, that there was more available to her than keeping Switch Donovan's house and raising his babies. When these wayward doubts made their way to her consciousness, she stilled them because she had a great deal invested in them not being true. After all, she had a husband who declared that he loved her. And she had a clutch of fine, pretty children to raise and a little house to raise them in. What more could a girl want?

But as the years passed, smudges and drips began to appear on the canvas of her self-portrait. She began to wonder more and more if she hadn't made a mistake. She loved her children, and she still loved her husband—although not as much as she once had—but she was not happy with her life in general. She had not obtained all that she had sought, or even most of it, and she certainly wasn't having much fun. She was a practical woman, however, and she knew that she was three children too late for second thoughts, so she took her problem to her only confidante, Aunt Jess.

"You could just shoot him," Aunt Jess said from her end of the phone. In truth, this was not a new suggestion. Millie had heard it from her aunt before, on more than one occasion.

"I don't want to shoot him. I just want him to stay home more." Besides, she didn't own a pistol.

"Shoot him in the leg. That'll slow him up."

"Are you going to help me or not?"

"Okay. Okay. Here's what you need to do. Write out a list of everything you are unhappy about. Then arrange the list, prioritize it so that the things you are most discontented with come first. Once you have done all of that, begin with number one, and work your way down the list resolving the problems. And I mean, really, really solve them. Don't move on to number two until number one is totally taken care of, until you have put it to rest."

"That's good thinking. I'll try it."

"And if you change your mind about shooting him, call me back. I'll come watch the kids for you."

Once Millie prioritized her dissatisfactions, she was surprised to find that the entry that had worked its way to the top of the page was *loneliness*. Specifically, she missed her husband. No, that wasn't right. She had had quite enough of the Switch Donovan who rolled in every three or four days, shaved, showered, had sex, ate, laid some money on the coffee table, patted the kids on their heads, told her he loved her, and left. It was like she was running a combination boarding house, brothel, and daycare center, and she was tired of it.

Millie was actually lonely for a theoretical construct. She was missing the company of the husband she wished she had found, the man she had always imagined she would wed. That husband would talk to her, hold her hand sometimes, play with the children, and help her plan and execute their lives together. So she told Switch that she wanted him to be home more often, believing that if he were there, the feeling of closeness would manifest itself, and the quality of family life for all of them would improve. She asked Switch to consider leaving his job at the railroad. It was dangerous work, and it didn't pay well, or at least not well enough for her husband to be gone as much as he was. He could earn just as much over at the sawmill and be home with her and the kids every night.

Switch balked at this idea, but she continued to make her desires known, and that fact plus the blinding headaches that began to afflict her every four days or so—migraines that coincided with her husband's conjugal visits—convinced Switch to agree to at least think about a career change. His acquiescence seemed to cure the worst of her headaches, and these were kept at bay by Switch's continued reassurances that he was thinking about it, that he was looking at other careers, that he had talked to the foreman down at the sawmill, that he was considering going back to school. In an earnest attempt to help him make up his mind, Millie prayed earnestly on a daily basis for her husband to cease being a brakeman, and those prayers drifted skyward like mists rising from a slow, green river at the breaking of the day.

Finally, her appeals worked their way to the top of the heavenly prayer list, past the cancers and algebra tests and foxhole entreaties, and a sign was sent from above in the guise of a freshly oiled switch on a rainy day over at the three-mile-long rail siding near Ft. Payne, Alabama. The railroad tracks were wet due to inclement weather, the switch mechanism was swimming in oil due to the declining level of pride extant in the American workforce, Switch's boots were slick, and he was in a hurry to hump the car—and a bit hung over on top of all that. Before he knew it, Switch had slipped under the wheels of the grain hopper he was riding down the siding. He experienced a brief instant of hard pain followed by a blackness that had never known light.

Millie had always known that Switch was just fair as a provider, and that fact had been somewhat confusing to her, because she had thought that railroad men made good money, earned, in fact, about twice what her husband brought home every week to their little house in Sequoyah. But Switch had always insisted on handling the business and the money, and he tended toward defensiveness when questioned about their finances. So, since Millie was a thrifty person anyway, she and her children had learned over the years to live on what Switch provided without complaint, and not to inquire too closely lest the founder of the feast become cranky and pout.

It was a workable system, and as such it was in use in at least one other household in the vicinity. Switch's *other* wife, Adele, was just about as happy in her home over in Sand Valley, Alabama, as Millie was in Sequoyah, which was to say that she, too, thought that railroad men made a better living than her particular one did. As a matter of fact, Switch only earned about half of what she thought he ought to. And she, like Millie, wondered why her hard-working man couldn't be home more. But Adele was an economical homemaker who knew how to take the bitter with the sweet, how to cajole a dollar into performing the work of two, and she and her four children all worked together to make ends meet. They lived at the base of the mountain near the town of Sand Valley in a doublewide trailer that Switch had bought upon his marriage to Adele fifteen years previously, five years before his nuptials with Millie.

After Switch died, no one was left to keep these balls in the air, and they began to drop like hailstones in a summer storm as they fell to the earth, bouncing once or twice before melting slowly away. Switch's tapestry of lies had been complex almost beyond belief, but it had relied on him for its inspiration and central support, and when he passed beneath the wheels of that hopper, his stories crumbled.

He had a life insurance policy as part of his benefits with the railroad, but he had never changed the designated beneficiary from his mother to either of his wives. Mrs. Donovan—the matriarch—lived in Birmingham, but she had been out of touch with her only son since he ran away at seventeen. So she didn't know that Switch had been twice married, or that she had at least two daughters-in-law and a minimum of seven grandchildren scattered across two states. And since she was unacquainted with these facts, she was unaware of the need to share the proceeds. But, to be fair, she most likely would not have, anyway, had she known, since she was not considered to be a generous woman by anyone who had the misfortune to know her.

When Switch had been among the living, he had arranged for both of his house payments to be deducted from his pay-check. Actually, the bank had insisted on this method of repay-ment before they would agree to extend the privilege of a mortgage on either domicile. But now that he was a card-carrying member of the legions of the fallen, each of his wives discovered that keeping their family's heads out of the weather was going to be an issue. Additionally, Switch had let the mortgage insurance on both of his residences lapse, so Millie found herself with three children, no husband, no income, and a house payment due on the tenth of the month, and with the exception of the number of children, Adele found herself in a similar situation.

Overall, though, Adele was in better financial shape than her junior partner. She had been the first wife, the alpha wife, so to speak, and she was the one whom Switch had told the railroad about. So Adele and her four youngsters were eligible for survivor's benefits and worker's compensation, which allowed them to live in a style to which they were not previously accustomed, although they became acclimated to their higher standard of living fairly quickly. Getting himself run over by that grain hopper had been just about the best thing that Switch had ever done for Adele's family, and after they got over the initial shock and grief associated with the loss—a process that was hastened considerably upon Adele's discovery that a whole other family was going through that same process less than forty miles away—mere words could not convey how much they appreciated his sacrifice for the greater good.

Millie was afforded the opportunity to meet her co-wife at Switch's funeral. There were twenty witnesses to that solemn event: Millie and her brood, Adele and her progeny, six rented pall bearers rounded up at the Salvation Army and outfitted in the thrift shop, the funeral director, a preacher, two grave-diggers, and a representative from the Norfolk and Southern who was not in a position to confirm or deny much, including the existence of the railroad, the day of the week, or whether or not he was actually there. After the ceremony, the bereaved widows spoke briefly while their children roamed among the monuments like sad banshees wandering the melancholy paths of eternity.

"You were married to Switch, too?" Millie asked. They eyed one another warily, like two prizefighters facing each other during the moment just after the handshake and right before the bell. Adele nodded. She looked like Millie would look in five years, and she always would. They could have been sisters, older and younger.

"How long were you married?" Millie continued. It was a morbid kind of curiosity, but she had to know.

"I was married to the lyin' bastard for fifteen years," Adele answered. "How about you?" She, too, needed the truth.

"We were married for ten."

"Are those young'uns his?"

"Every one of 'em."

"They're good-lookin' kids."

"Thanks. So are yours. Do they belong to him, too?"

"Every one of 'em. Looks like I don't need to tell you that Switch liked to screw and he didn't believe in rubbers."

"Oh, I remember. He told me he was a Catholic, and he said that if he wore a rubber he would go to hell. When we first got married, I didn't mind because I wanted children, anyway. Once we hit three in five years, though, I sort of had to take matters into my own hands." She gave a rueful smile and a small shrug before continuing. "Maybe the fact that I've been secretly on the pill for the last five years will get him there, anyway. To hell, I mean."

Millie wasn't sure why she had shared these details. It was as if she were talking to a fellow survivor of some large disaster, an earthquake, perhaps, or a tsunami. As each of Switch's lies had revealed itself over the days of mourning, her regard for her former husband had dropped a notch or two, and he hadn't been that highly placed on the pedestal to begin with. Her feelings for him had slipped from vestigial love to disgust with herself for being so gullible, so that by the time of the funeral, Switch was little more than the warden in a bad dream of a decade-long prison term. "I hope it does, anyway. I'd like to give *him* a surprise for a change." Millie had been wishing her departed husband a long and bad eternity for a little over three days now. It was the least she could do.

"He was funny like that about birth control," Adele answered in kind. "It seems like he would have been more worried about dancing in the fires of hell because he was a cheatin' son of a bitch who had two wives. I'm not a real big churchgoer—never have been—but to me, it seems like being married to two women at the same time is a lot bigger sin than wearing a condom. You know what I think? I think he just didn't like to wear them, and he made all that goin' to hell stuff up to cover his tracks. Anyway, you notice that my youngest is nine? After four kids in six years, I sorta figured out like you did that what he didn't know wouldn't hurt either one of us, so I started takin' the pill, too. With any luck at all, maybe he ended up in hell twice. Once for you, and once for me."

Adele chuckled at the thought. She seemed to have moved past the stunned phase of their joint and peculiar situation as well.

"I'll tell you something," Millie said. "I think maybe somewhere deep down I always knew that there was another woman. Too many things just didn't add up. Looking back now, I feel pretty stupid. I should have seen it. I should have at least asked a few more questions. I didn't, though. Maybe I just didn't want it to be true, so I hid my head in the sand. Anyway, I used to sometimes wonder how it would be if I ever came face to face with *the other woman*. You know, like that big scene they always put in the movies." She smiled ruefully. "But now I'm standing next to you, and it turns out that *I'm* the other woman." She shook her head. "You must really hate me for marrying your husband. I'm sorry. I didn't know. I swear I wouldn't have, if I had known."

"Ain't this some shit?" Adele asked as she offered Millie a Marlboro. "Lord, girl, I don't hate you. How can I hate someone for doing the exact same thing that I did? Sure, I married him first, but hell, you didn't know about me. And I never knew about you, either. But I sorta wondered sometimes, too. And you know what? Don't neither one of us know if we're all there is. For all we can tell, there might be two or three more wives scattered up and down the main line, bless their hearts, and ten or fifteen more kids, poor things. Think about it. How often did he come home to your house?"

"Once or twice a week."

"Same here. So, where do you think he was all the rest of the time? Sleeping in the yard foreman's shack? I doubt it, unless the foreman was a forewoman. We could be the tip of the iceberg." She laughed bitterly. "He wasn't worth killing,

Raymond L. Atkins

but if I had him here right now, I'd kill him anyway." She lit her smoke. "Sorry, no-good bastard," she muttered.

"I'd help you," Millie replied. "My aunt told me to shoot him years ago."

"Your aunt is a smart woman."

"I should have listened."

"And guess where I'd shoot him first?"

"Same place I would," Millie said. They smoked in silence a moment. Then she spoke again, but quietly, as if she were talking to herself. "I'm glad he's dead." She took a deep drag from her borrowed cigarette and let it out slowly. Her statement had surprised her, but it was the truth. Switch had betrayed her, had made a mockery of the decent life she had tried to build on top of the ruined foundations of her own childhood. Everything he had ever said to her was now suspect. His love for her had been a sham. His life was a lie, and that made her life a lie by association. And now he had left her with three children to raise and no money to raise them with. Being run over by the grain hopper had been too good for him.

"Honey, everyone who ever knew him is glad he's dead," Adele responded. With five years seniority, Adele was certainly entitled to her opinion, and she wasn't shy about sharing it. "You're glad, I'm glad, the railroad's glad, his sorry-ass mama's *real* glad, all them kids over there are glad, or at least, they will be soon enough." She took one more puff before flipping the butt into Switch's grave. It landed on his casket and burned slowly on the lid, an erstwhile candle lit in honor of a philandering scoundrel. "He was the horniest son of a bitch I ever knew," she eulogized, "but he ain't getting' too damn much now, by God." She seemed to draw satisfaction from that fact. The two women were quiet for a moment, each with her private thoughts. Then Millie spoke.

"I don't know what I'm going to do. He was a lying bastard, but at least he made the house payment." She took a final drag from her cigarette as well. Then she sighed and tossed it into the grave. It came to rest beside Adele's on their departed husband's coffin. "I've got children to feed, and I'm not sure how I'm going to do it. We were just getting by, as it was." She rubbed the back of her neck.

"You and me are sort of in the same boat," Adele said. "I'm not sure what my next step is, either." She took a half pint of Jim Beam from her old brown pocketbook, unscrewed the cap, and took a sip. Then she offered a taste to Millie, who wasn't much of a drinker but who took it anyway. It had been a long week. The liquor burned a bit on the way down, but it seemed to fortify her. "Switch wasn't much," Adele continued, "and that was bad luck we shared. Some women find good men. We each found half of an asshole. He made fools out of us, and we could have done plenty better than we did. But the good part about not losing much is that he won't be that hard to replace. We'll find men—good men, or at least better than we found before—and we'll be all right. We just need to be sure we find two different men this time. Or if we settle on the same one again, we need to make damn sure he's rich and he's sterile."

"You can have him," Millie replied. "I think I might be through with men."

"You might change your mind about that."

"Anything's possible."

To her credit, Millie hung on financially for several months after Switch's interment. She began caring for the children of several of the working mothers in her neighborhood, and because of her hard work and her frugality, she started to believe that she might be able to keep her house. Then the bank sent a letter informing her that the balloon payoff for the second mortgage was due. This was news to Millie because she hadn't realized that she had a second mortgage. Millie explained her situation, and the bank sympathized with her plight but said their hands were tied, that the money had been lent and must be repaid. The house was eventually repossessed and was bought on the courthouse steps by Gilla Newman's son, Stanley, to add to his portfolio of rental properties. He allowed Millie to stay on in her own home, but now she was a renter, not a buyer.

After she became a widow, Millie began to receive assistance in the form of small checks mailed to her by Aunt Jess, thirty dollars here and fifty there as she could spare it. One time Aunt Jess even won five hundred dollars on a scratch-off lottery ticket and sent the entire windfall to her niece. But then she was killed in a car accident, and Millie was left with no family besides her own children. As is often the case among the living, Millie hadn't realized how much her aunt meant to her until she was gone.

Millie was an attractive woman, and, unfortunately for her, the new landlord thought so, too. So even though Stanley Newman was a married man with two children at home, he took a shine to his new tenant and began to make overtures. Millie resisted his advances for a variety of reasons, any of which on its own should have been sufficient. Most important to her was the fact that Stanley was a married man. She had been within spitting distance of two married men in her life— her father, Stu, and her half-husband, Switch—and neither had instilled in her a desire to risk getting too near a third, lest unfortunate circumstance occur. Millie was a compassionate person who would not willingly put anyone through the pain she had suffered. She had been appalled to find herself the unintentional other woman, and she would never cast herself in that role again. And finally, as she had indicated to Adele, Millie wasn't particularly interested in securing a replacement man. Admittedly, she had only tried the one, but she had to say that it hadn't worked out that well. So she worked a long day, every day, caring for a pile of children—her own as well as those of other women—and when bedtime came, the only horizontal activity she was interested in was sleep.

Stanley Newman was stubborn, however, and he was not accustomed to taking *no* for an answer. Using a line as old as philandering itself, he told her that he was in the process of leaving his wife. He told her that they had been unhappy and that the divorce preliminaries had begun.

"I think I love you, Millie," he had said.

"You have a perfectly good wife at home," Millie replied. "It's a fine, big home, and your wife's a nice woman. You have two beautiful children with her. What you need to do is go there right now and love her. That's what you signed on to do when you married her." They were facing each other through her locked screen door. It wasn't much protection, but it was all she had at the moment.

"She doesn't understand me," he whined, falling back seamlessly on additional time-honored material.

"Well, Stanley, it's a shame that she doesn't understand you. But I do." She had known exactly what was up when she looked out the window and saw him standing there, freshly shaven with a bouquet of roses. Anyone who had spent any time at all in Sequoyah knew that Stanley Newman was a womanizer, just like his father before him.

"How would you like a rent reduction?" he asked, changing tactics.

"You sweet-talking man! I would love a rent reduction. Air conditioning would be great, too, and a refrigerator that won't let the milk go sour in three days would be amazing. But I won't screw you for any of it."

"C'mon Millie. Don't be this way. I just want to talk."

"I don't have to talk to you, Stanley. I just have to pay you rent." Thus she managed to keep her landlord at bay. And she kept the lights turned on, the water flowing from the tap, shoes on her children's feet, and food in their bellies. It was a hard lot, some days, but it was the lot she had drawn, and she did not often complain.

Chapter Nine

On his way to Millie Donovan's house, Early stopped at the Jottem Down Store in Sequoyah and picked up three sacks of groceries. He bought flour, eggs, milk, beans, ground beef, two big boxes of cereal, cans of hash and beef stew, a pound of coffee, and candy and other assorted goodies for the kids. He also obtained some cash. He had a tender spot in his heart for people in trouble.

"You got a sweet tooth today, Early?" asked Webby Barrier, proprietor of the Jottem Down Store, as he gestured at the candy. Webby was a hunched, warty man with wispy hair, watery pale-green eyes, and a web of skin between each thumb and forefinger. If a frog could turn into a grocer, it would favor Webby Barrier.

"The candy's for Millie Donovan's kids. So's all the rest of this stuff." A thought occurred to Early. "How much is Millie's bill?" As was the case with most rural storekeepers in the South, Webby let many of his customers buy on the credit until payday rolled around. But sometimes paydays were delayed by circumstance, and if everyone who owed a dollar on the book came in and paid up, Webby could look forward to spending the remainder of his warty years in relative luxury.

"Lord, Early, to be honest, I don't even know how much she owes. She would pay it if she could, but she can't. She just can't seem to get a break, and I don't have it in me to let them children go hungry." Webby shrugged, looking embarrassed.

Early was touched by his kindness. "Try to get it totaled the best you can, Webby. Make a guess about the stuff you left off, too. The next time I come in, I'll settle it up."

"It's pretty big."

"Doesn't matter. Get it ready. I'll be back in a day or two to take care of it."

Early left the Jottem Down and drove slowly through town. He wasn't stalling, exactly, but he was thinking over his course of action. He had been pumped up when he left Hugh Don Monfort's beer joint, but now that he was in the vicinity of Millie Donovan's house, he was hesitant. He hadn't seen Millie in some time, and although he was certain she needed the help, he wasn't so sure how she would react to him barging in with groceries and cash.

He came to the stop sign at the intersection of Railroad Street and Main and sat, drumming his fingers on the wheel. He remained a moment, stretching his neck this way and that to relieve the pent-up tension. Then he took a deep breath, let it out slowly, and made his left turn. He was thinking too much, he decided. Either she would welcome the help, or else she would run him off. Either way, he was going to make the gesture. He drove to the end of the dead-end street. Millie's was the last house on the right.

Upon his arrival, Early was greeted by a yard full of children. Millie's three were there as well as a selection of kids she was babysitting. Early was immediately able to pick out the Donavan children from the crowd. Switch had been a rogue, but he had been a handsome one, and when his handsome, roguish genes had combined with Millie's good-hearted, attractive ones, they made pretty children.

Early got out of his truck and was immediately surrounded by the younger children in the yard. The oldest girl, fourteen-year-old Lisa Marie, was obviously in charge, and she attempted to keep order as he handed out Moon Pies, Baby Ruth candy bars, and cartons of chocolate milk to general acclaim. Once the children were happily snacking, he waded through the pack with the remaining two bags for Millie. She met him on the porch, looking surprised. She also looked like she'd been crying. Her eyes were red and her cheeks puffy.

"Early? Early Willingham? My God, how long has it been?" She smiled tentatively. "It's not that it isn't good to see you, but you're about the last person in the world I was expecting to drive up." She took his hand. "Actually, I was sort of thinking Austell Poe might be coming for a little visit."

Early grimaced unintentionally. "Hey, Millie. Hugh Don told me about your troubles. I thought I'd bring the kids some candy and see how you were doing."

She averted her eyes and took one of the sacks from him. They went inside.

"Set it on the table, Early," she said. He did as he was told before taking a good long look at his hostess, whom he hadn't seen up close since before her husband left suddenly for parts unknown. She was about twenty years his junior, a compact person who stood no more than five-and-a-half feet tall. She had green eyes, short black hair, a nose with a bit of an upturn, and a pretty smile that used her entire face as its canvas.

Early had known her all of her life. He had been friends with both of her parents back in high school, and he had stood at their wedding. Later, Patsy and Stu had fallen out of favor with him over what he considered to be their neglect of their own child, but Millie had still attended Camp Redemption many times on the Early and Ivey free plan. To Early, she was like the daughter he never had. Later still, after her folks died, she had worked at the camp as a counselor for four of her teen years. She had been a good camp counselor, although she did have a tendency to try to miss the occasional Sunday morning preaching at the chapel.

But time had written its tale on her in bold strokes. She still had that pretty smile, but now it was a touch weary, a smile that seemed to remember how but not always why. After ten years of marriage to Switch Donovan followed by five years of penury that included fending off the occasional advance by Stanley Newman, Early thought it was a miracle that she bothered to smile at all.

"How are you doing?" he asked. He knew it was a stupid question, but he had to break the ice somehow. Millie started to speak but found herself unable to. Tears began to stream down her cheeks, and before Early could think of any words of comfort, she buried her face in his shirt and began to cry as they stood there in her kitchen. She was wracked with hard, bitter sobs, and Early gently patted her head and said "There, there," letting her get it all out. He didn't know what else to do. Finally, after several minutes, she slowed to sniffles and gulps. When she backed away, there was a wet circle as big as a pie plate on his shirt. He handed her his handkerchief.

"I'm so sorry," Millie said, sniffing. "I've never done that before. I didn't cry when Patsy and Stu got blown up. I didn't cry when Switch got run over by that grain car, and I damn sure didn't cry at his funeral, although I did sniffle a bit when I found out about his financial arrangements. I didn't even cry when Aunt Jess died in the car wreck. Not in front of people, anyway." She dabbed absently at the spot under his pocket. "I don't know what's wrong with me. It's been happening all day. I guess you could say that, after all these years, I've had just about all I can take. I didn't mean to mess up your shirt."

"Don't worry about the shirt," Early said. " Dry your eyes and talk to me. Tell me what's going on. Tell me how I can help."

Millie took a moment to finish composing herself. Then she sat and gestured at a chair for Early. "How am I doing?" she said as she took a chair across from him. "Not all that hot. I have three children and no husband, and I didn't have much of one even back when I had one. I'm broker than I've ever been, which is saying something, because I swear it seems like I've been allergic to money my whole life. I wouldn't sleep with my landlord, so now I have to move. I don't have a car that runs, or any relatives, or any place to go. There's no food in the house except what you just brought, but at least now I can give the kids some supper without begging Webby Barrier for more credit. That man's a saint."

Early nodded. He couldn't argue with that.

Just then, a child ran in, one of the many that Millie kept for others. Early didn't recognize him and wondered who he belonged to. He had scraped his elbow and was howling like a coonhound on the scent. Millie took him in her arms and kissed him where it hurt. Then she rocked him in her lap a moment until she had made it better. Finally, she sent him on his way. Early found himself wishing she could solve her own troubles so easily.

"Whose kid is that?" Early asked. He thought he could recognize most of the children in town, but this boy rang no bells.

"He's Sarah Blansit's nephew from Gulfport. He's just visiting for a couple of weeks."

"That explains it," he said. "Sorry. Go ahead."

"I did have five hundred dollars that Hugh Don Monfort gave me, but I offered that to my new landlords as a back payment on the rent, to try to buy some time." Mille shook her head. She got up and rummaged through the grocery bags he'd brought. "They took the money, and after they wrote out a receipt and thanked me, they told me I was still in arrears, and they are tossing me out on my ass anyway. It's not that I didn't owe them the money. I owed them every bit of it and a lot more besides. It's just that I got my hopes up when they took a partial payment. I let myself believe that things were going to be okay for a little while, that maybe I had some time to come up with a plan." At that moment, she found the two hundred dollars that Early had tucked in the sack, and she

Raymond L. Atkins

began to cry again. "But I'm out of time," she said, "and things are not going to be okay."

"Please don't cry," Early pleaded. He had not intended to be there when she found the money, and he had certainly not wanted to upset her with the gift. Crying females were a problem for Early. When he heard one, he became anxious. His head would begin to hurt and his palms to sweat, and he would do most anything to make a sobbing woman stop. It was a compulsion.

"Damn it," she said. "I'm sorry, Early. I can't help it, and I don't know what I'm going to do. I'm so tired of living like this. I'm not a bad person. I don't think I've ever done a really bad or hurtful thing in my life. So why does it just keep coming?"

She crossed her arms on the table, leaned her head forward, and bawled for all she was worth. Early sat with his jaw clenched and watched helplessly. She was in a tough spot, a tenuous situation that the groceries and cash he had brought could not even begin to address. Even the larger sum that Hugh Don provided hadn't done her a bit of good. As Millie had just pointed out, she wasn't a bad person. It was true that she had the worst luck he had ever seen, and her taste in men was worse than her luck. But she didn't deserve a lifetime of misery because she was luckless and a poor judge of character.

Suddenly, Early knew how to make her stop crying. The idea had been tickling at the edges of his consciousness since he had left Hugh Don Monfort's beer joint, and now it came into full focus.

"Millie," he said gently. She didn't acknowledge him. She was there in the room with him, but she was also far, far away. "Millie," he repeated, "look at me. Please. I have something I need to talk to you about."

"What?" she asked in a near whisper as she slowly raised her head. She seemed distracted, almost angry, as if her guest

137

had intruded upon an interlude of grief, a sad and private moment.

"I want you to hear what I'm going to tell you. Are you listening?"

She nodded, and then she looked him in the eyes. "Go ahead," she said.

"I'm going to come back tomorrow with the camp bus. We'll load up your kids and your things, and we'll move you."

She shook her head and sighed with despair. "Early, you are a good man, and I appreciate the effort, but it's like I told you. I don't have anywhere to go."

"Yes, you do. I want you to come up to the camp. We'll move you and the kids into one of the cabins. You can stay as long as you need to. Stay until you get back on your feet. Stay until next year if it suits you. You've spent I don't know how many summers out there, and you know that valley like the back of your hand. You used to love it there, and you can't tell me you don't think it would be a good place for your kids to live now. For a while, at least."

Millie looked at Early in confusion.

"What are you saying?" she asked. "Do you want me to come be a counselor again?"

"No. Not a counselor. Business is bad, and we're not having camp this year, so the place is pretty much deserted. I just want to help you and your kids and give you a place to live."

Millie looked at him warily now. He could see that the idea held appeal for her, and it gave her hope for the first time in weeks. But at the same time, it looked like she thought the proposition was too good to be true. It was almost as if she were afraid for the idea to be real.

"People don't just help," she said cautiously.

"Sometimes they do."

"What will Miss Ivey say?"

"Ivey's the one who sent me." In a way, that was the truth. Ivey had placed them both under a divine mandate to help the needy. And if a woman with three kids who was about to be evicted didn't qualify as needy, then Early needed to buy a dictionary, because he wasn't sure what the word meant.

"I'll be back in the morning," he said. "We can get it all done in a day. Which cabin do you want?"

"Early, I can't let you do this."

"Why can't you? Don't be a hero. I have plenty of room and you need somewhere to go. It won't cost me one thin dime to have you and the kids stay in a building I already own."

Actually, Early figured that the proposition would end up costing him a fair amount over the long haul, starting with the grocery bill down at Webby's, but the Lord loves a cheerful giver, or at least, that was the rumor that Ivey was spreading. "Anyway," he said, "I had already decided to move *some* woman and her kids into the camp, so it might as well be you and yours. I won't have to learn so many names this way. Now tell me which cabin you want."

She didn't answer for a moment. She looked at him again, and this time Early saw relief, gratitude, and hope. He also saw a trace of shame, but they had plenty of time to work on that. Then she dropped her eyes.

"I always liked Nathanael," she said quietly. "It's nice and large, and it has the best fireplace." She looked up and smiled a bleak smile. "That deer head hanging above the mantle is kind of creepy, though. No matter where you go in the room, the deer looks at you."

"He does that because he has a bad attitude. He didn't really want to end up over the mantle." A memory flitted by, and Early smiled. "I remember running you out of Nathanael one Sunday morning." He had been making his rounds and had discovered a small flock of counselors conducting an impromptu round of spin the bottle in front of said preserved mammal, which had indeed cast its glassy, baleful gaze upon them all. "You didn't seem to mind the deer head then."

"No, he was looking at us the whole time, and I minded it. But I was busy at the moment, and Miss Ivey's preaching was worse than the deer head, anyway. Come to think of it, she was kind of like that deer. Whenever she preached, it always seemed like she was looking right at me."

"She was looking at you because she thought she knew what you'd been up to. Still, Ivey's preaching wasn't so bad."

"If it wasn't so bad, how come you made your rounds even when everyone was in chapel?"

"A man can't be too careful when he's in the Bible camp business," he replied with dignity. "The world holds you to a higher standard. Anyway, Nathanael it is. And you know, that deer is an heirloom. He was killed by one of my long gone kinfolks so that several other long gone kinfolks could eat. But I'll take him down if it'll make you happy."

It did look a little creepy, come to think of it, and he didn't want to scare her children. They were probably jumpy enough already due to the changes going on in their young lives. He hoped that a new, better time was in store for them. He wondered briefly how Ivey would feel about the additional tenants but figured he'd find out soon enough, since his first stop after he left Millie's place would be the Washed in the Blood and the Fire Rapture Preparation Temple, where he would collect his sister. He stood up. "I'll see you in the morning," he said.

Millie walked over and gave him a hug. "Thank you," she said.

"It's nothing," he responded. Then he stepped onto the porch and down the steps, worked his way through the mob of children, and climbed into the truck. He waved from the cab and started the motor. Millie stood on the porch and looked appraisingly at her unexpected benefactor. Then she smiled and called to her children.

Early made slow work of the drive to the church, hoping as the miles sauntered by that Ivey had not received any countermanding orders from on high while he was gone to town. The die was cast, and the poor were about to be among them. He knew in his heart that he had done a fine thing by helping Millie, and the warmth of her gratitude lingered with him.

He intended to tackle the subject of the impending short-term adoption of Millie and her family just as soon as Ivey got into the truck, but his plans changed abruptly when he arrived at the sanctuary. Ivey was standing in the parking lot when he pulled up, which was unusual. She was generally the last one out of the building. Several cars were still parked on the gravel, indicating that the weekly deacon's meeting was not yet concluded. Early had a sense of premonition. He stopped the truck next to his sister. She snatched the door open, hopped in, and slammed it hard behind her.

"Take me home!" she said, clearly agitated.

"What's wrong?"

"I can't talk about it." She was fussing with her pocketbook, smoothing the wrinkles from her dress hem, and otherwise fidgeting.

"Try." Early shifted the transmission into park, but he left the truck running with the air conditioning on high.

"'How long shall I bear with this evil congregation, which murmur against me?'" she said. "Numbers 14:21."

"Ivey, damn it, I don't want to hear any verses right now. Tell me what the trouble is. Why were you standing in the parking lot? Why aren't you inside with the deacons?"

"Saying *damn it* is a sin. And I quit the church. I'm not a deacon anymore, so there's no sense in me being at the deacon's meeting. Now you know what's wrong. Take me home."

"Now I know what happened, but you still haven't told me what's wrong. What do you mean you quit the church?" Ivey would no more willingly quit the church than she would voluntarily cease to breathe.

"Early, I clearly remember teaching you how to speak English. I quit the church. I left. I am no longer a member of the Washed in the Blood and the Fire Rapture Preparation Temple."

"Why?" Early was perplexed. Ivey had been a founding member. She had bought and donated the little piece of ground where he'd stopped the truck, and she had literally wielded a hammer and saw alongside her fellow parishioners to help build the church. She was the life's blood of the congregation.

Ivey sighed. Then she began speaking quickly, as if she wanted to get it all said before she lost her nerve. "Avis Shropshire came to second preaching today. He picked a good day for it, because the Word was heavy on Brother Rickey. It was like the man was on fire, I tell you, and about halfway through the sermon, Avis got a strong dose of the Spirit. He fell out and talked in three or four tongues, including one I've never even heard. I swear, Early, if I ever saw a man heaven-possessed—and I have—it was Avis! And you should have seen him after the service. He was so happy. It was like the weight of the world had been lifted from him. He said he had felt the hand of Jesus during Brother Rickey's sermon. He said he was going to bring his whole family back next week, and that they would join the church and start tithing. He said he had heard the call, and that he had found his church home. I was so proud for him! It was a blessing for all of us to see Avis receive the Lord." She frowned. "But then at the deacon's meeting later, after the congregation had gone home, Brother Rickey called for a vote to close the membership rolls to new

142

members. And the vote was six to one to close them. I was the only one to vote against the idea."

"What was that all about?"

"You know good and well what it was, and it makes me sick to say it. Avis Shropshire is a Negro man, and he's married to a Mexican girl. Brother Rickey said we had gotten along fine without *them*—meaning Mexicans and Negroes, I suppose—at the church for a long time, and he reckoned we could just keep on getting along fine without them. He said he had nothing against them personally—which was a lie—but they had their own churches to go to, and that was where God wanted them to go. That made me mad, so I asked him to show me the verse that said that white people shouldn't go to church with Mexicans and Negroes. He looked at me a minute, and he didn't say a word. So I quoted Romans to *him*. I said, 'For there is no difference between the Jew and the Greek: for the same Lord over all is rich unto all that call upon him. For whosoever shall call upon the name of the Lord shall be saved.'"

"Good for you."

"It didn't do a bit of good! It was like he didn't even hear me. Brother Rickey told me that Avis Shropshire wasn't a Greek or a Jew. Then he just turned his back and called for the vote. Do you know why he did that?"

"Why?"

"Because that's all he could do. There is nothing in the Word about not letting Negroes and Mexicans join this church! I know it, and Brother Rickey does too!"

Early just shook his head. Brother Rickey was one of those mean and stupid people Charnell had talked about. "God must like stupid people," he said, "because he sure made plenty of them." It was one of his favorite sentiments, and unlike Brother Rickey, Early believed he could back up his point of view with Scripture.

"Hush," she said. But she didn't disagree.

"I'm sorry, Ivey. I know how much the church means to you."

"I love this little church, but what they're doing isn't right, and I can't be a part of it. I told them that, and they just smiled at me like I was simple and went ahead and voted anyway."

"You know what? I bet Brother Rickey's vote is against the law. I bet they can't do it."

"That's not the point. It probably is against the law, or it ought to be if it isn't. But it's all ruined for Avis now. That's the thing. Would you want to go back to a church after it had voted you down? Would you want your wife and children to go there after they had been told that they weren't good enough? Avis got the Spirit right there in that sanctuary. He got it preached into him by Brother Rickey and fell out right there on that floor. Now he's going to find out that he's not welcome."

"See, this is the very reason why I don't go to church," Early said, as if a point long contested had finally been clarified.

"You don't go to church because you'd rather drink beer with Hugh Don Monfort."

"Well, that too," he admitted. Then he noticed that something was missing. "You forgot your covered dish." His sister was always at the front of the line when it came to bringing food to an event or a gathering, but it wasn't like her to let a dish get away. She had once tracked down and recovered a missing Tupperware cake carrier that had inadvertently made its way to Chillicothe, Ohio.

"I'll just leave it," she said quietly. "I don't want to go back in there and see them again. Let's just go home."

Early knew she must be upset if she were willing to leave her Blue Willow tureen. It had been owned by their mother, and by her mother before that.

"I'll go get it," he said, opening his door.

"Don't you dare get into a fight in church," Ivey cautioned.

"I won't."

"Promise?"

"I promise. I'm just going to get the dish. I won't be but a minute." He walked across the parking lot and through the door. Up at the front of the church, Brother Rickey Lee sat in the first pew, and with him were his five brothers in racial purity, Trace McBrayer, Jackson Dillon, Palmer Strand, Odell Cooper, and Arthur Haney. They all looked slightly guilty, as if they had been caught talking about someone. Someone like Ivey, for example, or maybe Avis Shropshire. Brother Rickey stood and smiled, but it was a Judas smile. He walked toward Early with his hand extended.

"Brother Early!" he said. "It's so good to see you in the house of the Lord." He stood there with his palm extended for a long moment, waiting for his guest to shake with him. Finally he seemed to understood that no clasp of brotherhood was forthcoming, and he stuck his hand into his pocket.

"Don't get too teary-eyed about it," Early growled. "I'm just here for Ivey's crockery."

"Oh, yes, the poor thing forgot it. I'm afraid she's losing a little ground, bless her heart. Still, old age comes to us all."

"It doesn't necessarily have to," Early said. Then he remembered his pledge to his sister. "Rickey, I've never had anything against you until today. You weren't exactly my cup of tea, but live and let live has always been my motto. But now I have something against you. You've upset Ivey, and I don't like it when people upset my sister. She told me why she left the church, and I'm surprised she didn't give you a good whack on the way out the door."

"Brother Early, as God is my witness, I didn't mean to upset Sister Ivey, and I don't mean to upset you, either. Things just sort of got out of hand. I would be more than happy to step out and apologize to her, if you think it would help. I already tried to tell her I was sorry once, but she wouldn't accept my apologies."

"She does tend to hold a grudge," Early allowed. "Don't waste your time going out to the truck. It won't do you any good. Maybe you can try her again in a couple of years, once this has all blown over. In the meantime, stay away from her. I mean that. And what the hell are you talking about, saying she's losing ground? She hasn't lost an inch in thirty years."

"Well, she ran out of here a while ago like she was on fire. She said she was quitting the church! Over Avis Shropshire, of all things! Of course, we won't hold her to that. She's always welcome here. But I thought her reaction might be a sign that she's getting a little confused."

Early really wanted to smack Brother Rickey, but a promise was a promise, and Ivey would be bound to find out. "Rickey, let me tell you how I want it to be."

"Please, call me Brother Rickey."

"I don't have any brothers. I do, however, have a sister. A damn fine one. And you aren't allowed to say anything bad about her. And I'm not just talking about today. I mean *ever*. She's a better person than you can even imagine, better by far than you and your running buddies over there, and I won't have you speaking ill of her, or telling lies, or spreading gossip. This is your only warning."

"I've already told you that we want her back."

"Is she welcome to bring Avis Shropshire with her?" Early asked.

"I think she may have misunderstood what we were saying about Avis."

"So Avis and his family are welcome here next week? That's great. I'll be sure to tell her."

"Well, no, not exactly. We all just felt that he might be happier among his own kind."

"Happier among his own kind? You mean human beings?"

"Early, I—"

"Americans?"

"What we meant was—"

"Georgians?"

"No."

"Sawmillers?" Early pressed, referring to Avis's job as a bucking-saw operator at the local lumber mill.

"No, you see—"

"Yeah, I see. I see just fine. Where's Ivey's bowl?" Brother Rickey silently pointed. Early retrieved the tureen. Then he walked back over to share a thought with the preacher. "Avis Shropshire is a big man. I don't know how you were planning on breaking the news to him, but don't worry yourself. He's a good friend of mine, and I'll tell him all about it when I see him in town." He smiled unpleasantly at Brother Rickey. "Are you a betting man, Rickey? Because I'm ready to put up hard cash that as soon as Avis hears that his pretty wife and his two little boys aren't good enough for the likes of you, he'll be down here wiping up the floor of the sanctuary with your sanctimonious ass."

"There's no call for that kind of talk!"

"I think there is. And remember what I said about Ivey. If I hear that you've been running your mouth about my sister, Avis Shropshire will be the least of your problems." Early exited the church and headed back toward the truck.

"Any trouble?" Ivey asked as she received her bowl.

"None at all," he replied. "Let's go home."

Chapter Ten

Early and Ivey rode back to Camp Redemption. He wanted to tell her about Millie Donovan and her children moving in, but the time wasn't right, so he decided to let it go until they got back home. He figured he could tell Ivey and Jesús over the evening meal. He decided to stick with what had happened at the church.

"Do you want to talk about it?" he asked.

"Hush, Early. I'm trying real hard not to sin right now, and I don't need you distracting me." Her eyes were closed and her brow wrinkled, as if she were concentrating.

"Unless you've got a bottle of gin tucked in your pocketbook, I don't see too much opportunity for sin here in the truck. I guess we could cuss a little."

She sighed loudly, opened her eyes, and cut them his way.

"I'm trying to not sin in my heart. 'Be ye angry, and sin not: let not the sun go down upon your wrath.' Ephesians 4:26. I'm working real hard at not having bad thoughts about Brother Rickey and the rest of the deacons, but they keep popping in anyway. They are not being good Christians. They know better—all of them—and I expect better from them."

"I guess not thinking about Brother Rickey and the boys is sort of like not thinking about a pink elephant."

"What's a pink elephant got to do with the church?"

"Never mind. Anyway, it's at least an hour until sundown, so you can let the bastard have it a little while longer. That way you can have your cake and eat it too."

"I swear, Early. You'll say anything. Especially when you've been to see Hugh Don Monfort. I don't know what's going to become of you after I'm gone. I don't know who will try to keep you from blaspheming, or who will pray for you when you blaspheme anyway."

"It'll be a while yet, so don't fret. You're going to live a long time, and I'm planning on changing my ways next week, or maybe the week after at the latest, so it's all going to work out fine."

"You don't know how long I'll live! None of us do. The Lord could call me home right now. Or He might just decide to bring *you* before the throne. You need to give *that* idea some thought. 'The days of our years are threescore years and ten; and if by reason of strength they be fourscore years, yet is their strength labor and sorrow; for it is soon cut off, and we fly away.' Psalms 90:10. I'm seventy-two. I've had my threescore and ten plus some. I could be at the pearly gates by morning."

"That's true. Or you could live thirty more years. Like you said, we don't know. So let's quit talking about dying."

"We all have to die."

"But we don't have to talk about it. It'll be bad enough just doing it."

They arrived at the turnoff for Camp Redemption and bumped along the dirt road to the Big House.

"I think I'll make us some supper," Ivey said as she opened the truck door.

"Why don't you let me scratch up something?" Early asked. "You've had a hard day. We can have a sandwich, or I can make something hot." He could warm up canned food and navigate cold cuts with the best of them.

"I don't want a sandwich, and I don't want to have to eat your cooking, either. I know you mean well, but you're a terrible cook. Just scoot for an hour or so and I'll have us a decent meal on the table. Go down to the lake and skip some stones. Leave me be with my thoughts and my pans. I'll ring the bell when it's ready."

Early nodded, grabbed a can of malt liquor, and did as he was told. He headed out the door and down the path. It was late in the afternoon, the magic hour, and the red orb of the sun appeared to rest on the peak of James Mountain to the west of the camp, casting a ruby hue over the landscape. He could hear the tree frogs as they began to warm up for their nightly serenade, heard the *reek...reek...reek* as it echoed among the pines. It always amazed him that a creature smaller than the end of his thumb could produce a sound that could fill the entire valley.

Early decided to check on Jesús and see if the boy wanted to go skip some stones. He arrived at the cabin and knocked on the door.

"You want to come down to the lake for a while?" he asked when Jesús told him to come in. "I can show you how to put a little English on your stone when you skip it." The young man was reclining on a top bunk in the center of the cabin, watching a movie on the television recently relocated from Early's room. The current scene contained three of the four requirements for adolescent films: martial arts, automatic weapons, and car chases. The fourth—voluptuous bosoms— would likely appear in time.

"Nope," Jesús replied. "I want to finish this movie."

"Why don't you come with me? I don't want you spending too much time alone." Early thought Jesús was probably missing his family, and he didn't want him to become depressed.

"Really, I'm good. I'll come to the lake with you later. What time is supper?"

"In about an hour. Listen for the bell."

Jesús nodded and went back to his film, and Early resumed his trip down to the water.

It was closer to full dark. The evening star had appeared, and Early tried to remember if it was Mars or Venus he was seeing. He thought he recalled that it depended on the time of the year, that in spring it was one of those planets and in fall it was the other, but for the life of him he couldn't remember which it was right now, or even if he had the correct astronomical facts. It bothered him that he was not as sharp as he once was. He supposed that time was marching on, that—as Brother Rickey would have said—he was slipping. Early stopped at the hollow tree and reached in for his pipe and something to fill it with. Then he meandered on down to the lake, made himself comfortable, and packed the bowl of his Dr. Grabow. He popped the top on the Schlitz malt liquor, took a long drink, lit up, and began to contemplate the complexities of the long day just past.

He considered his sister and her difficulties with the brethren at the church. Just the thought of Brother Rickey got Early's dander on the rise, and he had to take two deep hits from the Dr. Grabow before his dander even pretended to settle down and behave. He was proud of his sister for standing up for Avis Shropshire, proud that she was a woman who lived her convictions rather than just talking about them. But he was also worried about her. It had been a traumatic interlude. Her beliefs were the stone foundation of her life, and they had not changed. She had faith enough for at least two, and that little church had been her anchor chain for many years. Early knew that she would miss it, that she was no doubt already feeling the hole its absence would leave in her life. Since it wasn't likely that she would begin to visit Hugh Don Monfort's beer joint with him on Sundays—which he had to admit was probably just as well—they would simply have to find her another church home soon.

More stars began to glitter and shine in the twilight. A warm, gentle breeze blew across the lake. Off to the north, Early noticed a white light that winked every five seconds or so. It was the marker light for the water tower up on Fox

Mountain. When he was in a contemplative mood, as he was beginning to be now, it reminded him of a lighthouse beacon, although he supposed they were much too far from the ocean for it to be of much use as a navigational aid. Maybe in a million years, give or take, when the mountains tumbled back to ruin and the waters once again flooded the land. Of course, by then, the light bulb would no doubt have gone out, and even if it didn't, there probably wouldn't be any ships around to see it anyway, because a million years was a long, long time.

Early took another sip and one last hit from the pipe before settling into a long rumination on the longevity of signal beacons and the viability of commercial shipping in the far distant future. It was a fascinating subject, and he examined each new thought as it emerged for its inherent intricacy and beauty. Presently, his musing was intruded upon by the clanging of a bell. At first he thought the sound of a channel buoy had traveled the long miles from the petulant sea. Then he realized he was hearing the dinner bell mounted on the weathered hickory post right outside the back door of the Big House. An hour or more had passed in a moment, and Ivey was signaling supper. He drained the last swallow of his malt liquor, tapped the cold ash from the Dr. Grabow, and headed toward the evening meal. He was quite hungry.

When he entered the kitchen of the Big House, a variety of aromas jostled for his attention. Ivey had heated up the remaining dumplings and placed them back into the rescued Blue Willow tureen in the center of the table. They waited there next to a platter of country-fried steak. Arranged around this centerpiece were crockery bowls containing pinto beans, creamed potatoes, slaw, and fried okra. She had piled fresh biscuits on a plate beside the scarred cutting board, and a tall pitcher of iced sweet tea waited on the countertop. The table was set with Ivey's nice china—her company dishes, as she called them—and the place settings were completed with the good silver resting on crisply starched white linen napkins. She had outdone herself, and, judging by her contented humming, she knew it.

"Are we expecting company?" Early asked.

"I just felt like cooking a big meal and sitting down to it like decent folks," Ivey said. "I think we'll enjoy it better than a sandwich and a warmed-up can of beans—not that it wasn't sweet of you to offer. Now, would you go down to Philip and get Jesús? It's time for supper."

"I figured he'd already be here," Early said. "Don't start without me." He eased a biscuit from the plate, stepped out the door, and walked toward the cabin. He chewed his biscuit as he walked, savoring the taste of buttermilk and butter. Halfway down the path he met Jesús, who was hurrying to supper.

"I'm hungry," he said as they met.

"Let's go get to it, then. Ivey's got enough food up there to feed an army, but between us we ought to be able to make a dent." They walked side by side to the Big House. The thought again crossed Early's mind that he had gotten used to having the boy around. Jesús seemed like he fit there, as if he had been at Camp Redemption a long while, like the cabins or the cookhouse. Perhaps his sister was right. Perhaps Jesús was fated to be with them.

"How'd the movie turn out?"

"Lame."

They entered the kitchen and took their places at the table. Ivey joined them and said grace, and although she normally tended toward long entreaties with the Almighty, annotated and cross-referenced prayers resembling dissertations in religion, she kept this one fairly short. She asked for blessings on the present company, and then she interceded on Brother Rickey's behalf—and on behalf of the remainder of the deacons as well—that their respective stays in purgatory be only as long and as painful as was absolutely necessary to accomplish their individual salvations. The food was still hot after the *amens* were said, and the three of them set to with relish. They were quiet as they loaded their plates and managed the first few bites. Then they settled into the meal and began to chat.

"How was Hugh Don today?" Ivey asked as she buttered a biscuit. Early supposed she would talk more about the happenings at the church when she was ready, once the risk of having sinful thoughts had passed. Or perhaps she had exhausted that subject and was ready to move on to more pleasant topics. It was always hard to tell where Ivey Willingham would travel next.

"He was watching soccer on TV," he replied as he cut a bite of country steak with his fork. Ivey had pounded it before cooking and had fried it slowly, and it was so tender that no knife was necessary.

"That doesn't sound much like him," Ivey said.

"I play soccer," Jesús noted.

"Are you any good?" Early asked.

"My team was in the finals last year."

"Maybe you can help us start a team here next year," Early replied. Then he turned back to Ivey.

"I think it's just a phase he's going through," he said as he reached for another helping of fried okra.

"Hugh Don needs a wife," Ivey observed.

"He's already had four," Early countered. Technically, Hugh Don had been married *five* times, but two of the marriages had been to the same woman, and the consensus around town was that those should only count as one. Her name was Chrissy, and she had been wives three and five as well as the precipitating factor in divorce number two, if one could believe the gossip down at the diner.

The first of the two ill-fated marriages between Hugh Don and Chrissy had ended suddenly during an argument over

Chrissy's Salisbury steak when she emphasized the point she was making—which was that she didn't give a damn how good Hugh Don's mama's Salisbury steak had tasted—by stabbing Hugh Don in the right thigh with a steak knife. The discussion had lost steam at that point, as if Hugh Don had conceded, but the marriage soon fizzled out as well.

The second sacred union with Chrissy terminated under similar circumstances, with the only differences being those of dish, weapon, and appendage. This time she *shot* Hugh Don with the twenty-two she kept tucked in the waistband of her panty hose, shot him in the left thigh during an animated discussion concerning the unfavorable comparison between Chrissy's and the senior Mrs. Monfort's fried chicken crust. As had been the case during their earlier altercation, Chrissy had not much cared what kind of cook her older rival had been, as evidenced by the gunshot wound and by her invitation to Hugh Don to just go live with his damn mama, if he missed her cooking so much. Unfortunately for Hugh Don, his mama was dead, so he was left with the sole option of eating hard-boiled eggs at the beer joint until he could get enough sherry into Maxine Turner to convince her to be bride number five, or perhaps six, depending on the numbering system employed.

"He needs a wife who won't stab him or shoot him," Ivey clarified, as if she had finally, after all that time, stumbled on the main problem with the bootlegger's relationships.

"That could be where he's going wrong," Early admitted. He thought that the same formula for marital happiness could be applied to all men everywhere. He had been slow to get over his own wife's departure to Opelika, but he had to confess that the emotional healing would have come much quicker had Brandy simply shot him in the leg before heading west.

"Chrissy's not a bad girl," Ivey said.

"No, but she's a bad cook. According to Hugh Don, she's a bad cook with a knife in her hand and a gun in her panty hose." It was a dire combination in Early's opinion, a guaranteed recipe for trouble.

"She's just spirited, is all," Ivey said.

"High strung," Early agreed.

Ivey did not approve of Hugh Don or his wayward lifestyle, and she certainly didn't like the fact that he seemed to be leading her baby brother down that same path. But as much as she would have liked to, she was never quite able to fault Hugh Don for getting stabbed and shot by his wife. Yet Chrissy had been her lifelong friend, and she certainly didn't want to blame *her* for the troubles the pair had experienced. The problem was compounded by the fact that Ivey had tasted the competing versions of both the Salisbury steak and the chicken crust in question, and Hugh Don's mama was definitely the better cook of the two women. Chrissy was a much better shot, however, and she had the added advantage of still being above the sod.

"Well, spirited or not, I think Hugh Don has finally gotten over her. He's sweet on Burton Turner's mama, Maxine."

"Maxine Turner? What does she see in Hugh Don Monfort?" She reached for the salt and directed her attention to Jesús. "Are you getting enough to eat, Jesús?"

He nodded, his mouth too full to speak.

"He gets her sherry at cost. Also, Hugh Don tells her what she wants to hear about Burton."

"Poor Maxine. It would be terrible to have a child go bad."

"It would be even worse to have one who was that damn stupid."

"Hush," Ivey said, but Early noted that she didn't disagree. He changed the subject as he spooned a fresh portion of creamed potatoes onto his plate and reached for another biscuit.

"I saw Millie Donovan today."

"You did?" Ivey asked. She looked startled, as if she had just seen the ghost of Hugh Don Monfort's mama walking past with a platter of fried chicken.

"Are you okay?" Early asked.

"I had a dream about Millie last night. I thought that it was strange at the time, because I haven't seen that girl since she was a camp counselor."

"Tell me about the dream."

"It was kind of crazy. I was watching it like it was a movie, but I was in it, too. It was summer, and we were swimming in the lake. The water was real warm, warmer than I've ever felt it, almost like a bath. Jesús was there, too. He was doing the backstroke. There were some other folks in the water, people I didn't know, some kids and a woman with black hair. And then we heard hollering. We looked over by the falls, and someone was drowning. It was Millie Donovan. I knew it was her when I saw her, even though I don't have any idea what that girl looks like these days. Anyway, you swam over to her. She was splashing and screaming, and she went down for the last time. But then you got there and dove down under the falls and pulled her back up. You saved her. You got behind her and calmed her down. After that, you swam to shore with her and pulled her out. She was coughing up water and choking at first, but finally she started taking regular breaths. Then she started to glow, and she sat up and spoke. She said, 'I will not hunger nor thirst, nor will the heat nor the sun smite me, for You who have mercy on me will lead me, even by the springs of water will You guide me.' That was Isaiah 49:10. It's one of my favorite verses. I didn't know Millie Donovan liked it too."

"Maybe you dreamed she said that one because you like it so much," Early suggested.

"I guess I know what I heard her say, and Millie is a grown woman who can speak for herself." Ivey was apparently still a bit testy from her recent experience with Brother Rickey.

"Okay. Sorry. Never mind. I just thought I'd mention it. What about the other woman? Any idea who she was?"

"I've never met her."

Early considered the dream and its implications. "Do you remember when you said that we were supposed to shift our ministry from the spiritual education of children toward the care of the needy?"

"I remember when *Jesus* said that we should take care of the needy," she corrected.

Actually they were both slightly off base, because a dead Chickasaw had said it, but Early wasn't going to argue as long as the conversation seemed to be going his way.

"Right you are. Well, Millie Donovan is about as needy as anyone I've ever seen." He described her circumstances to Ivey in detail: the loss of Switch, the shared widowhood with Adele, the abject poverty, Stanley Newman and his wandering libido, the house repossession and subsequent rent increase, the unpaid grocery bill at the Jottem Down.

Jesús eavesdropped in silence as he attempted to do justice to the supper before them, but every now and again he shook his head in disapproval when a particularly unhappy fact was shared.

When Early finished, Ivey spoke with fervor. "Now I know what the dream was about! That poor woman. Those poor, pitiful children. Early, we have to help her and her family." An unpleasant thought seemed to cross her mind, and she frowned as she continued. "And you wanted to sell half our valley to Gilla Newman, after what his boy has done to Millie. I hope you see what kind of people the Newmans are now."

Early choked on a bite of creamed potato. He coughed and took a drink of tea. "Ivey, I've always known what kind of

Raymond L. Atkins

people they are. Everyone who has ever met them knows what kind of people they are. Even people who *haven't* met them know. You can just look at them and get a pretty good idea. They're the kind of people who end up with all the marbles generation after generation, because to them, marbles are the most important things. They're the kind of people who would sell their own mama if the market price was right. I wasn't endorsing Gilla when I brought that subject up. I don't like him, and I've never trusted him. I like his boy even less. I was just letting you know about his offer."

"Well, just so we're clear, I don't want any of Gilla Newman's marbles, or any of his money, either. And that goes double for Stanley. 'Hell and destruction are never full, so the eyes of people are never satisfied.' Proverbs 27:20."

"You took the words right out of my mouth. And I promise you I'll never sell the valley to the Newman family. Just forget I ever mentioned it. Now, can we get back to Millie? I've already made up my mind about what I think we ought to do about her, but this is a fifty-fifty proposition, and I want to hear what you think." He wasn't being disingenuous, necessarily, but he was hoping that Ivey might suggest what he had already offered.

"What does Jesús think we should do?" she said, looking over at their young ward.

He looked up from his plate in surprise, his eyes wide, a crumb of cornbread resting casually on his chin. "Huh? Don't look at me! I'm just visiting here myself. I'm the hired man. I don't know the lady. You guys do whatever you want to. It's your camp, and it was your dream."

"You have to be the one to decide who we help," Ivey said to Jesús.

The boy looked confused. "Why?" he asked.

"Humor her," Early said. He knew better than to argue with Ivey when she had that angelic tone in her voice.

159

"I don't know. You could give her some money, but I know that money is tight, and it sounds like she needs a lot of it. I guess if you really wanted to help her, you could move her and her kids into one of the cabins, like you did with me. That way she'll have a place to live. You already said you weren't going to be using them this year, so there'll be lots of room." He shrugged and looked at Early as if wondering if he had gotten the correct answer.

"I knew it!" Ivey said. She clapped her hands together once for emphasis. "I just knew it." She looked at her brother and pointed a fork in his direction. "We have to move Millie and her kids into one of the cabins."

Early slowly chewed his dumplings as he mulled his sister's dream and her subsequent actions. The Lord did indeed move in mysterious ways. He had wondered since leaving Millie's house if he had done the right thing, and how his sister would take the news. He hadn't thought that she would mind, but it had been a fairly generous offer to make unilaterally. Now, it looked as if his invitation hadn't been news at all, that it had all been foretold in Ivey's dream. Apparently, Early's spur-of-the-moment trip to the destitute woman's home had, in fact, been part of the larger plan, and he had merely been the messenger, the errand boy sent to deliver the invitation.

"I was hoping you'd feel that way," he said, "because I already invited her. I was going to tell you when I picked you up from church, but, you know, it didn't seem like the best time." She nodded, and he continued. "In the morning, Jesús and I will go over there in the bus to bring them here. I don't have any idea how long they'll be staying. It won't be a permanent arrangement, but it could be for a pretty good while. It depends on how long it takes her to get back on her feet. Anyway, I let her pick out the cabin she wanted, and she chose Nathanael. So I guess we need to step over there after supper and spruce it up." The cabin had been sitting empty since the previous camping season.

"It will be a labor of love," Ivey said. She was beaming. "We'll make it nice for her and her family."

Early looked at Jesús. "How about it? Are you ready to start earning your keep?"

"Just let me eat these last few bites," Jesús said.

After supper, they all adjourned to Nathanael, and over the course of the next three hours, they took over the former camp counselors' duties—sweeping, mopping, washing, and dusting everything within reach. While Early and Ivey turned the mattresses and began to make up the beds, Jesús announced that he was going outside to wash the exterior glass.

"That boy is a hard worker," Early noted as he snapped a sheet and tucked a corner.

"He's that," Ivey agreed, but she seemed preoccupied as she smoothed the wrinkles. She worried with the linen until it suited her.

"What's on your mind?"

"I can't get Brother Rickey out of my head. I swear I don't know how I could have been so wrong about someone. And the deacons! I've known some of them since they were just boys. How could I not see their ugliness?"

"Screw Brother Rickey and the deacons he rode in on."

"Early!"

"Sorry, Ivey. That one just slipped out. I don't know what to tell you about the gang down at the church, except to say that it's real easy to pretend to love thy neighbor when you're in an all-white congregation. Same way it's easy to say you love the poor when everyone around you has a little money. Talk is cheap until someone like Avis Shropshire comes along and calls your bluff. When he did that, Brother Rickey and the deacons had to put their Bibles where their mouths were, and they couldn't do it."

"Well, it makes me sad."

"I know it does. But don't worry about it anymore. What's done is done. Anyway, I've had an idea I want you to hear."

"What's your idea?"

"When word gets out at the church that you've quit, and why you did, some of the faithful—the *real* faithful, that is— won't be very happy. I wouldn't be surprised if several of them quit too. You're very popular, while Brother Rickey is, well, Brother Rickey. When parishioners start bailing out, we need to be ready with an alternative."

"I don't see what you mean."

"We have a church right here that seats 140 people," he said, pointing in the general direction of the chapel. Through the window they saw Jesús leaning in to clean a stubborn spot on the glass. "And we've got the best preacher in the state right here, too." This time he pointed at Ivey. "We can start having services next Sunday. You can preach to me and Jesús for starters, and Millie and her kids. We'll ask Avis Shropshire and his family if they want to come, too. That's unless he's in jail for strangling Brother Rickey. Before long, we'll have a church full of folks." Ivey's eyes had gotten wider as he spoke. She looked like a child on Christmas morning.

"Do you really think so?" she asked.

"I guarantee it. I think we ought to give the church a good name, too, like maybe the Get Right or Get Left Rapture Preparation Temple." Early had once seen that phrase on a marquee outside a one-room sanctuary in Leesburg, Alabama, and he had always thought it had a nice ring, in a clever-yet-ominously-threatening way.

"I think everything but the name is a wonderful idea," his sister replied. He started to object, but she held up her hand

and continued. "Why don't we just call it the Camp Church?" She smiled at Early as she spoke. "It really is a good idea."

"Now you're talking," Early said. "Within a year they'll be lined up out to the highway to hear you preach. You'll put Rickey Lee out of business. By the time you're finished with him, he'll have to turn the Blood and Fire into a convenience store."

Ivey smiled in spite of herself. Then she frowned. "Oh my goodness! Early! I just thought of something! If I die in my sleep tonight, the church will inherit my side of the valley. Remember, I left it to them in my will."

Early had always though it was an iffy idea, anyway, to leave 200 acres of prime mountain real estate to a round preacher and his one-horse church—and then to count on his inherent good judgment and sense of Christian charity—but her half was her half, and Ivey was entitled to do with it what she would. But now that she had changed her mind, it wouldn't be difficult to adjust her post-mortem wishes.

"No problem," he assured her. "I'll get with Charnell tomorrow and have him change the will. In the meantime, it's very important that you don't kick the bucket. I don't want you riding in cars, flying in airplanes, or even going upstairs. You'll be putting me in a bad spot if you leave me with Rickey Lee as my neighbor."

"You don't think you could love him?" Ivey asked with a sly smile.

"I don't even think I can work my way around to liking him," Early replied.

"You know you're supposed to love your neighbor. 'Love worketh no ill to his neighbor: therefore love is the fulfilling of the law.' Romans 13:10."

"I guess I'm going to have to work on that."

Chapter Eleven

The next morning, Jesús and Early left Camp Redemption on their errand to gather Millie Donovan and her brood into the fold. They had begun the day by removing the rear seats from the camp bus to make room for the Donovan family belongings, and now Early was in the driver's seat while Jesús sat on the bench directly behind him. Early sipped a steaming cup of coffee while he drove. His passenger nursed a can of Mountain Dew. They rode quietly, each with his own thoughts. It was a dazzling spring morning, bright as a new dime in the hand of a smiling child, and the sounds of birds chattering drifted about in the gentle air. Signposts and mailboxes rolled past as they motored toward town on their thirty-minute drive. The trees and vines along the roadside had opened their buds, and hues of pink, white, yellow, lavender, and pale blue added color to the morning. Tendrils of kudzu snaked up utility pole guy-wires and slowly climbed the trunks of trees.

The bus, a GMC by birth, was twenty-five years old. It had begun its career in the Sequoyah school district, where it had faithfully carried children hungry for knowledge for fifteen years. Early had bought the conveyance—complete with broken crankshaft and two flat tires—for $500 at an auction sale around the same time that Bill Clinton was splitting hairs as to the definition of sex. After Early installed a junkyard motor and six new tires, he painted the venerable vehicle, and it became serviceable transportation for many busloads of camp children. This morning, the bus was performing community service as a humble moving truck.

"Hey, Early," Jesús said as he leaned on the aluminum bar between them.

"Hey."

"What was the deal last night when Miss Ivey wanted me to decide whether or not Millie Donovan should move in with us?"

"It's kind of complicated." The bus body shifted as Early took a long left-hand curve, the local version of the ubiquitous Deadman's Curve. There were actually two of them on this stretch of highway, known respectively as Deadman's Curve and The Other Deadman's Curve. Early had been successfully leaning into both his entire life, although some of his fellow citizens had not fared so well. There were five small, white crosses sadly standing watch at Deadman's Curve, and six more down the road at The Other Deadman's Curve, mute testimony to the dangers of high speeds, low bids, slick tires, and, sometimes, just plain bad luck.

"Whenever grownups say something's complicated," Jesus said, "they usually shut up right after they say it. Does that mean you're not going to tell me?"

"No. I'm going to tell you. It just means I don't quite know where to begin, because it truly is complicated. Let me see. You know that Ivey is a very religious woman, right?"

"I'll say. She makes my mama look like an atheist, and Mama goes to church every day."

"Well, because Ivey is so religious, or at least I've always assumed it's because of it, sometimes she has visions. Actually, I suppose they're more like dreams, because they usually happen when she's asleep. Anyway, in these dreams, or visions, or whatever you want to call them, dead people talk to her. Most times, the dead people who come to her are folks she used to know, like our mother, our father, or one of our other relatives who has passed away. But there have been times when total strangers have appeared to her. She has no idea who they are." A thought occurred to him. "And it's not even always dead people. Every now and then it'll be an angel, and a couple of times it has been people who are still living, like with her dream about Millie. But whoever or whatever comes to see her, sometimes they tell her the future. Other times, they tell her about things she needs to know in the present. Every now and then, they give her a task to perform, like a sacred quest or a project." Early looked up into the mirror above the windshield and saw doubt etched on his passenger's face. Early realized how crazy it all sounded, and he didn't blame the boy for his misgivings. It was a lot to take on faith.

"Do you think she really has them? The visions, I mean?"

"Oh, she definitely has the dreams. Whether or not they mean anything is another question."

"You said the ghosts give her projects?"

"Maybe *project* wasn't the best word I could have used. I'll give you an example. Camp Redemption got built because of one of her visions."

"You built the whole camp because of one of Miss Ivey's dreams?"

"No, I built the whole camp because my sister asked me to, and because I've always tried to give her what she wanted. But the idea for it came from one of her dreams."

"No way!"

"Way. And the part you'll really like is that, nine times out of ten, when she has one of these dreams—or visions or revelations or whatever—what she says is going to happen does happen, or whatever she says we should do works out fine. Look at Camp Redemption."

"That is so cool!"

"I have to agree with you. She's a pain in the neck and then some most of the time, but it is pretty cool."

"But what about her telling me to decide? What was up with that? She was looking at me so hard, it scared me. I didn't want to say anything, but I was kind of afraid not to."

"Here's the story about that. After I told her that we couldn't afford to run the camp this year, she had one of her dreams. In it, a dead Chickasaw Indian came to her and told her that our ministry at Camp Redemption wasn't over just because money was tight, and that we needed to shift our focus toward helping people in trouble. In that dream, Robert Corntassel said that we would know who to help, because Jesus would tell us. The next thing I knew, I had found a kid named Jesús sleeping in one of the cabins, and he told me that he could use a bite to eat." Early glanced in the mirror to see the boy's reaction. "It's your name. Jesús. She thinks you're part of the prophecy. And that's why she thought you were the one who would tell us who to help. I don't want you to get a big head over this, but to Ivey, you're a sign from God." He looked back to his driving.

"I like the sound of that," Jesús said. "Who is this Robert Corn-whatever guy?"

"Robert Corntassel. That was the dead Chickasaw's name."

"Sweet! I like his last name. Do you think he came from one of the mounds?"

Early was somewhat surprised at how easily Jesús was accepting the facts about Ivey and her unusual skills. He had expected a bit more resistance. "I don't know if he did or not. It's possible. There are a lot of Indians out there."

A couple of minutes passed as Jesús absorbed this information. Then he spoke again. "Early, I don't mean anything bad by asking, but is Miss Ivey kind of crazy?"

"It's a fair question, and I wish I could give you an absolute answer. There have been times when I thought she must be insane. I mean, there are dead people coming to her in dreams. There are angels who are on a first-name basis with her. That's all incredible stuff, and it would be awful easy to dismiss her as a total wacko. She's been like this her whole life, or at least the part of it I can remember, and I guess I don't notice it as much anymore. The way she acts, the dreams, the visions, all of it just seems normal to me. But realistically, yeah, it's entirely possible that she has a loose connection or two. That's certainly easier to believe than the alternative, which is that she is some kind of prophet. But whatever is going on, there's no getting around her track record. She's been right a whole lot more than she's been wrong, and even when she misses the mark, it's more like we didn't understand the message, that the information was there but we misread it."

Jesús gave this explanation some quiet consideration as he sipped his can of Mountain Dew. "What should I do if she asks me to decide on something else?" he finally asked. "What am I supposed to say? What if I tell her to do the wrong thing? Last night I just sort of guessed at what the answer should be. I don't even know Millie Donovan, but it seemed like helping her was the right thing to do. I know I was pretty glad when *I* got some help. I had a fifty-fifty chance, so I went ahead, and I just got lucky and picked the right answer, the one you wanted to do, anyway. But I don't want to screw up and choose the wrong thing." His face clouded, the burden of prophecy weighing upon him.

"Just do what you did last night, and you'll be all right. My sister's a good-hearted woman who has always tried to do the right thing. I've never known her to cause anyone harm. You've got a good heart, too. If she asks you a question, just tell her what you think. You can't go wrong telling the truth. As for whether she's crazy or whether she's a prophet, I don't know. She is what she is. What I do know is that we were waiting for a message from Jesus, and then you came trotting up the road. Think about that. It could be a coincidence, or it could be something else. Most miracles could be called coincidences if you view them objectively, if you look at the act and leave the hallelujahs to the preachers."

"What about Jesus walking on water?"

"Well, that could have been really shallow water and really thick soles on His sandals."

"Healing the sick?

"People get well for no reason all the time."

"Feeding the multitudes?"

"Good public relations."

Early was always on shaky ground when it came to miracles because, truth be told, he didn't believe that they existed. But he wanted to. He wished he had it in him to take it all on faith, to accept unexplained cancer cures and water walks and bleeding palms and all the rest as the miracles they were purported to be, but when it came right down to it, he could always come up with a better explanation than divine intervention, a more plausible explanation than magic from beyond the clouds.

Even when it came to Ivey, his own personal live-in prophet, he could never quite make the complete journey to being a true believer in miracles. A part of him always hung back at a spot where perhaps the light was a little better and examined each occurrence through the harsh lens of reality. Ironically, even as he looked, he realized that it took as much faith not to believe as it did to accept something blindly, that both points of view required belief in something larger, be it God, coincidence, the randomness of the universe, science, or mere blind luck.

They rode in silence a while, cruising Highway 56 as it curved in and out like a snake along the base of the mountains. The thoroughfare followed the path of least resistance as it traversed the lowlands, sneaking between ridges and cutting through swales. It essentially retraced the route first taken into the area by the original inhabitants as they walked the wilderness, and subsequently by the Spanish, the French, the English, and Seaborn Willingham, his ailing bride, and his wagonload of red-headed, rowdy boys.

The road was the artery that kept the community alive, and it lead them straight into town. As Early and Jesús motored onto Main Street, the traffic signal turned to red, so Early slowed the bus to a stop, and then they sat while absolutely no traffic journeyed perpendicular to their line of travel. First one, then another motorist eased in behind them. Soon a line of six vehicles waited for the signal to blink to green.

They were being detained by Sequoyah's only traffic light, the physical manifestation of the level of fiscal responsibility demonstrated by the town's mayor, Gilla Newman. It was one more light than the traffic situation in Sequoyah merited, but state grants for unnecessary signals had been plentiful the year it was acquired, and Gilla just had to have it. The four-way stop signs it replaced were unceremoniously snatched from the ground, and a new age in traffic control was ushered in.

"How long is this light?" Jesús asked after two minutes. "I'm dying back here." Apparently the Mountain Dew had run its natural course. As for the signal, once it had clicked to red, moments seemed to elongate into hours, as if the selection of drivers sitting there drumming fingers, lighting smokes, and reading newspapers had somehow been shifted to an alternate universe in which time slowed.

"It'll change in one more minute," Early said as he glanced at his watch. He looked on in amusement at the *Got Jesus?* billboard that cast its long shadow over Billy's Chevron. Early did indeed have him, and the boy was getting restless.

"But there haven't been any cars coming the other way!"

"There never are," Early replied. "The big lightning strike of '03 gave this signal a mind of its own."

"Why don't we just run it?" Jesús asked. Early pointed over to their right. The town's police cruiser was tucked up beside the Jottem Down grocery store. The traffic light was unnecessary and foolish, much like the local policeman, but Austell Poe would ticket anyone who challenged its authority, or his. They were kindred spirits: one biological, the other something quite different. But in that corner of the world, red was red, green was green, revenue was revenue, and the law was the law. Plus, Austell was still on the lookout for the camera thief, and woe betide that miscreant should he or she ever be apprehended.

The camera thief had struck the previous year, a month to the day after Gilla Newman installed traffic cameras at the intersection. The recession had not yet fully reared its ugly head, and state grants for unnecessary traffic cameras to be installed at equally useless signal lights had been available for those willing to execute the proper paperwork. Gilla Newman was a visionary, and he positioned himself at the head of the line for this exciting new technology. Mayor Newman arranged for Sequoyah's traffic cameras to be installed under the pretense of a safety initiative, but in fact the move was a poorly veiled attempt to raise revenue for the town, which needed additional income primarily so it could pay its mayor.

The plan began to develop difficulties when Sequoyah's Electrical Department—Trace McBrayer and Booger Wheeler—installed the devices over a rainy weekend. Trace was a fair hand when it came to replacing bulbs in the street lights, hanging the town's four Christmas stars in September and removing them in June, and jimmying faulty receptacles down at City Hall, and Booger was pleasant company as well as a reliable pair of hands to steady a ladder, but the pair were clearly out of their league when it came to installing and programming two automatic cameras designed to stand guard at a capricious traffic signal. The four hands were willing, but the two minds were weak.

For starters, Trace couldn't read English all that well, thus the installation instructions written in what seemed to be German were a true mystery to him, a Teutonic riddle with no apparent solution. And Booger couldn't read at all, although in his defense, he had never claimed he could. Still, if he *had* possessed that arcane skill, he *might* have read that the control board for the new system needed to be kept dry, and if he had acquired *that* information, he *may* have subsequently mentioned to Trace that he, Booger, had dropped that mysterious electronic component into a puddle. Instead, he wiped the control board on the leg of his pants before handing it over, so it was not a particularly surprising development that, when installed, the cameras took pictures of every car that entered the intersection, regardless of whether the traffic light was green, yellow, red, or completely burned out. Dozens of tickets were generated and mailed, but unfortunately, most of these citations went to law-abiding citizens, honest taxpayers who had paused for the full three minutes before being fined seventy-five dollars for entering the intersection under the green light.

This indiscriminant photography of innocent motorists continued until the night before Thanksgiving, when an unknown local Samaritan—one who apparently owned a ladder and who *could* read German—stole the cameras right off the poles. Upon opening his front door the next morning, Gilla Newman was greeted with a flash that blinded him for several moments. After his sight returned, Gilla—ever the optimist—opened the door once more, and again the flash took his vision. He stumbled through the house with his hands over his eyes before nearly jerking the back door from its hinges as he attempted to make his escape. It was at this point that he found the other purloined camera, which caught a fair likeness of him as he threw his arms up over his head and fell out into the yard. Warrants were issued that morning for the phantom photographer, but he or she refused to surface and claim credit for the episode, even though Charnell Jackson put out the word that he would defend the scofflaw at no charge, all the way up to the Supreme Court, if necessary. The cameras were removed from Gilla's front and back porches and went into the shed behind City Hall with the town's lawn mower and the four obsolete stop signs, mute testimonials to the generally declining level of respect for the law.

Back at the traffic light, Early nodded at Austell in his police cruiser. "That's why we don't run the light. Austell would give his own mama a ticket if she ran this light." As a matter of fact, Austell had once done just that, but the judge was a reasonable man and had thrown out the case in the name of decency. "You know, it's still kind of early, and Millie may not be ready. After the light turns green, what do you say we stop and kill a few minutes at the diner? I could use another cup of coffee."

Ivey had placed a large breakfast before them at the Big House that morning—French toast, sausage links, and scrambled eggs—so Early wasn't hungry, but he didn't want to arrive at Millie's while she was trying to dress the kids, or while she was still in her bathrobe. The family had a big day ahead, and Early believed they should be allowed the time to compose themselves. Plus, it was about the time of day that Charnell Jackson liked to stop at the diner for his breakfast, and Early wished to confer with him on the matter of Ivey's will.

"You own the bus," Jesús said simply, "and you're driving. I could use a bite, anyhow." Early couldn't imagine where Jesús was going to put it, but through the years he had seen more than a few young men eat as though they were hollow. Maybe the boy was preparing for a growth spurt.

"Listen, if anyone asks, I want you to tell them your name is John Smith, and you're a counselor I hired to help me this summer." Early had given the matter some thought and concluded that the likelihood was slim of anyone realizing the true nature of Jesús's presence as a runaway among them. He figured that as long as he was reasonably prudent, none of the local folks would be any the wiser.

"That goes for while we're in town as well as when we get back to the camp," Early continued. "If Millie or one of her kids wants to know, you're John Smith. Have you ever been to Tallahassee?" Jesús indicated that he had. "Good. You're John Smith from Tallahassee. Throw in a few Tallahassee details, just to keep it realistic. State capital. Florida State University. That kind of stuff. Can you remember that?"

"Got it. You're sure about that name?"

"I'm sure. Just don't forget and accidentally say your real name, or mention Apalachicola, or that you ran away or anything."

"I won't."

The light finally changed to green, allowing them to ease two blocks up the main street before they took a right into the parking lot of the Jesus is Going out of Business Diner. Early parked the bus beside Charnell Jackson's bright red 1984 Cadillac Sedan DeVille. According to its owner, the vintage motorcar was the last model Cadillac had ever built that was worth driving. Early knew it was Charnell's Caddy because of what seemed like an acre of white vinyl covering the vehicle's roof. Additionally, the car bore a prestige license plate with the word LAWPUP emblazoned on it.

Charnell had always wanted to purchase LAWDAWG in honor of his occupation and his years at the University of Georgia, but prestige license plates were sold on a first-come, first-served basis, and someone took that name long ago. He had been willing to settle for LAWDOG as a fallback, but it, too, was already riding on the back of a barrister's vehicle. Finally, in desperation, he had filled out the forms and plunked down the cash for LAWPUP before someone grabbed it up as well, leaving him with the as-yet-unclaimed LAWMUTT or the ignominious LAWHOWN.

Jesús—aka John Smith the traveling camp counselor from Tallahassee—and Early exited the bus and walked to the front of the diner. The doorbell tinkled as they swung the screen door wide and entered the dining area.

"Morning, Early," Candace Shellnut said. She and her coffee pot followed the pair to Charnell's table. Jesús and Early took seats opposite the lawyer, who was using his final bite of toast to chase the last of his cheese omelet around a platter full of ketchup.

"Hey, Candace," Early said. "Just some coffee for me."

She looked at Jesús and raised an inquiring eyebrow.

"Could I get hotcakes and bacon?" the boy asked, holding up his second can of Mountain Dew to indicate he was good on the drink.

"What kind of syrup you want, hon?"

"Just some extra butter, please."

Candace nodded and headed back to her station at the cash register, where she called the order through the window to her husband, Anderson. "Cakes and sowbelly," she hollered. "Cow butter on the side."

"Comin' right up," Anderson piped.

Back at the table, Jesús was undergoing a long appraisal from the jaundiced eye of Charnell Jackson. Finally, the attorney cleared his throat and spoke to Early.

"Who's the kid?" He asked this with characteristic bluntness, and although he had directed this inquiry to the elder member of the pair opposite, it was the boy who answered.

175

"My name is John Smith, and I'm a counselor from Tallahassee that Early hired to help him this summer." Jesús delivered this spiel in a monotone, as if he were reading the line from a note card. Early put his head in his hands and sighed. The next time he kept a runaway kid, he would make sure he got one who could lie with competence.

"Nice," he said to Jesús.

"What?" the boy asked.

"Tell me you didn't do what I told you not to do," Charnell said to Early.

"In all honesty, I can't tell you that," Early replied.

"Shit," Charnell muttered.

"*What?*" Jesús asked Early again.

"Nothing," Charnell replied as he handed the boy a five-dollar bill. "Would you mind going to get change from Candace over there, and then play some songs for us on the jukebox? Play whatever you want, as long as you don't play any of that rapping shit, and as long as you do play number B24."

That particular song, "Coal Miner's Daughter" by Loretta Lynn, had been Charnell's favorite for many years. The first time he heard it, he, Early, and Hugh Don Monfort were at the beer joint drinking, respectively, Budweiser, Schlitz malt liquor, and Pabst Blue Ribbon. When the song came on the radio, Charnell had listened silently to every note, and toward the end of the rendition, there had been a tear in his eye. Then he had sighed, arisen, and exited the beer joint.

"Don't worry, I've got his keys," Early had told Hugh Don. "He can't go anywhere without his car."

"He must be taking a leak," Hugh Don replied, reassured. Twenty minutes later, however, the lawyer had still not returned. Their subsequent search turned him up about a mile-and-a-half down the road, headed in a generally northerly direction. He was making for Nashville, and he had the full intention of declaring his love to Miss Loretta once he arrived.

Jesús tucked the bill in his shirt pocket and arose to perform his task. "Which way to the bathroom?" he asked. Early pointed toward the facilities. Jesús departed, leaving his elders looking at one another over a wide expanse in points of view.

"Sometimes I think you're as crazy as your sister," Charnell began conversationally. He made a steeple with his fingertips and looked at his table companion.

"Sometimes I am. It sort of runs in the family, like red hair or living up in the valley, although I didn't get the red hair. But this is not one of those times. How the hell can you eat eggs with ketchup? That's some nasty business."

"How the hell can you *not* eat them with ketchup?" Charnell asked. "By the way, if you get caught with John over there, I don't know you."

"Sure you do. You know me just fine, known me all my life. And you knew I wasn't going to send him back to his father. What I need you to do now is figure a legal way for me to keep him. Since you think I'm crazy, you might brush up on my insanity defense, too, just in case I do happen to run out of luck and get caught with him. I would like to avoid jail while I'm doing the right thing. It would be like getting a bonus." Charnell grunted as Early continued. "Anyway, I told him to hold a low profile and pretend that his name was John Smith. I have to admit he wasn't that convincing, but I'm going to work with him on his presentation. He either can't lie worth a damn or he's screwing with me. Personally, I think he's screwing with me. He's got a touch of the wise-ass gene. That might be why I like him so much."

"He's definitely screwing with you. You know, Bob Jones would be a better phony name than John Smith. Craftier. Lots more subtle. Fool a lot more people using Bob Jones."

"Thanks."

"Now," Charnell said, "tell me again why you want to keep him. And don't give me that *it's the right thing to do* line. I have defended several currently incarcerated people who, when it came right down to it, were guilty of nothing more than trying to do the right thing. It didn't save them, and it won't save you. Sometimes doing the right thing will actually piss off a judge. What, you think I'm kidding? I'm telling you, they're not normal people. Judges, I mean. They're not like you and me. Some of them are okay, but some of them are mean and stupid, and a few are just plain nuts. And it's really hard to get rid of a mean, stupid, *or* crazy judge. Excuse the pun, but they are sort of laws unto themselves. So what you need to do is pretend that I am the judge, and that you're looking at big trouble if you can't get me to see things your way. While you're at it, pretend for argument's sake that your lawyer is on my—the judge's—bad side, and be extra convincing."

Early considered this request. "How many judges have you pissed off?" he inquired. "Tell you what. Never mind answering that. I don't want to know. As for your question, the last time we talked, doing the right thing would have had to be sufficient, because it was the only reason I had. But I really like the kid. I've only known him a few days, but I care about him. I want to see him come out okay. For sure I don't want him to be beaten to death by his father. You know how I am with people I've just met. It takes me a while to get used to folks. Sometimes I never take a shine to them. Like Gilla Newman, for example. Or his boy, Stanley. Or his father, Mr. Frank. He's been dead ten years, and I still don't like him. But with Jesús, it's different. I'm feeling very paternal toward him."

"Nobody takes to Newmans, so don't lose any sleep over it. Taking to a Newman would be like taking to the clap. Some things you just can't get used to. But I'm with you on the rest of it. You like him and want to keep him, *and* you want to do the right thing. That might not be good enough, but that's what we've got. I'll start researching the law books. There must be a loophole in there somewhere big enough for you and the kid to hop through."

"Thanks." A thought occurred to Early. "Remember that I'm temporarily out of business. I have no income, and I didn't exactly have to burn off the extra cash back when running a camp was being good to me. So, since I can't pay you anyway, what do you think this is going to cost me? Oh, and will you take a two-party, out-of-state returned check as a deposit?"

"You make an old man want to cry. Tell you what. I'll do whatever legal work comes up with respect to Jesús—"

"It's John now."

"No, it's Jesús. If you try to hide him by changing his name, it makes you look guilty."

"I *am* guilty."

"That's just a technicality. Most people are guilty of something. The trick is not to look like you are."

"Okay."

"Plus, if you try to hide a Hispanic kid by changing his name to John Smith, it makes you look guilty and stupid."

"Which is bad?"

"Real bad. The only thing that judges hate more than a guilty defendant is a stupid defendant. You roll them both together into one defendant and you've got real trouble. You might get the death penalty."

"I see."

"Never forget that most judges think that if you weren't guilty, the police wouldn't have picked you up in the first place. So just call him Jesús and let the dice roll where they roll. As for the rest of my fee, I'll take care of whatever comes up for free."

"I was just kidding about not paying you. I'll come up with the money somewhere. I can't let you work for free."

"Let me finish. It won't cost you any money, but you have to let me come live at the camp for a while."

"You've got a house. A pretty nice one, the last time I looked. Why in hell would you want to come live in a Bible camp?"

"Two or three reasons. First off, I'll be close to my sweetheart. We'll sit in the swing on the Big House porch while we watch the sunset and grow old together. Second, I'll be near my favorite fishing hole and my best fishing buddy. You and I can get into some of those big bass you're always telling me about."

"Uh-huh. And?"

"Finally, and to be honest with you, this is the big one, I am about to not have a house anymore. Or very much money, either. It's all gone. Or just about all of it, anyway."

"What are you talking about? Everybody knows you're loaded." The general consensus around town was that Charnell had more money than Carter had little liver pills, which was to say he had plenty.

"Well, I have to admit it. I was loaded. But now I'm a poor but honest country lawyer. Do you know what a margin call is?"

"Not really. Something to do with the stock market?"

"It's a special name they have in the financial world for paying the piper. I speculated heavily in oil futures. In other words, I bet that oil would be worth a certain amount on a certain date, and it turns out that it was worth a great deal less when that black day rolled around. To put this into perspective, you have to understand that it is nearly an impossibility to lose money on oil. It's kind of like losing money on sex. In theory, it can't happen, sort of like gravity can't quit holding these coffee cups to the tabletop. But I managed to anyway. Some of us were just not meant to play the market. There's a sucker born every minute, and my mama was in labor for three long days. So, since oil has no apparent future, financially speaking, neither do I."

There was a momentary silence, a stillness that was broken by the opening notes of Miss Loretta's "Coal Miner's Daughter." Charnell smiled a rueful, preoccupied smile.

"Damn, Charnell," Early said. "I don't know what to say. Like you said, I didn't even think it was possible to lose money on oil. I mean, they call it black gold, for Christ's sake."

"Neither did I, and neither did my broker. I would question him closely on the subject, but I can't seem to get him on the phone."

"Maybe he jumped from a window."

"I have an alibi."

"Or hung himself."

"We can only hope."

"And you're really broke?"

"Broke as a joke. Broke as a spoke. Broke as the Ten Commandments. Give me a minute, and I'll think of some more."

"That's okay. I got it. You're broke. How much did you lose?"

"Enough to give me chest pains, but not enough to kill me outright, although it was touch and go there for a while. Anyway, my fee for legal work with the kid will be room and board. I need to lay low and rest up, in a manner of speaking."

They paused a moment as Candace brought Early's coffee and Jesús's second breakfast. She topped Charnell's cup as well. The break in the conversation continued momentarily as Charnell watched Candace's tight skirt retreat.

"Sweet Lord have mercy on us all," he said slowly. "Mm, mm, mm."

They were quiet for a minute as Early digested the information concerning his attorney's economic misfortune. The news these days was chock full of disaster stories from the financial circles, tales about people who had lost their life savings in the stock market, grim anecdotes about 401(k)s losing half their value or more. But the unfortunates who had suffered these reversals had been strangers, names without faces. Now the Wall Street plague was hitting closer to home. Charnell was as slick as they came, and if it could happen to him, then no one was safe from ruin.

Early had no issues with Charnell taking up residence at the camp. They had plenty of room, and it was a good way to pay legal fees. Plus, if times got really tough, Charnell would bring with him a working pair of hands, which could come in handy if they all ended up harvesting aluminum cans by the right of way. Early extended his right hand and shook Charnell's.

"Welcome to Camp Redemption," he said. "You might be interested to know, now that you are among the needy, that your coming was foretold." Early believed that, as a courtesy, people who were mentioned in prophecy should be notified of that fact, just in case they wanted to take a shower, dress up a bit, and put on a tie.

"Bless Ivey," Charnell said. "She takes good care of me."

"Of course, it's starting to get a little crowded. First Jesús, then Millie Donovan and her kids, and now you. We'll put you in the Big House, unless you'd rather have a cabin."

"Millie Donovan?"

"Millie's got a serious case of the outs. She's out of money, she's been out of luck for a long time, and she's about to be put out of her house. I'm on my way over there now to move her and her kids to the camp." Early still felt good about his decision. It was another of those right things to do. "She'll be staying with us for a while."

"Damn. Poor Millie. I've always liked that girl. She asked me to take a look at her finances when Switch died, and I did, but there wasn't a thing I could do. That boy had it screwed up so bad, nobody could have fixed it." Charnell shook his head as he remembered. "It sounds like it's a good thing I'm getting in early, while there's still a nice selection of places to sleep. I'd hate to end up bunking in the stable with your crazy horses."

"The horses probably wouldn't be that wild about the idea, either. Jimbo is kind of particular about the company he keeps, and Betsy would just as soon bite you as look at you." He and Ivey did not run an equestrian establishment, but they had acquired two horses over the years—Jimbo from Hugh Don Monfort, who had received the animal as payment of a gambling debt, and Betsy from a man who'd died without making arrangements for her. They kept the horses around mostly because Early liked them. Besides, he didn't know what else to do with them.

The campers were allowed to pet and feed them, and those who could ride were occasionally permitted to do so, but mostly the horses were at Camp Redemption because they had nowhere else to be.

"Betsy is an insane horse," Charnell said.

"But I got her cheap. And anyway, she's a sweet animal with everyone else in the world. It's just you she bites. She likes the taste of lawyer, I guess. I hear ya'll taste sort of like chicken."

"Stupid horse."

"Anyway," Early said, changing the subject, "I'm sort of hoping you're the last needy person we have to put up for a while. I still have a date with damnation if I have to sell half the valley to Gilla Newman in order to feed everyone, and since your oil went south, his is the only offer on the table again. I guess I should have taken you up last week. I've got plenty of room for everyone, but we might all be eating beans and cornbread on a regular basis."

"As long as we don't have to eat that damn horse," Charnell muttered. "Beans and cornbread are tasty, especially if Ivey's the cook. And if it's any consolation, the check apparently would have bounced if I had gone ahead and paid you for half the valley. Then you would have had to hire me to sue me for the money. My heart wouldn't have been in the case." Charnell's voice was suddenly sad. "Speaking of Ivey, she called me right before you came in. She wants me to come out to the camp this morning. She said it was very important that she saw me today, but she wouldn't say why. Do you know what she wants?"

"She wants to change her will. I was about to bring it up, but she's in a hurry, I guess. She has fallen out with the Washed in the Blood and the Fire Rapture Preparation Temple. Now she's afraid she's going to suddenly keel over before she gets the will rewritten. Brother Rickey Lee is out."

Charnell raised his eyebrows. "The last I heard, she just loved that boy. To hear her tell it, he was the next best thing to the Second Coming. Kind of like Jesus, but with gravy stains on his shirt. I disagreed with her decision to leave her half of Willingham Valley to him in the first place. But she wouldn't listen to me. I forget who—it might have been Abraham—but some biblical person had come to her in her sleep and told her to leave a million dollars' worth of land to the church, and I couldn't talk her out of it. What made her change her mind?"

"Brother Rickey and the deacons have pissed her off over the question of admitting minorities to the church."

"No shit? Hah! I'd like to have seen the looks on their faces when they realized they'd just thrown away some prime real estate."

"They don't know. I think she wants it to be a surprise."

"Hell hath no fury," Charnell noted.

"Yeah, I expect they'll think twice before they call her a senile old lady next time."

Jesús arrived back at the table, sat, and began to butter a pancake. The music from the jukebox drew to a close. Then, in a little burst of déjà vu, the opening bars of "Coal Miner's Daughter" floated once again through the diner.

"I didn't recognize any of the songs," Jesús said to Charnell as he folded a piece of bacon into his hotcake, forming a miniature breakfast taco. "Bunch of lame, country tunes I've never heard of. So I just played your song five times."

"This boy has a head on his shoulders," Charnell noted. He tapped the tabletop with his right hand in time with the music. "He knows how to think on his feet. He'll go far."

"Ivey and I like him," Early confirmed. "And he's already gone pretty far. When are you going to move to the camp?" Upon hearing this, Jesús paused mid-chew and looked at Early. Then he shrugged and began to butter another hotcake.

"I've got some business to take care of today. But first I guess I had better go see what Ivey wants in her new will. Then I've got some other things to attend to. Signing some papers. Hiding some assets. Hunting down and shooting my broker. That kind of stuff."

"Can you hide assets?"

"Are you kidding? I can hide them better than anyone."

"That's not what I meant."

"I know what you meant," Charnell said, but he did not elaborate.

Early shrugged. He supposed if he had no direct knowledge of any of his friend's shenanigans, he couldn't be called to testify. "So you'll be on out tomorrow?"

"Probably late in the day, depending on how everything goes and whether or not I get arrested. Don't tell Ivey I'm moving in. I want it to be a surprise."

"It's kind of hard to surprise her, but I won't say anything." Early looked at Jesús. "Are you ready to go?" he asked.

"I'm ready." He took his last bite of pancake and swigged it down with the rest of his Mountain Dew. Both Early and Jesús stood.

"We've got to go move Millie," Early said as he placed a tip on the table and picked up the check. He grabbed Charnell's bill as well. "I'll see you tomorrow."

"That's not much of a tip," Charnell noted as he nodded at the gratuity.

"It's all you can afford," Early replied.

"I'll be there," Charnell said. Early nodded, and Jesús followed him to the counter, where he settled up with Candace and waved at Anderson in the back. Then the two of them headed to the bus. As they walked across the gravel parking lot, Jesús began to question Early.

"What's a broker?"

"Apparently it's someone you pay to lose all of your money for you." Early was one of those lucky folks who literally lived in his portfolio, and he had never found it necessary to seek guidance on the road to poverty. It had always been a well-marked trail, one that any self-respecting Willingham could find with both eyes closed, like a horse locating a water hole in the badlands. "You hire him, and he makes you broker." This gag was met by momentary silence. "Get it? Broker?" Early was never one to resist telling a bad joke, and he liked acknowledgement if not outright acclaim for his efforts.

"I got it," Jesús said. "Do you really think that Mr. Jackson will shoot his broker?"

"Not fatally." *Or at least not intentionally,* he thought. Charnell was a notoriously bad shot. Once while participating in the American Legion turkey shoot held each Thanksgiving on the football field behind the high school, Charnell had missed both the target and most of the embankment behind it and had instead shot the War Chief, that fierce wooden mascot who had for long years been the totem for the Sequoyah Indians. With marksmanship of that caliber, any attempt at winging his broker could have a tragic outcome, just as it had for the War Chief, who was now missing three feathers, part of his nose, and most of his tomahawk, all for the crime of standing silently on top of a grassy berm, woodenly minding his own business while waiting for the next ball game to begin. Early hoped that Charnell's financial advisor fared better even though he deserved worse, but he knew there were no guarantees in life, and he supposed that time would tell. "By the way," Early said, "the whole John Smith deal is off. Just be yourself."

"Good. I didn't think it was going to work."

"Well, yeah, the way you did it, it was a terrible idea. I almost called Austell Poe and turned you in myself. Anyway, Charnell said to just act normal and leave the worrying to him. I still don't want you to talk about Apalachicola, or how you got here, or why you had to run, but you can be Jesús."

"I had less to remember back when I was John Smith."

Chapter Twelve

After their breakfast meeting with Charnell Jackson, the subsequent trip to Millie's place on the cul-de-sac on Railroad Street took only a few minutes. As they pulled up in front of the house, Early cut the wheels sharply to the left and pulled all the way up on the curb across the street. Then he cut the steering wheel hard in the opposite direction and backed across Millie's front yard until the emergency door at the rear of the bus was just a short stride away from the concrete front porch. He switched off the ignition and he and Jesús stepped out. The Donovan family stood on the porch. The children were freshly scrubbed and lined up like three stepping stones, left to right, tallest to shortest, oldest to youngest. Millie was positioned off to one side, and she smiled briefly at the moving crew.

"Hello, Early," she said. She looked at him momentarily, then at her children, then back at him.

"Hey, Millie," he replied. Although it was still early in the day, the air was warm in spite of the gentle breeze that tugged at their hair as it blew from the west. The ensuing moment of silence was just long enough to be uncomfortable, although Early could not quite fathom why. Finally, he broke the pause by placing his hand on his companion's shoulder and introducing him to the assemblage on the porch.

"Millie, kids, this is Jesús. He's working for me as a caretaker out at the camp this year." Jesús nodded and waved. Then he busied himself by looking down at his shoes. Apparently, reticence was in the air.

"Hello, Jesús," Millie said. "Let me introduce my children. This is Lisa Marie, my oldest. Everyone thinks I named her after Lisa Marie Presley, but I didn't. I just liked the name." Lisa Marie rolled her eyes. Then she and Jesús each caught the other's glance before quickly looking somewhere else. Lisa Marie was a younger version of her mother, a fifteen-year-old carbon copy minus the bumps, bruises, and stretch marks, complete with short, dark hair, a pretty smile, and green eyes. Millie continued the introductions. "Next to her are Iris Anne and Bliss. Iris Anne is thirteen, and Bliss is twelve."

Although there was a year between them, they were close in size and appearance. They each had long, dark, curly hair tied in the back, and both wore faded jeans and t-shirts. Iris Anne wore glasses, and Bliss had a habit of squinting, as if she needed a pair as well.

"Are you guys ready to load up?" Early asked. "I brought some boxes and big plastic garbage bags from camp in case we needed them." Millie nodded, but her children swayed like stalks of corn in a prairie breeze. It was obvious they weren't sure what to do next.

"Boxes and bags are good," Millie said. "We don't have that much furniture, but we've definitely been short of stuff to pack in. It's mostly just clothes and dishes and such."

Early stepped to the back of the bus and opened the emergency door. He began to transfer empty boxes to the porch. Jesús went to the front of the bus, reached in through the open door, and removed the carton of black garbage bags. When he arrived back at the porch, he walked up the three concrete block steps and shook several bags open with quick snaps. Then he handed one to each of the Donovan children. They stood immobile, looking at the garbage bags in their hands and the growing pile of empty boxes before them. They seemed confused and perhaps a bit dazed, as if they had heard of boxes and garbage bags at some point during their short lives but had never thought to encounter them.

Millie clapped her hands a couple of times before speaking briskly. "Okay kids, come on, now! Let's get busy and pack our things. We've got a lot to get done today!" Slowly the children began to move.

"Jesús, why don't you help out with the packing, too?" Early suggested. "Once it's all packed up, you can bring out the loaded bags and boxes. I'll put them onto the bus." Jesús nodded, seemingly happy to have a task to perform. Early noticed that the boy had casually come to rest near Lisa Marie. She opened the screen door and shooed her sisters into the house. Then Jesús held the door for her as she entered. He went through behind her, leaving Early and Millie by themselves on the rickety porch.

"I'm sorry the kids are acting so skittish this morning," Millie said. "They're all pretty nervous about moving, and they're a little bit shy on top of that. I guess you could say they're kind of in shock, even though they knew that this was coming. This old house is not much, and that's a fact, but it's the only home they've ever had. I talked to them last night about moving. I told them about you and Miss Ivey and what nice folks you are, and about what a great place the camp is. They're all looking forward to coming to Camp Redemption, and I know they'll all be fine in a little while. They're good kids."

"I'm not worried about them. I know they'll be fine. And it's understandable that they're having a bad day of it. I've lived in the Big House my entire life, and it would feel strange for me to leave my home, too, particularly if I was going to live with people I didn't know. So don't give it a thought. They'll loosen up as soon as they get used to me and Ivey and to the whole idea of moving. Tell me about you. How are you doing today? This has been your home a long time, too."

"To be honest, I'm not that upset. Not right now, anyway. I might get a little teary later. I don't know. But a lot of things went wrong for me in this house, a lot of plans went bad and a lot of hopes sort of just died of old age. Or maybe it was malnutrition. But either way, I don't guess I'll be too sorry to see the last of it. It wasn't the house's fault, but still, it does have a way of reminding me about some things I'd rather just forget." She was quiet a moment. "Besides, it's a dump. Always has been. I tried to make it as nice as I could, for the kids' sakes and for mine, but it's just a board house at the end of a dead-end street. It needs paint, it's cold in the winter and hot in the summer, and the busiest railroad track in North Georgia runs through the back yard." As if to punctuate that sentiment, the rumble of a slow freight train came to their ears from the track fifty yards distant. They waited as the horns blew at the crossing at the other end of the street. This break was known by the local residents as the Railroad Street pause, and few conversations in that part of town were finished without at least one of them.

"Well then, let's get you loaded up and out of here," Early said after a minute or so. The engines were far down the track by then. "The sooner we go, the sooner you can start forgetting."

"That sounds good. But first I want to tell you something." Millie had moved past Early and positioned herself between him and the door. She stood there in her blue jeans and looked up at him.

"All right."

"What I want to say is that I can never thank you enough for saving us."

He noticed the faint shine in her eyes. "Don't even mention it," he said,"All I'm doing is letting you stay in an empty cabin. Anybody with any decency would do the same."

"I don't think so. Decency seems to be in real short supply these days, and regardless of what you say, you're saving us from I don't even know what. Until you came in here yesterday, I didn't have anywhere to go, and I didn't know what I was going to do." She held the tips of her right index finger and thumb so that the light of the morning sun barely shone through. "We were this far from living at the Salvation Army if we were lucky, or from sleeping under the highway bridge over the Echota if we weren't. And we haven't had a great run of luck around here lately, so it probably would have been the bridge. And we would have had to walk to the bridge, at that, because I don't have a car that will start. I didn't even have supper for the kids last night until you showed up with your bags of groceries."

"It was nothing," he protested quietly.

"It was anything but," she replied simply. "I have a confession. I've never been very religious. I wasn't raised that way, and I think you have to be raised to it before you truly take belief to heart. Faith isn't something you can all of a sudden decide you're going to have. So I'm kind of ashamed to admit this, but I prayed yesterday, and I mean to tell you that I prayed hard. I prayed to the good Lord to save my children from being put out on the street. I was on my knees right there in the kitchen. I prayed until my head hurt and my legs went numb. I had just asked God to give me a sign when I heard your old truck door squeak and slam, and the kids started hollering for candy." She was quiet again for a moment. She looked at Early, and there were tears in her eyes once more, but this time they were joyful, and her eyes sparkled. "I want you to know that I will never forget that you brought my children a treat. That you had enough regard for the poor things to stop and buy them ten dollars' worth of sugar. I swear I won't forget that, not even if I live to be a hundred."

Early was humbled by her thanks. "I don't know," he said, trying to lighten the mood. "If you live to be one hundred, you might get a touch forgetful." He thought it best not to offer any comment about his new status as one of God's signs from above, and he made himself a mental note to oil the door hinges on the truck at the earliest possible moment. There was no sense in tipping people off when he was about to save them. He took a deep breath, patted Millie on her shoulder, and went to work. He had a bus to load and a struggling family to relocate, and he was burning daylight.

Moving the Donovan family made for a busy day. But it wasn't a normal day, or a normal year for that matter. This year, Early's campers were a runaway kid from Florida, a destitute woman and her family from Sequoyah, and an irascible lawyer who had lost all of his money betting on a no-lose proposition. He didn't count the dispossessed creepy deer head he had moved at Millie's request, because even though it was between homes, it had always resided somewhere in the valley.

Millie and her family were installed in Nathanael along with their handful of belongings, mostly clothing, personal effects, and a television. During the move, it became apparent that the furnishings in the house weren't worth the trouble of moving. The various pieces had been cheap to begin with and were now ravaged by wear, time, and the effects of children. They sagged and leaned, with stuffing hanging out at odd seams and duct tape strategically placed where necessary.

"All the cabins are furnished," Early reminded her. "So you don't need this furniture. And when you get ready to move, we'll figure something out. I don't want to make you feel bad, but if we take some of those beds apart, I don't think they're going to go back together. One of them is actually nailed to the wall. And the mattresses have seen better days."

"My new landlords will have to pay someone to move it all out," Millie pointed out.

"Well, you gave them five hundred dollars just the other day. If it costs them more than that to get rid of it, they can send the bill to me."

And so they left all the furniture where it sat.

The bus ride to Camp Redemption was uneventful. Early drove the GMC, and each of the children occupied a separate seat with the exception of Jesús and Lisa Marie, who shared a bench and engaged in quiet conversation. Millie sat in the seat behind Early, and once or twice during the trip when he looked into the mirror above the windshield, he caught her with a smile on her face. He was happy to see that her worries were eased, and he was secretly proud that he had been the one to make it happen.

Once they arrived at the camp and made decisions about who was going to sleep where, the Donovan family began to go about the business of converting a cabin into a home. The two younger children claimed a bunk and a footlocker for themselves in the central sleeping area. When they all noticed that there were plenty of extra beds, each chose a backup bunk as well, just because they could. This was the height of luxury to children who had not known such before, and Early shared vicariously in their pleasure at the extravagance. Nathanael was a large building, the largest of the cabins on the north side of the lake, and the family fit with ease, even with the additional turf that the younger children had staked.

Millie occupied the counselor's bedroom at one end of the structure, and Lisa Marie, at the age when privacy was desirable, gladly took the small game room at the other end.

"Your kids are settling in fine," Ivey noted as she, Early, and Millie stood by the door to the cabin and viewed the housewarming. Ivey had been a whirlwind the entire day. She loved tending other people's children. It was her ministry, and she was in her element. She had folded clothes, settled disputes, unpacked boxes and bags, hung pictures and posters, and offered the occasional spiritual advice when warranted.

"They do seem to be doing great," Millie replied. She turned to Ivey and took hold of both of her hands. "Miss Ivey, thank you so much for taking us in. And for helping us get settled, too. I told Early, and now I'll tell you. You have saved my family. I can never repay the debt I owe you both. Thank you." She blinked a tear and buried Ivey in a hug.

"'The one who despises their neighbor sins,'" Ivey said in a muffled voice. "'But if I have mercy on the poor I am happy.' Proverbs 14:21." She patted Millie's back as she returned the hug.

"She means *you're welcome*," Early said to Millie. To Ivey he said, "You despise Gilla Newman, and he's sort of your neighbor. As a matter of fact, you despised his daddy, Mr. Frank, even more. And you're not too wild about his boy, either. Of course, none of them are poor, but technically, they *are* your neighbors." He thought about it a moment before offering a short addendum. "Well, the live ones are, anyway." Mr. Frank had choked on a communion wafer some years back and had gone to his reward, such as it probably was.

Ivey frowned at Early but said nothing. She was caught dead to rights in a sin, as guilty in her way as Hugh Don Monfort was every time he sold a can of beer or a bottle of whiskey, and there was little she could say in her own defense.

"Don't you worry," Millie said, coming to her aid. "I despise Stanley Newman so much that the good Lord won't even notice your feelings about him." She pointed to the empty spot above the mantle as she directed her next comment to Early. "And thank *you* for moving that deer head. I was hoping you would remember." She shivered involuntarily. "That thing has always given me the worst case of the willies."

"He wanted to put it in the Big House with me, but I put my foot down," Ivey said. "I don't need *wildlife* watching me while I am trying to cook. It's bad enough with Early looking over my shoulder all the time."

"Where did it end up?" Millie asked.

"Right now it's over in Simon." Early replied. "I'm not sure where its new home will be."

"Its new home needs to be in the dumpster behind Simon," Ivey noted.

"Are you kidding? That head is a piece of history. It's way over one hundred years old. It's our heritage."

"It's a piece of a dead deer," Ivey replied, "and I have to agree with Millie. That thing has always been creepy." Given the long and exotic list of Ivey's nocturnal visitors, Early had to concede that if anyone were qualified to spot creepy, it was his sister. "I've got to go finish cooking supper," she continued. "We'll be eating in about an hour. Early, please make sure everyone gets there on time. I want us all to eat together like a family, and I hate to serve a cold meal."

She stepped out of Nathanael and headed back to the Big House. Early walked out onto the porch and sat in one of the rockers. It had been a tiring day, and his weariness was beginning to catch up with him. He thought briefly and fondly of a pipeful and a Schlitz malt liquor down by the lake, but with the crowd and the excitement, he knew it would be impossible to slip off unnoticed. He sighed. It would have to wait. Maybe he would get an opportunity later, after all the children were down for the night. Soon he heard the screen door squeak, and Millie joined him. She sat in the rocker next to his.

"Hey, Millie," Early said. "Busy day."

"I'll say."

"It may take a day or two for you to settle in, but the hard part is over with now."

"We'll all be sore tomorrow."

"I haven't seen Lisa Marie in a while. Is she in her room?" When Lisa Marie had found out that she was to have a room to herself for the first time in her young life, she hugged both her mother and Early.

"No, she has gone for a walk with Jesús."

"They seem to be hitting it off." He chuckled. "We may have a case of puppy like going on there. Ivey will be having chapel this Sunday. I suppose I'll be resuming my normal patrol duties. Still, it shouldn't be too hard to keep track of just two. It was only when the hooky players got up into double digits that I had trouble staying on top of the romance in the air." He cast a sidelong glance at Millie, and she managed a sheepish smile as she looked away.

They rocked quietly on the porch and watched a pair of cardinals at the bird feeder, the male with his fancy red plumage, showing off and causing a fuss, and the female with her sensible brown frock, quietly pecking at the sunflower seeds, looking at her mate with an expression that suggested she wished he would just hush and eat. The sun had dropped low to the mountaintop west of the valley. Soon it would be dusk. Early was wondering idly if Anderson and Candace Shellnut would be interested in adopting the creepy deer head as a wall decoration for the diner when Millie broke the silence.

"Do you ever still walk down to the lake and have a pipeful of marijuana?"

The question caught him off guard. "How do you know about smoking at the lake?" he asked. He had always been careful with his habit, and he assumed his vice had remained a secret. Charnell knew, and Hugh Don, but until now, he thought that was the extent of the list.

"The last year I was a counselor, I saw you slip out of the Big House one night late. I couldn't sleep, so I thought it would be fun to follow you to see what you were doing. You stopped at the dead tree on the trail, then went down to the lake and had a smoke. Later, after you had gone back to bed, I sneaked a pipeful myself. It was the first time I ever smoked marijuana. It was kind of odd that after all of those years living with Patsy and Stu—the two biggest dope heads in the free world—the first time I ever got high was at Bible camp. I have to tell you that I liked it quite a bit. I probably had a genetic predisposition to the stuff. Anyway, I knew right off why it had caught on."

"I'm sorry," Early said. He felt ashamed. "I don't know what to say. I can't remember a single time I've smoked when camp was in session. It would be too easy to get caught when kids are here, and I never wanted to set a bad example for any of the children who attended camp. I must have broken my own rule. Maybe I had a really bad day or something. Maybe Ivey was onto me about a prophecy." Early felt the need to explain, and he wanted her to understand.

"You didn't break your rule. It was between sessions, and Miss Ivey had let me stay an extra weekend. You didn't even know I was here. I never told anyone, so your dark secret is safe. But I have to confess that I sneaked down to the lake several times after that night. I used to love the relaxed, floaty way it made me feel. I would smoke a bowl, then lay back and look at the stars until they started to fade away at dawn. It was the best summer I ever spent here. As a matter of fact, it was the best summer I ever spent, period."

"I feel bad about this," Early said. "I should have set a better example. You were just a kid, and I had a responsibility to help you make good choices."

"You did set a good example. You taught me that you didn't have to be perfect to be a good a person. You taught me that it was possible for a responsible adult to have a little fun and still be a responsible adult. I really didn't mean to upset you. I don't even know why I brought it up. It's not like I've been studying on it all these years. I guess it was just the setting, and you sitting there, that reminded me of happy times. Please, just forget I even asked. It's not important."

They sat quietly for a moment. Then Early spoke. "You're a grown woman now, but in my mind it's like you're still just a kid. That's the way my brain works, I guess. I freeze people in time. Most all of the kids who ever came here will always be youngsters to me. I occasionally run into some of them as adults, but I don't really see them as they are now. So when you asked that question, just now, for a minute I felt like I was talking to an eighteen-year-old version of you. And I felt guilty and defensive. Do you see what I'm saying?" She nodded. "The answer to your question is *yes*," he continued. "I do still like to go down to the lake from time to time. You're welcome to join me whenever you want to."

"That would be nice," she said. "But only if you really don't care. To be honest, I'm sort of looking forward to another hit or two. I got married the year after that summer, and I've been too poor to indulge in any bad habits since." She laughed and shrugged. "It's probably just as well that I married Switch. If I'd had any money, I might have ended up like my parents."

"You're not making me feel better," he said.

"Let's gather up the children and herd them to the Big House," she suggested. "It's getting close to supper time." They stood, and she faced him. After a moment's hesitation, she smiled, and he did the same. Then they turned and went back inside.

Millie Donovan and her brood had been living at the camp about two weeks before she and Early found a chance to continue their discussion concerning Early's bad habits. It was a Tuesday night, and Early had eased down to the falls, both because he felt the need to spend time with Dr. Grabow and because he needed time to himself. Charnell had moved into the Big House the day after the Donovan family took up residence in Nathanael, and he and Ivey had been yammering at each other pretty much nonstop ever since. There was no acrimony in this pastime—indeed, they seemed to enjoy one another's company tremendously—but the noise level was higher than Early was accustomed to.

Charnell's establishment of residence at the Big House had been fortuitous in more ways than one. In addition to providing companionship for Ivey, Charnell addressed a lingering concern that had plagued Early. Ever since he had cancelled camp, Early had been worried about the Willingham Valley cash flow. And with the addition of each extra mouth, that concern had increased. But along with his Cadillac, his suitcases, and his greasy fedora, Charnell had also brought several mason jars full of good, cold, hard cash on moving day.

"A lot of folks keep their money in banks," Early noted.

"If you put your money in a bank, it exists," Charnell replied. "This money doesn't exist." He handed a quart-sized jar of well-preserved currency to Early. "Let me know when that runs out, and I'll give you another one."

"I'd have put you on retainer a long time ago if I'd known about this."

"There have to be special circumstances before my clients get put on the fruit jar plan."

"Ah."

So while Ivey and Charnell watched Tuesday late-night television, Early sat on his bench down by the falls and tamped his pipe full of sweet dreams. There were no lights on anywhere in the camp. Even the pole light down by the road was out, and he had made his way by celestial navigation, moon glow, and memory to his spot by the lake. It was after midnight, so he was not worried about being caught with the smoking gun, or in this case, the smoking pipe. He lit the Dr. Grabow and took a long, slow drag. He held the hit for seven Mississippis, then exhaled and repeated the process. He popped the top of his Schlitz malt liquor and had a sip. It was a fine evening to contemplate the higher mysteries. The fireflies were up late, and they flickered and danced over the surface of the lake like drunken demons. Suddenly, Early heard a twig snap behind him. He coughed and swore, and he was still trying to stuff the lit pipe into his jeans pocket when he heard Millie Donovan speak.

"It's just me, Early. Don't catch your pants on fire." She sat next to him on the bench, took the malt liquor from his hand, and sipped. "I seem to have a knack for catching you smoking pot."

"You scared the bejeezus out of me," he said. His heart was pounding. "I thought one of the kids had snuck up on me for sure." She handed him the can of Schlitz, and he took a long drink.

"If you worry so much about being caught, why don't you just light up at the Big House instead?"

"The view down here is much better. And Ivey has a nose like a coon dog. That's the reason I hide my stash in the tree."

"She can smell the pot?"

"She can smell the sin."

"What about your Schlitz malt liquor?"

"In Ivey's hierarchy of worldly transgressions, sipping a cold malt liquor at the end of a hot day is way on down the list. It's an allowable offense, as long as you don't enjoy it too much and provided you don't forget to feel bad about it later."

"Well, anyway, you don't have to worry about any of the kids tonight. They're all asleep. They had a big day." Millie and Early listened to the falls and watched the moonlight glint from the water's surface. Presently, Millie spoke again. "Do you mind if I have a puff?" she asked.

"Help yourself." He handed the pipe to her. Her first hit produced a fit of coughing, but she was game and determined, and by her third toke, she was handling herself like a refugee from the sixties.

"It's kind of like riding a horse," she remarked. "You never forget how, once you go to the trouble to learn."

"Like riding a bicycle," he agreed.

"I don't know about that. I never learned how."

"Bless your heart," he said. "But no matter. Think of a horse that has two wheels instead of four legs, and you've sort of got the idea." She handed it back, and he took a draw from the pipe and a sip from the can. "How did you know I was down here?" he asked.

"I just had a feeling you might be. I went to bed when the kids did and fell right asleep, but I woke up about an hour ago and couldn't drop back off. I tossed and turned for a while, and then I thought to myself, *I bet Early's down at the lake.* It just seemed like that kind of evening. So I slipped on some clothes and came down to see. And here you are."

"I needed to treat my glaucoma, and Charnell and Ivey were being loud and annoying, so it seemed like a fine time for a stroll."

"You have glaucoma?"

"No."

"Miss Ivey and Charnell are loud and annoying?"

"It's the oddest thing. They're both just a bit hard of hearing, but I never really noticed it before now. If you get them together in a room with some background noise, they start getting louder and louder. After all the times I've seen them together over the years, you'd think I would have noticed it before."

"Why do you think they never got married?"

"Where'd that come from?"

"I'm just curious. Usually, people who have dated for a long time end up getting married."

"I asked Charnell about it once. After he told me to mind my own damn business, he had a few more beers and loosened up enough to tell me the story. He said he's asked her to marry him several times over the years. He even bought her a ring once. But he said it was the great sadness of his life that she always said no. According to Charnell, whenever he asked, she was adamant on the point that she was married spiritually to Jesus, and that if she were to wed Charnell, she would be married twice, and that would be a sin."

"So she won't marry him because she considers herself already married."

"Right."

"To a member of the Trinity."

"Yep."

"But she's been dating Charnell since before I was born."

"Exactly."

"So when she's on a date with Charnell, she is sort of fooling around on—"

"God, basically. It's complicated. To be honest with you, I don't think she's ever just sat down and thought about it all the way through to its logical end. That's not the way her mind works. And she's not going to hear it from me. I don't think she'd take it all that well if she realized she was a cosmic floozy. That's the kind of information that could ruin her whole day."

"What does Charnell think about beating Jesus' time?"

"Charnell gives three-to-five most days that he's going to hell anyway, so he says he could care less. He says he loves Ivey and always has, and if he has to be the boy toy on the side, then that's what he'll be."

"Strangely, of all the images that jump to mind when I think about Charnell Jackson, boy toy isn't one of them."

"I know what you mean." Maybe it was the ears.

They sat quietly and comfortably as they finished sharing the Dr. Grabow and the can of malt liquor. Early had a small, pleasant buzz, and from the contented sigh that came from Millie, he assumed that she, too, had enjoyed the smoke.

"I feel very…nice," she said.

"Should I pack the pipe again?" he asked.

"Lord, no. You're going to have to carry me home as it is."

"Well, it's not that far, and you don't look that heavy." He gestured at her with the bag of pot and the pipe once again.

"Oh, what the hell," she said. "I haven't gotten good and ripped since before I was married. A girl's got to let her hair down from time to time, don't you think?" As a response, Early loaded about half a bowl and relit the pipe. They shared it in silence. Then, as he liked to do, he eased his head onto the back of the bench and watched the stars.

"There is a line of bright flashing lights like strobe lights all along the mountaintops," Millie noted. "They stretch as far as I can see. What are they?"

"Those are cell phone towers. I like them because they look like the masts of old sailing ships. If you look at them during the day, you'll see that they have crow's nests up near the top. I don't know why that appeals to me so much, but it does. Maybe because it's something very old combined with something brand new."

"What are the crow's nests for?"

"I don't know a lot about cell phone towers, but I guess they're for technicians to stand in while they work on whatever it is they work on up there. Kind of on that same subject, my father's brother used to be the guy who changed the flashing red lights in radio and television towers. This was back in the fifties and sixties. He was a young guy, real small and wiry, and he would scoot up those towers like a chimpanzee. My father said he was fearless. But he couldn't fly, apparently. He missed his step while working on a tower up on Signal Mountain, Tennessee. He fell sixty feet and landed on a rock, and that was it for Uncle Eldon." There was a long silence. Then Millie began to laugh, as if he had told a great joke. "What?" Early asked.

"I'm sorry," Millie replied, still laughing. "That was a really great story, Early. I'm serious." She wiped a tear.

"Then why are you laughing?" He was truly confused.

"I don't know," she said. "Poor Uncle Eldon. He couldn't fly..." They sat and watched the towers flash under the canopy of night. Presently, Early heard his companion begin to snore. It was a wonderfully pleasant scene, and he briefly considered smoking another pipe, but he decided against it. He knew he needed to get his partner in sin home before one of her children awoke and missed her. So he stood, stretched, and stashed his supplies in his pocket. Then he shook Millie's shoulder gently.

"Millie, wake up."

"Mmmph..." She swatted at his hand and slid down to a prone position on the bench. He shook her once again.

"Come on. Time to go home."

"Uh, uh," she murmured. Then she began to snore once again. Early sighed. He sat her up on the bench. Then he stood her up and carefully bent down and draped her over his right shoulder. He felt protective of her at that moment, as if she were a child, and he knew it fell to him to see her home and to keep her from harm. He quietly carried her up the trail and back to Nathanael, and once there he eased open the door and slipped inside with his burden. She never stirred as he silently placed her on her bunk. Then he tiptoed back out into the night and quietly closed the door behind him.

Chapter Thirteen

Summer came to Willingham Valley like an old friend wearing strange new clothes, and it brought with it both the familiar and the novel. The daytime weather was hot and humid, but the nights were cool, and there was no rain to speak of that long season. As was normally the case in summer, children wandered the grounds of Camp Redemption, but the young folks hiking the trails and swimming in the lake were fewer in number, and they were permanent features on the landscape rather than temporary visitors just passing through.

Additionally, there was church on Sunday and Wednesday, but instead of these services being held solely for the benefit of Bible campers and camp employees, they were the scheduled worship rituals of the newly formed Camp Church, of which Ivey was the preacher, deacon, and caretaker. Led by Avis Shropshire and his family, a small exodus of disaffected but faithful rapture preparationists had wandered the wilderness from Brother Rickey's church toward Willingham Valley, and now fifty or so worshippers sat in the pews every time Ivey rang her bell, opened her doors, and banged on her pulpit.

During the course of the summer, Ivey had five visions. This was not a remarkable record in and of itself. She often had her dreams and prophecies in series, and these periods of increased activity were sometimes followed by quiet interims in which no representatives from the golden land came to see her. There was no set pattern, so it was not unusual for her to have five visions during such a short span. The difference this year, though, was in the enigmatic nature of the revelations. Normally when a messenger came to Ivey, the sacred memorandum was clear to her. But that was not the case with these latest revelations. Now, it was as if the messages were not meant to reveal but rather to confuse or otherwise disguise the truth. In Early's opinion, they were not unlike many of the parables he had read in the New Testament, their arcane meanings buried under layers of obfuscation and hyperbole.

The first of Ivey's summer visions came soon after Charnell Jackson moved into the Big House. That development had surprised Ivey, but she acted as pleased as a schoolgirl at her first prom. Indeed, when her longtime companion took up residence, it seemed as if Ivey became less fractious than usual. She and Charnell had not exactly grown old together, but they had certainly aged in close proximity to one another, and she seemed to find it a comfort to have her lifelong friend near to hand, like a favorite dog-eared book or a frayed heirloom quilt.

But two nights after Charnell arrived, Vester Willingham visited Ivey. He was normally a quiet, pleasant shade—not much trouble at all, really, just as he had been in life—but on this occasion, he was wild-eyed and unkempt. When Early came down to the kitchen the following morning, his sister was already at the table. She was dressed, the coffee was made, and the biscuits were browning in the oven, so it appeared she had been up for some time. She seemed unsettled, and if he didn't know better, he would've sworn that something had frightened her.

"Morning," Early said. "Sleep well?"

"Daddy came to see me last night," she answered. Early noticed a quaver in her voice, and she was paler than usual.

"Was he mad because you're shacking up with Charnell?" Early asked.

"Behave yourself, Early. We're not shacking up. We're living in the same house."

"Sorry. Poor word choice. How's Daddy doing?" Early poured a cup of coffee and added two spoons of sugar.

"Not too good," she answered vaguely.

"Tell me about it." He warmed her coffee while he had the pot handy. Then he sat beside her at the table.

"He looked really bad, like he had been sick."

"Well, Ivey, he *is* dead." There was no avoiding the fact. Vester Willingham had been gone a long time.

"Still, he wasn't right," Ivey replied in a distracted manner, almost as if she were talking to herself. "He hung around a little while, not saying anything at all. And then he quoted Matthew to me. 'And then shall many be offended, and shall betray one another, and shall hate one another.' That's Matthew 24:10. I know it like the back of my hand, but I don't know what he meant by it. I heard the words as plain as could be, but I can't for the life of me figure out why he said them." She looked at her baby brother, her business partner and confidant. "There's no reason to even *have* a vision if you can't figure out what it's supposed to mean. It doesn't make sense to have one if you don't know why."

Early couldn't agree more. It seemed a pointless exercise to host a visitor from the far shore unless some type of useful information was gained during the visit. "What else did he say?"

"Not one single word. In all my years, I've never seen anything like it. He never made another sound. But he stood there the rest of the night, just looking at me with a sad expression on his face. Sometimes he floated over to the window and stared out like he was looking at the road, like he was waiting for someone. Then he would come back over to the bed again." She caught her brother's eye. "It kind of scared me, and Daddy has never frightened me before, living or dead. I finally got up and came down here so he would go away and leave me alone, so he would quit looking at me." She gazed over at the oven. Then she arose. "I think the biscuits are ready."

"Sounds like a creepy visit." Early took a sip of his coffee. It was hot, strong, and sweet.

"I hope I didn't hurt his feelings. He *is* our father. But I couldn't stand him looking at me anymore. And I don't like it that I don't know what he was trying to tell me. What do you think it means?"

"Lord, Ivey, I don't know. You're the resident expert on this kind of stuff. Maybe it had something to do with Brother Rickey and the boys over at the Blood and the Fire. That was a kind of betrayal. They betrayed their faith, and they betrayed your trust in them. For sure they betrayed Avis Shropshire." Early was not one for regrets, but he wished he had popped Rickey Lee upside the head when he had been granted the opportunity. Life was short, and another chance was not guaranteed.

In Early's studied opinion, the management of the Washed in the Blood and the Fire Rapture Preparation Temple were each and every one a waste of good dumplings. He and Hugh Don Monfort had recently passed a pleasant hour exploring that very issue, and they had agreed that there wasn't a thing wrong with the group that a short head start and a high-power rifle wouldn't cure. Hugh Don had even offered to burn the church to the ground. He further proposed to let Early have the option of deciding whether or not Brother Rickey should be inside during the blaze. All Early had to do was give the word and buy the marshmallows. It was a fine offer indeed, but Early declined, although he appreciated the rain check Hugh Don had extended in case he changed his mind.

"It was a betrayal for a fact," Ivey said. "A big one. A going-to-hell one, if you want to know my opinion. But it's behind us now. Why would Daddy come all the way down here to tell me about something that's already happened? There's nothing I can do about it. I can't change it or prevent the deacons from hurting Avis Shropshire's feelings. That's already done. I can't make them love their neighbor if they won't do it, no matter what the Bible says on the subject. And it says plenty." She looked as if she were about to back up her assertion with a few examples, but Early beat her to the draw.

"I don't know what to tell you, Ivey. It does seem like our father wasted a long trip. You know what you ought to do? You should pray on it, and maybe it'll come to you. Maybe you'll figure it out." It was a puzzle, but Early didn't plan on giving the matter too much more attention, because he knew that Ivey would worry with it until she had figured it out to her satisfaction. Inferring relevance and meaning from arcane incidents had always been a strength of hers, a divine gift.

By the time Ivey's second vision occurred, the month of June was past and a hot and muggy July was on them like a morning fog clinging to bottom land. It was the Fourth of July, Independence Day, and Early and Ivey had brought all the residents of Camp Redemption down to the lake for a picnic and an afternoon of relaxation. They enjoyed a lunch of cold fried chicken, potato salad, baked beans, and fried pies. Subsequent to the celebratory meal—and in honor of cramp prevention—Ivey enforced the customary one-hour delay before allowing the youngsters to enter the water. The swimming embargo may or may not have been an old wives' tale, but there was no arguing the fact that not one single person under the age of eighteen had ever suffered a cramp and drowned on Ivey's watch, and she intended to keep it that way. The hour dragged slowly by with many complaints from would-be swimmers, until Ivey put the matter into perspective.

"My mama used to make us wait *three* hours," she told Millie Donovan's youngsters. They looked appalled at this new information.

"No way!" said Lisa Marie.

"It's true," Early said. "You could die of old age before Clairy Willingham would let you get into the water. She'd make you wait three hours even if you were on fire. Still, I never got a cramp." He had to admit it.

Finally, Ivey allowed Millie and her children to go swimming in the cool, green water of Lake Echota. Charnell wasn't much of a swimmer, so after lunch he climbed into his Caddy and drove over to Hugh Don Monfort's place for a cold beer and a boiled-egg chaser. It was a hot day, and Early was considering a swim, but in the meantime he skipped stones away from the swimmers and toward the falls. The idea of getting into the water held some appeal, but he suspected if he got into the lake now, he would likely be relegated to diving duty. Millie's younger two loved to climb onto his shoulders and dive into the water. Early liked to play with the kids, but a little diving duty went a long way, especially when the diving platform was over fifty and prone to spells of sciatica.

Ivey, the designated matriarch of the idyllic scene, was busy napping on a blanket in the warm, patriotic sun. Suddenly she sat up, confusion etched on her features like fine filigree. She looked first to the left and then to the right. She shook her head, cupped her hands to her mouth, and yelled for her brother. Early glanced over his shoulder at the sound. Then he dropped the remainder of his smooth stones and came running.

"What's wrong?" he asked as he trotted up.

"Mama came to see me just now," she replied. She sounded agitated almost to the point of anger.

"Was she sick like Daddy?" Early asked.

"Early, she's *dead*," Ivey explained patiently, as if her brother were limited in his understanding of the nature of mortality. Early stood corrected.

"Yes, I remember," he muttered. Sometimes it was difficult being Ivey's brother. But he plowed forward regardless. "What did she say that got you so stirred up?"

"'I must work the works of him that sent me, while it is day: the night cometh, when no man can work.'" She spoke the words dramatically. The syllables were dark and full of omen, and the very air around them seemed to chill.

"That's from John, isn't it?" he asked. The verse had a familiar ring.

"John, ninth chapter, fourth verse." She looked at Early. "It's a portent about death. Brother Rickey used to call it the death verse."

"Screw Brother Rickey," Early interjected. It was a conditioned reflex, a Pavlovian response that he could not control. "Sorry," he said in anticipation of Ivey's reaction.

"I should hope so! Anyway, I was taking my nap and minding my own business when all of a sudden I felt a breeze on my face. I looked up, and there she was. She wouldn't look at me at all. She said what she said—and she only said it once, just like Daddy did when he came to see me—and then she drifted away." Ivey pointed east, where, presumably, heaven lay.

"Just settle down. I don't think it's about a particular death," Early said. "To me it's kind of like she was telling us to stick to the right path, to stay on the old straight and narrow highway, because sooner or later, we all have to die. That's a whole different message. It's more like a general reminder to behave rather than a specific prediction about any one person's death. It might even make a good sermon."

"I've preached on that very point many times. It's never a bad idea to remind folks that they need to have their houses in order. You'd probably remember the sermon if you had been paying attention. But you didn't hear Mama. I did, and this was different. She was talking about imminent death. Someone's going to die." She was adamant.

"How do you know that for sure?"

"How do I know that water's wet and the sky is blue? I just know. But what I don't know is whose death Mama was predicting, and that makes me afraid." She shivered, and Early saw goose bumps form on the backs of her arms.

"Ivey, you don't have to be afraid about dying."

"Oh, good Lord, Early! What are you thinking? I'm not afraid for me! I'm ready whenever He is. I've been ready for years. But what if it's a warning about one of these poor children, here, or their mama? Or even you, for heaven's sake?" She looked over her shoulder, as if the angel of death might be slipping up at that very moment, coming in on tiptoe, holding the scythe over his head so it didn't drag in the gravel. Then she lowered her voice. "It could even be a foretelling about Charnell. I love Charnell Jackson, and I'll tell you right now I'm afraid for *him* to die. I've gone to my knees and prayed hard for that man every day for over fifty years, but what if that wasn't enough to save him? Heaven just wouldn't be the same without Charnell." She shuddered as she contemplated the idea. "That's what I'm worried about." Early sat beside her on the blanket and put his arm around her shoulder. He couldn't help thinking that heaven wouldn't be the same *with* Charnell, either, although he didn't share that musing with his sister.

"And you don't have any idea about who Mama was talking about?" he asked instead.

"Not a single clue. Last month, Daddy warned me about a betrayal. Now, Mama has come to warn me about a death. Something bad is going to happen, Early. Right here in our valley. Here at Camp Redemption. I can feel it in my bones, and if I can't figure it out and maybe stop it, then someone's going to be betrayed, and someone's going to die."

"Maybe it'll be Brother Rickey or Gilla Newman," Early said, trying to put a positive spin on the moment that would perhaps cheer Ivey up. Maybe one would betray the other, which would lead to them shooting each other.

"Maybe it won't," came her morose reply. She was having none of his words of comfort.

"Try not to let it fret you."

"How can I not let it worry me? This is not a maybe. I'll tell you one thing. We're going to be double-safe around here until I can figure this out."

"Does that mean we can't shoot off the fireworks once it gets dark?" Early had a feeling that the pyrotechnic display was about to be cancelled in the name of public safety. He had driven over to Alabama for the fireworks and had come home with an impressive array. He knew that the kids and Charnell would be disappointed if Ivey forbade their use.

"Yes," Ivey confirmed. "And get those children out of the water. They've been in there long enough, and there's no use in tempting fate. They could all be working up leg cramps right now."

Ivey's third brush with revelation came on July 16, Charnell Jackson's birthday. During the adult portion of that celebration, Charnell broke out a dusty bottle of Glenfiddich single malt whiskey that he claimed was between fifty and sixty years old. That may or may not have been the case, but it was smooth regardless, and before long there was more of it inside the revelers than in the flask. Even Ivey had a small tumbler of the amber fire, and she sipped at it from time to time in honor of the birthday boy.

"Drink up!" Charnell said loudly. "We don't want the damn lawyers to get their hands on this, too!" The damn lawyers had been having their way with Charnell and his tired old assets all summer, and he had become fussy as a result.

"Charnell, *you're* a damn lawyer," said Millie Donovan, who had imbibed more than one small tumbler of the whiskey.

"That's true, darlin.' But I'm a *good* lawyer. A *decent* lawyer. A lawyer with compassion and integrity. And I was out of law school and practicing good, decent, compassionate law while these blood-sucking bastards were still dragging on their promiscuous mamas' tits. Curse them *and* their promiscuous mamas' tits." He held up his glass in solemn salute to his black-hearted adversaries and their sainted but lascivious mothers' bosoms.

"Charnell!" Ivey said. She was frowning and rubbing her temples, as if her boyfriend's outburst had given her a headache. "You shouldn't curse people, even if it is your birthday! And you shouldn't refer to their mothers' chests, either." She took a deep breath before she continued with a disgusted tone in her voice. "And saying *tit* is a sin." Early wasn't so sure about this last admonition, although the first two pieces of advice had been relatively sound.

"You're right, Ivey," Charnell said, abashed. "I got carried away. I don't know what I was thinking. I apologize." He bowed low in an exaggerated manner and swept his arm before him. "It must be the whiskey."

"Whiskey or not, you need to get your mind *off* of strange women's bosoms and get your mind *onto* the Lord," Ivey noted ominously. "And once you get it there, you need to keep it there."

"Yes, ma'am," came his humble reply. "Will you forgive me?"

"I will forgive you," she said, but her voice had dropped to a whisper. "But only because it's your birthday. Anyway, I'm not the one you should be concerned with. You need to be asking the Lord for His forgiveness..." Her voice trailed off. Then her eyes seemed to bulge before rolling back in her head.

She slumped face forward onto her plate of cake. Her forehead hit the table with a loud thunk.

"Ivey!" Early and Charnell chorused. Chairs flew back and tipped over as they both jumped to their feet. Each man came around the table from the opposite side. Early grabbed his sister's wrist and checked her pulse. It was strong and steady. Charnell snatched a placemat and began to fan her. Millie Donovan hopped up and scooted to the sink. She grabbed a clean dishcloth and turned on the cold water tap.

"Her heart's beating fine," Early said tensely. His mind went to the death his departed mother had recently foretold, and he shivered in spite of himself. "And she's breathing okay," he continued. He had taken several first aid courses over the years in acknowledgement of his responsibilities as a camp owner and keeper of children, but most of his experience had tended toward removing splinters, cleaning scrapes, and bandaging cuts. Strokes ran in the Willingham line, and he wondered if maybe Ivey had suffered one. He searched his memory for the symptoms that would signal one.

"Did she have too much Scotch?" Charnell asked. He was hovering and ill at ease. "She's not used to drinking."

"She only had a sip or two," Early replied. "I don't think that's the problem. I'm worried that she might have had a stroke." He raised her head gently and felt her skin. It was warm to the touch, but not excessively so, and it didn't feel clammy. He took both of these factors to be good signs. Millie handed him the cool compress she had prepared, and he carefully bathed the cake from his sister's face. Ivey was unresponsive at first. Then her eyelids fluttered. Finally they opened, and she looked in momentary confusion at the concerned crowd.

"Are you okay?" Charnell asked. His voice was a decibel or two louder than his normal roar. This was a condition brought about by too much good Scotch blended with an overload of worry.

"I'm fine. Except that my head hurts, and you're hollering at me." She put her hand to the small goose egg growing in the center of her forehead. "What happened to my head?" Then she looked at the table. "What happened to my cake?"

"You passed out and hit your head on the table," Early explained. "And you sort of landed in the cake, too." He took her pulse again. It was still fine. He had finally remembered some of the early warning signs of strokes, and he intended to check them off one by one, just to be safe. He had already noted that she was not slurring her words, and her memory seemed unimpaired. "Can you see all right?" he asked her.

"I had a vision," Ivey replied.

"No, Ivey, I mean are you seeing okay in *this* world?"

"I see just fine," she responded.

"How many fingers am I holding up?"

"Two fingers and a thumb."

"Can you move all of your limbs? Any tingling or numbness?"

She raised her hands and wiggled her fingers. "I'm fine," she said. "Really. And you'll never guess who came to see me just now. Not in a million years."

"Who came?" Early asked.

"Robert Corntassel."

"Who is that?" Millie asked. She was somewhat familiar with Ivey's extracurricular activities thanks to Early and Charnell's descriptions, but this was the first she had heard of the elusive Chickasaw from the cemetery.

"He used to own the valley years ago, back before the Willinghams came here," Ivey said. "He foretold the coming of Jesús."

"How's his back?" Charnell quizzed as he took a dram of Scotch to steady his nerves.

217

"Can we get back to Ivey passing out?" Early asked.

"It still gives him trouble on cold mornings," Ivey replied to Charnell, oblivious to her brother's fears and moods.

"I don't like him poking around here," Charnell said. Then he turned his attention to Early. "Remember what I told you about him. He's fishing for a settlement. I guarantee it." The ancient barrister was sitting beside Ivey, stroking her hand.

"I think everyone here must be totally insane," Early said. "We need to quit worrying about Robert Corntassel and take Ivey to the doctor."

"I'm not going to the doctor," Ivey calmly replied. "You know I don't believe in them ever since they killed Mama and Daddy."

"A car accident killed our father, and a heart attack took our mother," Early noted. He hated to contradict his sister, but he deemed these particular facts pertinent.

"I know what I know," Ivey said as she crossed her arms. It was one of her favorite arguments, concise and difficult to counter.

"Excuse me," said Millie. "I really hate to interrupt, but if Robert Corntassel is dead, how can he be fishing for a settlement?" She looked at Early quizzically. "What kind of settlement would he be fishing for? What good would money do him?"

Early sighed, and then he explained as best he could given the nature of the facts. "Charnell thinks Robert Corntassel might be considering legal action because he hurt his back in the valley that we now own."

"But he's dead!" Millie exclaimed again.

"Tell *him*," Early replied, pointing toward Charnell, who was back to fanning Ivey with one of the placemats.

"Degree of animation doesn't matter," Charnell said. "Dead people sue and get sued all the time. One of the people suing me right now is dead—hopefully dead and in hell—but dead for sure. If I could lay my hands on the other two bastards that are after my hide, they'd be dead, too, although I'd hate to end up doing them a favor."

"How can killing them be doing them a favor?"Millie asked.

"A lot of people don't know this," Charnell replied, "but under certain circumstances, being dead actually enhances your case. It gets the judge and jury on your side. You get the sympathy vote. I can't tell you the number of times I've advised a client that they'd be better off from a legal standpoint if they were dead." He took a gulp of his Scotch, belched, and then took another. "Pardon," he said.

"Can we at least get back to Ivey's vision?" Early asked, casting away all hope for a prompt medical follow-up. Perhaps it was the Scotch, or maybe it was the personalities of the crowd, or it could be that his sister had simply cried *wolf* one too many times, but whatever it was, Early knew he was not in control of the situation, and it was unlikely that he would regain the upper hand anytime soon. He decided that a good fallback plan would be to keep an eye on her. He looked at his sister. Except for the bruise on her forehead, she seemed fine. "What did Robert Corntassel have to say for himself?" he asked.

"Well, first he told me he was glad to see me, and then he asked how you were."

"I'm good."

"That's what I told him. Then he quoted Scripture. 'And, ye fathers, provoke not your children to wrath: but bring them up in the nurture and admonition of the Lord.' That's Ephesians 6:4, and before you even ask me, I don't have any idea what it means." She held out her hands as if to demonstrate that there was nothing up her sleeves but skinny arms and abundant faith.

"Maybe Robert was just passing on some general child-raising advice," Early said, but it was a half-hearted attempt that he knew Ivey would discount. "We have kids living here now." Of course, none of them actually had fathers on the premises, so it could be something else altogether, or more likely nothing at all. "What do you think about that idea?" he asked Ivey.

"I think I have had visions since before you were born, and I've always known who they were about and what they meant. Now I have had three in a row that I can't completely understand. Maybe I've lost my gift. Maybe the Lord is angry at me for something." She shrugged, but she seemed more resigned than upset.

"I'm sure that's not it," Early said. "You've got to be one of His favorite people in the whole world." Of course, Early thought, that was no guarantee that she would always escape the heavenly gaze. Job had once been highly placed, and just look what had happened to him.

"Don't you worry yourself," Millie said. "It'll come to you." She gave Ivey a small hug.

"Don't let it get you down," Charnell boomed.

"I have a headache, and I'm going to bed," Ivey replied. She slid back her chair, arose, and headed up the stairs.

"Go with her, Charnell, and keep an eye on her." Early was still worried that she might have had a light stroke, or that she had suffered a concussion when she struck the tabletop. "Talk to her. Read to her. Don't let her go to sleep for a while." Charnell nodded, grabbed the Glenfiddich, and headed for the loft. Early looked over at Millie, who had reclaimed her seat next to him.

"It's not too late to move out," he noted conversationally. "I'll bet there are normal camps out there somewhere that would take you in."

"I don't want to move out," she replied. "I like it right where I am. And anyway, I think maybe normal is not as common as you think."

It was another month and a day before Ivey received any additional messages, but she made up for this paucity by having two of them on the same day. The first came via an unusual messenger, or at least an uncommon one, although in Early's opinion that disclaimer could be placed on all her visitors, since they were, after all, not of the normal world of man.

"Seaborn Willingham came to see me last night in a dream," Ivey announced one Monday morning. She and Early were sweeping out the church after a full Sunday of use.

"You're getting a lot of traffic this summer," Early noted as he swatted at a cobweb clutching a rafter. As near as he could remember, this was the first time Seaborn Willingham had made the trip back to high Georgia. In that regard, it was a momentous day.

"You know, he didn't look at all like that picture in Daddy's book," Ivey replied as she polished the oak pulpit. Vester Willingham had inserted several photos and drawings of ancestral Willinghams into his history of the valley, including a stern-faced rendition of Seaborn Willingham, the patriarch of the clan, that had reportedly been drawn by an itinerant artist in exchange for a plate of beans and some corn bread. "As a matter of fact, if you had red hair, he would've looked a lot like you. I didn't even know who he was until he told me his name."

"Good genetics," Early commented as he stalked a particularly recalcitrant dust bunny with his broom. "I'm curious to hear what Seaborn had to say." It wasn't that often that one got to hear the thoughts of a two-hundred-year-old patriarch.

"What *didn't* he say? I'll tell you one thing. That man was a talker. He kept me up half the night! He asked me how the family was doing, and what all was going on in the valley. He told me that Mama and Daddy sent word that they were fine, and to remember what they'd said to me when they were here. Then he asked me the strangest question." She was on her knees now, wiping down the baseboards. She apparently became so absorbed in this task that Early was finally forced to break the silence.

"Which was?"

"Oh. He asked me if I had seen Robert Corntassel hanging around the valley. He said he was looking for him. I told Seaborn that he had been here twice. Seaborn seemed kind of sad when he talked about Robert. He said he bore his portion of the sins of the ages because of the way he had treated Robert. Then he quoted me a verse from Psalms: 'The wicked plotteth against the just, and gnasheth upon him with his teeth.' That's Psalms 37:12." Ivey stood and smoothed her skirt. Then she stretched her back before taking a seat in the front pew. She was again silent as she studied the wooden cross on the front wall of the church. It was hand-carved black hickory, and family legend held that Munroe Willingham had originally fashioned it as a grave marker for his departed wife and children after the diphtheria epidemic had claimed them.

"Ivey," Early said. She startled.

"Huh? Oh, sorry. I was just thinking about how simple and beautiful Munroe's cross is."

"It is a wonderful old cross," Early agreed. He sat beside his sister. "You don't seem upset about Seaborn's message. You must know what it means." He hoped so, anyway. If his sister could decipher the message, then things might be getting back to what passed for normal in Willingham Valley. They could put from their minds the enigmatic messages from

222

earlier in the summer, just will them to depart the earthly plane and trouble them no more.

"I do. Before Seaborn left, he told me the story of how he came to own Willingham Valley. It was so sad."

"He bought it from Robert Corntassel, didn't he?"

"That's what we always heard from Daddy, but that's not what really happened." She looked at her brother, and there was a tear on her cheek. "Seaborn Willingham killed Robert Corntassel and took the land. He hit him in the back with a mattock. Then he buried him in the cemetery and stole the valley. It was just like it said in Psalms. The wicked plotted against the just."

"The wicked will do that. You've got to keep an eye on them all the time."

"I wish I didn't know about Seaborn and Robert," she said. "I've always loved the valley. Now I don't feel the same. I still love it here, but I feel bad, too. Bad and sad at the same time. Do you know what I'm saying?"

"I think so. But don't let it worry you. It happened two hundred years ago, and you didn't have a thing to do with it. Anyway, that explains why Robert's back hurts all the time. Whatever you do, don't tell Charnell about this. It'll just get him stirred up. He'll want to depose Seaborn, and that might be hard to arrange." She nodded, and Early continued. "So Seaborn came back to confess his sins? Is that what this was about?"

"I think it was, but he didn't come right out and say that. I think maybe he also came to apologize for what he'd done. When he left, he told me he was heading for the cemetery to see if he could find Robert. Why else would he be looking for him, except to apologize to him for killing him and stealing his land?"

"Maybe Robert has more property."

"Hush, Early."

"Sorry." Early had no solution for her question. He wondered why his ancestor had chosen here and now to clear the air. He wondered why his sister's current vision dealt with the past and not the future, which was the customary focus of the divine gaze. He wondered why Seaborn and Robert hadn't just gotten together in heaven over a couple of beers to iron out their differences. And, of course, he wondered why he was wondering about any of this, given the strong possibility that his big sister was harmlessly insane.

Ivey's fifth and final visit from beyond came that night. As he later related to Early after he awakened him for advice, Charnell discovered her mid-vision, so to speak, when he slipped down the hall and tapped on her bedroom door to wish her a good night. He heard her voice but not her answer, which he assumed was something along the lines of *come in.* He had been quite surprised to find her fully asleep while sitting up in her bed, engaging in discourse with no one he could see. Charnell watched this one-sided conversation for a moment before heading up the hall to Early's room.

"Early! Wake up!" Charnell whispered loudly as he snatched the bedroom door open.

"Huh?" Early asked sleepily. Then his reflexes fired and he came fully awake. "What's wrong?"

"Ivey's having a prophecy! She's sitting up in her bed, talking to someone who isn't even there."

Early yawned. "She always talks to people who aren't there," he said. "You ought to know that by now. Go back to bed."

"I know it, but I've never seen it before. You have to admit, it's kind of weird. Like in *The Exorcist* or something. Come help me wake her up."

"I don't want her awake. I want us asleep." He heard Charnell fumbling for the floor lamp by the door. "And don't turn on that light." Charnell turned on the light. The installation of a lock on his bedroom door climbed to the number-one spot on Early's to-do list.

"Come on!" Charnell said.

"Let me find my robe," Early replied to Charnell's retreating back.

When Early arrived at his sister's room, he found Charnell sitting in the bedside rocking chair, looking worried. He had switched on Ivey's reading lamp, and in that half-light he appeared even older than he was. Ivey, on the other hand, looked rested and serene, and the light from the lamp made her appear to glow. She sat in her bed and conversed fluently with a blank spot on the wall just above her picture of Jesus talking to the little children.

"What language is that?" Charnell asked Early.

"I don't think it's an actual language. It's a tongue she talks in when communicating with her informants. This is only the third time I've ever heard her having a vision, but it sounds the same as it did before. That's also the tongue she talks in when the Spirit comes on her in church. In over fifty years, you've never seen her fall out and talk in tongues?"

"I've missed that."

"You need to tighten up, Charnell. This kind of stuff is regular business around here. You better get used to it."

"What should we do about Ivey?" Charnell asked.

"I'm all for leaving her alone. She's been doing this her whole life without any help. But if you insist on waking her up, wait until she gets through talking. Maybe that will mean her vision is over."

"Do you think these visions are real?" Charnell asked. In all of the time they had known each other, he and Early had never actually discussed this particular subject. But it hadn't been because it was off-limits so much as it simply hadn't come up. Ivey was who and what she was, and they both had always acknowledged that fact and stayed away from their personal beliefs about her nature. But standing in a half-dark room in the middle of the night watching her talk in tongues, it seemed an eminently reasonable inquiry, a question that begged an answer.

"They're real to her," Early responded, "and if we wake her up in the middle of one, we'll catch hell for days. But I don't know if they are actually happening or not. Logic tells me that she's not talking to dead people from heaven, but logic can be wrong, so who the hell knows? What about you? What do you think?"

"I think they're real."

"Really?" Early was truly surprised. He had expected a little more cynicism from Charnell. "You think she is in touch with heaven? You think she's receiving a prophecy right now?"

"I think she's in touch with beings from another realm. I don't know if it's angels, or just your garden-variety ghosts, or creatures from another dimension, but I don't think she's nuts. She's a religious woman, so her mind processes what's happening to her in terms she's comfortable with. But it's definitely happening. She's psychic, or clairvoyant, or something like that. I guarantee it."

"And you believe this because?"

"Mostly because I have to," Charnell admitted. "You have to believe in the people you love. If you don't, you can't really love them."

"That's as good a reason as any, I guess."

They sat and watched her until, finally, after another ten minutes or so, her discourse drew to a close. Her head again rested on her pillow. Early was about to suggest that they just tiptoe out and leave her be, now that the excitement was over, when her eyes snapped open and she turned her head in their direction.

"Early! Charnell! What's the matter? Is there a fire?" Ever since she was a child, whenever she awoke in the night, her first question always concerned fire.

"No, Ivey," Charnell said. "We heard you having a vision, and we came in to check on you."

"Lord, I'll say I had one!" She caught Early's eye. "I've never had one quite like it before. Do you have any idea who came to see me?"

"Tell me who came, Ivey."

"Switch Donovan," she replied. "The very man!"

"Switch Donovan came to see you," Early stated flatly. "Millie's dead husband. The Switch Donovan who got run over by a train."

"It was him!"

"I don't want to put too fine a point on this, but unless I have really misunderstood how the whole deal works, Switch shouldn't be in heaven to begin with." He looked at Ivey. "Am I missing something here?"

She shook her head. "No, you're right on the mark. I asked him the same question, because I knew that he had two wives and all, and that he had gotten up to a good bit of other trouble while he was here, too. He said he remembered being cut in half by the wheels of that train car. He told me that it hurt really bad at the time, and that it's not much better now, and that he's been hanging around the railroad yard ever since."

"So hell is a railroad siding in Fort Payne?" Charnell asked. "That doesn't sound so bad." He looked relieved.

"It doesn't sound like streets of gold, either, with all your friends and loved ones waiting for you," Ivey pointed out.

"That's true," Charnell conceded.

"What, exactly, did Switch want?" Early asked, now that one of the great mysteries of eternity had been resolved.

"Well, he asked how Millie and the kids were—"

"I'll bet."

"—and then he quoted some Scripture to me. He said, 'Marriage is honorable in all, and the bed undefiled: but whoremongers and adulterers God will judge.' That's Hebrews 13:4."

"So Switch Donovan is giving marriage advice?" Early asked. "That's just great." This particular vision was getting on his nerves. He supposed that sometimes dead people could just hit a person all wrong.

"Well, he *was* a pro," Charnell noted helpfully.

"There was more," Ivey told them. "He also said 'Two are better than one; because they have a good reward for their labor.' That's Ecclesiastes 4:9. I just love Ecclesiastes."

"He'd know about two being better than one, too," Early said. He looked at his sister. "What's it all mean, Ivey?"

"I think it must mean we're going to have a wedding."

"Who's getting married?" Early asked.

"Switch didn't say."

"Switch Donavan is as useless as tits on a bull," Charnell said.

"Never speak ill of the dead," Ivey warned.

"It's okay, Ivey," Charnell said. "I said the same thing to him when he was alive."

228

Chapter Fourteen

September arrived windy and cool. This blustery weather was unusual for the ninth month of the year, which normally resembled summer more than fall, and which generally favored the dog days of August more than it did the pleasant nights of October. But change was flapping in the winds of North Georgia like a red flag at dawn, and the inhabitants of Camp Redemption found themselves squarely in its path. Later in his life, whenever Early looked back on that outlandish season, he had to admit that everything happened just as it had been foretold. Ivey had spent the summer talking to the ghosts of Willingham Valley and mining them for information. In retrospect, the revelations she received should have been sufficient warning. But the trouble with hindsight is that it is always as clear as a mountain stream, whereas foresight is often hazy, like the hour before the dawn over a lowland meadow.

During the course of the summer, the adults of Camp Redemption decided that the four children of the valley would be best served in a home-school environment when fall arrived. This was the most obvious solution to the Jesús problem, which was still unresolved. Charnell had looked into that matter thoroughly and had been unable to devise a legal strategy that would guarantee the boy's safety while satisfying all the other requirements of the complex scenario. He had proposed several avenues of action, but each had brought at least some chance that Jesús would end up right back where he started, or that his mother would be deported, or that his siblings would land in foster care. And since Early was not willing to accept these outcomes, Charnell's final word on the matter had been to lay low and hope for the best.

So the plan was launched to establish the Camp Redemption School. Millie called the county school system office and discovered the rules and procedures for home schooling—which were surprisingly few—and once the paperwork was done, she and the other adults began their preparations. They set up a classroom for Jesús and the Donovan children in the back of the Camp Church. Early was slated to teach math and science, Charnell was lined up for social studies, history, and civics, Millie was the designated English teacher, and Ivey would, of course, teach religion.

After buying the supplies and books and then writing and distributing the teaching plans, the adults realized than at least one of the instructors would be a better mentor for the children if he engaged in a review of the subjects he was to teach.

"There's a lot more damn history now than there was when I was a boy," Charnell growled.

"That's because you're a blaspheming old man," Ivey replied gently. "Consider it the blessing of a long life. Now hush and read your teacher's manual."

"And a lot of what's in these books they sent us is *wrong*," he continued. "I know. I was there."

"Hush and read your teacher's manual," Ivey repeated.

In addition to Charnell's historical dissonance, they discovered that religion was not even on the state's required schedule of subjects. But Ivey would have none of that.

"It's a sign of the end times," she said to Early in an ominous tone as she looked at the prescribed class list.

"We'll add some religion courses," he said. "I promise we'll add them." It had been his intention all along to slip religious studies into the schedule without mentioning to Ivey that the state did not actually require this instruction. What she didn't know wouldn't hurt her, and by keeping her in the dark he had hoped to avoid any unpleasantness, such as, for instance, Ivey insisting on the secession of Willingham Valley from the Godless state of Georgia. But she had found out anyway—perhaps through divine revelation—and had come straight to Early.

She flipped through the high school science book before stopping at page one hundred. She stabbed her finger at the bold heading, the one containing that most hated and feared of all words, *evolution*. "I haven't seen our Lord and Savior's name in here one single time, but I notice that Mr. *Darwin* made it into the book." Her finger tapped the dark print, further emphasizing her point. "They even have his dog in here," she went on. Early glanced, and sure enough, his sister had circled the word *Beagle* with a red felt-tip marker.

"*Beagle* was the name of his ship."

"And that's supposed to make me feel better? At least you can pat a dog."

"Ivey, I said we'd add religion." They were an unemployed Bible camp, after all. "I promise you'll get equal time, and you can run your classes any way you want to. I can't help it that the state doesn't make it mandatory to teach religion. All we can do is take care of what happens here."

"I tell you, it's a sign of the end times," she repeated, but she seemed somewhat mollified.

Plans have an inherent tendency to go awry, and such was the case when Jesús went missing on the first Tuesday in September. It was the inaugural morning of school, and Early was in the Big House preparing to teach his lesson when Millie rushed through the door. As soon as he saw the expression on her face, he knew that trouble was afoot.

"Jesús didn't show up for school," she began. "He didn't come to English class. I sent Lisa Marie to look for him, and she can't find him anywhere." She hesitated before telling him the rest. "And the camp bus is missing."

"What?" Jesús had stolen the bus? He hadn't seen that one coming.

"He's run away, Early. He's taken the bus and gone."

Early sat down slowly and gave this new development some thought. Jesús had seemed happy all summer. He had worked hard and played hard, and he had indicated that he liked living in Willingham Valley much better than he had ever liked living in Apalachicola, which wasn't surprising, given that no one in North Georgia had left him for dead on a country road. He got along well with Ivey and Millie. He thought Charnell Jackson was a hoot, and the aged barrister thought that he was a fine lad as well. Jesús was close friends with Early, or at least Early thought he was. And as for Lisa Marie, well, Jesús was smitten by her. There was simply no other word for it. He had a bad case of Lisa Marie Donovan, and only time would tell if he recovered. So why would the boy run off? And where would he go? Early knew he was missing a piece of the puzzle. He firmly believed in the maxim that when the facts didn't make sense, it usually meant that all the facts weren't in.

"Lisa Marie," Early said emphatically when the solution came to him. "We need to talk to Lisa Marie. Jesús wouldn't have gone away without saying goodbye to her. I'm surprised he didn't take her with him, and I'm sure he told her where he was going."

Millie nodded excitedly. "You're right! I should have thought of that. And she was a bit quiet this morning, now that I think back. Come on. She's over at the chapel with Ivey." The pair crossed the grassy courtyard and entered the church. Sitting in the back pew were Lisa Marie Donovan, Charnell Jackson, and Ivey Willingham. It was a small camp and a smaller school, and news got around fast.

Millie sat next to her oldest child and addressed her quietly and calmly, but there was a layer of steel in her voice as well. "Lisa Marie, we need to know where Jesús is, and we need to know right now."

"Mama, I don't know where he is. I swear to you on a stack of Bibles." She sounded sincere, and that stumped them for a moment. Early had been sure that she would know where the missing camper was, but apparently he was mistaken. Finally, Charnell cleared his throat and stepped into the breach. He stood, hooked his thumbs in his braces, and looked at her hard for a moment. Then he asked one simple question.

"Do you know where he's *going*?" This time, there was a long, uncomfortable silence. Charnell nodded to himself. He hadn't successfully lawyered for over fifty years without bothering to learn how to phrase a question, and apparently Lisa Marie was not willing to risk even one Bible on this one's answer.

"Lisa Marie," Millie said quietly but insistently. "We need to know where Jesús went. You know we don't want anything but the best for him."

"I can't tell you, Mama. I promised I wouldn't. I can't break a promise." A tear rolled down Lisa Marie's cheek.

"Promises are sacred things," Millie allowed. "But you know you shouldn't have made this one. I want you to tell us about Jesús."

Early could see that the young lady wanted to do the right thing, even though it was difficult to do so with a promise hanging over her head. Her emotions were obviously striving with one another. Finally, she spoke.

"He's gone to Apalachicola. He took the bus and he's gone down there to get his mama and his brothers. He left last night after everyone went to bed. He told me he'd be back tonight." She had said it loudly and in a rush.

"He went to Apalachicola," Early repeated, as if the words were a phrase spoken in a foreign language. Charnell grimaced, Millie turned pale, and Ivey began to pray quietly.

"Yes, sir."

"Did he have some kind of plan to get them out once he got there?"

"His mama knows he's coming, and she's supposed to have his brothers ready to go when he gets there. His daddy works at night and sleeps during the day. Jesús is going to slip them all out while he's asleep. Then he's going to bring them back here." She stood a bit taller now, and she looked relieved.

"So his mother is in on the plan?" This made Early feel better. At least Jesús was in league with an adult.

"Yes, sir. He's been talking to her all summer."

Here was news.

"What? I haven't noticed any calls to Florida on the phone bill. How's he been doing that?"

"Email. They've been emailing ever since he got here."

Early grimaced. He had allowed Jesús to use the computer in his office since he had arrived. He had seen no harm in the practice, but he hadn't even considered the possibility of email.

Lisa Marie turned to her mother. "Mama, I feel sick. I need to go lay down." Millie nodded. She thanked her daughter for her honesty and gave her permission to join the rest of the Donovan children over in Nathanael.

"Ho-lee shit," Charnell said after Lisa Marie had gone. He glanced in Ivey's direction to see if an apology was in order, but she was distracted by the news and had not noticed his transgression.

"I couldn't have said it better myself." Early sighed. A delicate and complex situation had just gotten more so, and he was unsure about the next step.

"We've got a fifteen-year-old runaway driving a stolen school bus to Florida and back with the intention of whisking his family out from under the nose of the man who tried to kill him." Charnell spoke in summation, as if he were presenting the facts of the case to a jury. "That's over four hundred miles each way, even if he doesn't get lost or take the back roads."

"I understand all that," Early replied.

"But there's no need for us to worry," Charnell continued, "because he's got his mama's permission to make the trip."

"Charnell, quit!" he said. "I get how bad this is!"

"Of course, since she's an illegal alien and all, her permission doesn't actually count here in this country. Not to mention the fact that she gave him permission to commit a felony."

"You're giving me a headache."

"As your attorney, I advise you to take four aspirins and leave town. At least there's some good news."

"What good news?" Early asked incredulously.

"The good news is he looks older than fifteen, so maybe he won't get stopped."

"He looks fifteen-and-a-half," Early pointed out. "Maybe."

"That's older than fifteen."

"I guess so. If all the nearsighted, stupid policemen in three states are on duty today, he might not get pulled over." This was apparently their one best hope.

"I told you it wasn't a good idea to teach him how to drive the bus," Ivey said reproachfully, "but you wouldn't listen to me." Judging by her gentle tone, she offered this observation as a simple matter of habit rather than out of condemnation.

"Well, if I had thought he was going to steal the damn thing, I wouldn't have taught him," Early responded automatically. Then he remembered himself. "Sorry," he said to Ivey. Then he glanced at Charnell. "What do you think we ought to do?"

The older man mulled the question before offering a surprising response. "I think we should give him until tonight, just to see what happens. Hell, he might just pull it off." He fished in his pocket for a slightly bent pack of cigarillos, removed one, and placed it on his lower lip, Bogart-style. He was looking for a match when Ivey spoke.

"I hope you don't think you're going to smoke that thing in my church." She folded her arms and glared at Charnell.

"Just one, Ivey? Please? It's been a stressful morning." He waited for her verdict with his kitchen match poised in mid-strike. She frowned, but then she relented.

"One, then. But don't make this a habit."

He nodded his understanding, and the matchstick flamed.

"Charnell," Early said, "I have to be honest and tell you that giving Jesús more time was about the last thing I expected you to suggest. Excuse me for being blunt, but are you crazy? We can't just let a truant kid cruise to Florida and back in a stolen bus that has Camp Redemption painted on it in tall, red letters." The man was a lawyer, for heaven's sake. He should know these things.

"Early, you're looking at this whole situation in the wrong light. You're seeing it as a problem, when what you should be doing is viewing it as an opportunity. What you need to do is consider our predicament in terms of probabilities and outcomes. Provided he hasn't already been caught—and I give that about a fifty-fifty chance, depending on how well you taught him to drive—the best thing that can possibly happen for all concerned is that he manages to snag his mama away from that wife-beating, child-abusing bastard. Think about it. If he makes it back here with her, we don't have a runaway on our hands anymore. What we have instead is a kid living with his mother, just like Millie's kids live with her. We are as pure as the driven snow and as legal as the Georgia Constitution."

"Well, I have to admit I hadn't thought of that." The outcome did have potential. Jesús moving his family—minus the father—into camp would solve a variety of lingering problems, and any negative issues that the solution brought with it would almost certainly be more manageable than the ones they were currently nursing along.

"That's why you have old Charnell here, my boy. To keep you thinking straight." An ash fell from his smoke to the floor, and Ivey glared at him.

"I have old Charnell here because he's laying low after he lost all his money on oil futures," Early replied.

"Smart ass," Charnell muttered. Then he continued, warming to his topic. "Not only should we give him until at least tonight to get back, but we should hit the highway and go run interference for him. You know, like Burt Reynolds did for Jerry Reed in *Smokey and the Bandit*."

"If only we had a black Trans Am for a chase car," Early noted, "and if one of us had good legs like Sally Fields."

"Millie's got good legs," Charnell pointed out. "But I think the car was a Firebird."

"Thank you, Charnell," Millie said.

"It was a Trans Am," Early said. "And we're not doing it."

"Okay. I guess you know what you want," Charnell said, but he sounded unconvinced. "Getting back to our scenario, if Jesús *can't* snatch his mama, the next best thing that can happen is that he makes it back without getting caught by the law. If that happens, then we're no worse off than we are right now. All we'll need to do then is keep him off the computer so he can't secretly email his mama anymore, put a long-distance block on the phone so he can't call her, and make sure we keep the bus keys hidden."

"You think we ought to tie him up, too?" Early asked.

"That'd be up to you," Charnell replied.

"We could try to help," Millie noted. "Now that we know she's willing to leave her husband, we can talk to her directly."

Early thought she might have a point. Certainly her idea had more promise than resorting to rope. And whatever happened, he didn't think that a return to the *status quo* was possible.

"Well, yeah, we could do that," Charnell admitted. "But let me present my final point. If he gets caught or has already been caught, we are truly and legally screwed. If that happens, we will have, as Ricky Ricardo once noted, *lots of 'splaining to do.*"

Early had a vision of a black Suburban roaring down the road to camp before skidding to a halt in front of the Big House. Doors would fly open, and out would leap lean and fit men wearing dark suits, Ray-Bans, and earpieces. "Freeze!" they would holler, and then all hell would break loose.

"I guess things can't get much worse than they already are," Early said. "So we'll wait until the morning, just to give him plenty of time to get back. But what if none of this happens? What if, come tomorrow, he's not back, either with or without his family? And what if he hasn't been caught, either? What are we going to do then?"

"I don't know what we'll do, Early," Charnell ruefully admitted. "I guess we could always pray for a miracle."

"I'll take care of that part," Ivey said quietly. "As a matter of fact, I'll go get started on it right now." She walked to the front of the church and sat in the middle of the first pew, directly beneath Munroe Willingham's old rugged cross. She clasped her hands and bowed her head.

Millie sighed and quietly stood. "I've got to go check on the kids and ground Lisa Marie for lying to me," she said.

"You know, she didn't really lie," Charnell said. "She told the absolute, literal, unvarnished truth. I feel kind of bad about boxing her in like I did, but we needed to know what she knew, and I have a talent for getting information out of people. So don't be too rough on her. She was trying to protect her boyfriend."

"I know it, Charnell, and I won't land on her too hard, but I do have to land on her a little. She knows how I feel about dishonesty. She was right there beside me while her daddy was lying to two different wives and seven little children. In my book, lying by omission is exactly the same as not telling the truth."

"You wouldn't make much of a lawyer," Charnel said with a grin.

"I know I wouldn't. But I'm trying to be a good mother and to raise good children, so I'll have to leave the lawyering to you. I know she was trying to help Jesús, but doing the wrong thing for the right reason is still doing the wrong thing. So there'll have to be some consequences."

Charnell nodded as she headed for the door.

As it turned out, luck was on their side, although Early had to concede that perhaps Ivey's entreaties for an acceptable outcome had reached the front office, in which case luck was not a factor. But whichever it was, good fortune or strong connections with influential friends, he was sitting on the front porch of the Big House a little after sunset that evening when the missing camp bus pulled up. It smelled like it was running a tad hot, and more smoke than usual came from the tailpipe. Additionally, there was a fresh and quite impressive scratch down one side. Jesús was behind the steering wheel, looking proud, defiant, and absolutely no older than fifteen even in the fading light. How he had made it to Apalachicola and back without being pulled over was beyond Early. Perhaps it *had* been a miracle, a direct intervention from above, and all the law enforcement officials in three Southern states had been stricken temporarily blind or inexplicably tolerant.

Behind Jesús sat a woman whom Early assumed was Isobel Jiminez. She was strikingly attractive in the muted interior lighting of the bus, with jet black hair worn to her shoulders, large dark eyes, and high cheekbones. Her complexion was the light caramel of calfskin gloves. Early couldn't determine her exact age but supposed that she was somewhere in her late thirties or early forties. He saw first one then another head of black hair pop up from the seat behind Isobel. He guessed that these belonged to Fernando and Diego, Jesús's brothers.

As he viewed the family, it occurred to Early—not for the first time—that Isobel might have a bone to pick with him since he had not revealed her son's location throughout the long summer. As it had turned out, the boy had been in touch with her the entire time, but Early hadn't known that, so he could take no credit for it. He believed that the reasons for his decision had been sound, that he had kept her son's best interests at heart. But he supposed that he would take his medicine without comment if Jesús's mother wished to dwell in the past. The door to the bus opened, and Jesús and his mother stepped down. The two small boys were too busy running up and down the aisle of the bus to worry about getting off.

"Hello, Early." Jesús seemed nervous, a condition that Early was in no particular hurry to ameliorate. Perhaps later, after the boy had stewed in his own juices for a suitable period of time. Eighteen to twenty months ought to be sufficient.

"Jesús," he said quietly, nodding. "I'm glad to see you got back safely." Early found that he was beset by conflicting emotions. He was relieved to see Jesús back home and safe, but he was angry that the boy had taken the bus and made such a risky journey. He could have been injured, killed, or arrested, or he could have simply vanished, never to be seen again. Additionally, Early was hurt that Jesús had not trusted him enough to include him in his plans. If he had known that Jesús was in contact with his mother and that she was willing to come to Camp Redemption, he would have gone with him, driven for him, and otherwise assisted in the rescue.

"This is my mother," Jesús said. "Isobel Jiminez. Those are my brothers on the bus." The horn blew as if to punctuate his statement.

"Hello Mrs. Jiminez." Early extended his hand and they shook. "It's nice to finally meet you." She gave him a frank but not unfriendly gaze. Her skin was laced with barely perceptible lines and patterns, like weathered ivory. These were worry lines, conceivably, or perhaps the telltale tracks left by the long days she had spent in the searing Gulf sun as she had worked the shrimp boats.

"It is good to meet you as well, Mr. Willingham," she said with a slight accent. "I have heard so much about you. Please call me Isobel."

"And you should call me Early."

"I want to thank you for watching out for my son, and for letting him live in your valley. Jesús tells me it is like heaven here. I think he must be right." Isobel smiled.

"It has been our pleasure to have him," Early said.

"When he sent me the message that you had invited me and my other children to come live here, well, I must tell you, it was like a dream had come true. I couldn't believe it." Early couldn't believe it, either. He was a better man than he thought. He nodded and smiled as Isobel Jimenez continued. "Jesús has told you that my husband is a bad man. That has not changed. But even I did not know how evil he really was, until I heard the story of how Jesús came to be here." She looked at her son, and tears filled her eyes. "My husband told me that Jesús had simply run away. He even showed me a note that he said Jesús had left. But he did not mention that he had nearly killed him. No. That part he left out."

Early could see where this was the sort of information that would likely be omitted from most conversations. Before he could respond, the screen door creaked and slammed, and Ivey and Charnell joined them on the porch. He took his sister by the arm and made introductions.

"Ivey, Charnell, this is Isobel Jiminez. She's Jesús's mama. Isobel, this is my sister, Ivey Willingham. And this is my attorney, Charnell Jackson." The two women smiled and shook, and Charnell doffed his fedora and offered his hand.

"I've been expecting you," Ivey said pleasantly.

As she and Isobel exchanged a pleasantry or two, Charnell leaned close to Early's ear to share an observation. "I'll be a son of a bitch," he whispered in a voice with a pitch and timbre similar to that of a tractor tire losing air. "Ivey prayed them right on into the landing pattern, and then she touched them down. I bet Jesús could've let go of the steering wheel and taken his foot off the gas, and the bus would've gotten here just the same. He probably could've ridden back there with his brothers."

All Early could do was nod. It was indeed remarkable.

"Jesús," Ivey said, "why don't you take your family over to Philip and get them settled in. And you'd better stick your head in and say hello to Lisa Marie. That poor girl's taken to her bed with worry about you. While you're doing that, I'll stir us all up some supper."

"Please let me help," said Isobel. She and Ivey seemed to have hit right it off.

"I won't hear of it," Ivey replied. "You've just ridden ten hours in a school bus. I'm sure you want to freshen up and get your boys settled in."

"You want me to drive them on over to the cabin in the bus?" Jesús asked Early.

"*Now* you're asking me if you can drive the bus?" Jesús hung his head as he swallowed this taste of comeuppance. Then he headed back for the driver's seat.

"He did not tell you he was going to use the bus?" Isobel asked. She was soft-spoken, but her words carried nonetheless.

"Well, no, he didn't. We discovered him gone this morning, and we were pretty worried about him. We had decided to give him until tomorrow morning to make it back. Then we were going to have to call the police. Not because the bus was gone, but because we were afraid for the driver. It's a long way to Apalachicola, and he hasn't been driving very long."

"He told me that you taught him to drive the bus and then allowed him to borrow it to come rescue us."

"I did teach him to drive, but he's too young to drive out on the highway. Not to mention the fact that he doesn't have a license."

"He said he told you he was sixteen and you helped him get a driver's license."

"Even if he had told me he was sixteen, which he didn't, and even if he'd had a license, which he doesn't, I wouldn't have let him drive by himself to Florida and back. You've just met me and don't know much about me, but you need to know that. I only taught him how to drive a few weeks ago, and he's never driven anywhere except on the roads here at camp. It's a miracle he made it."

"Halleluiah!" said Ivey.

"Not now, Ivey," said Early.

"I am so sorry," said Isobel. "I did not know." A look of distress crossed her features. "Does this mean that you did not invite me and my other boys to live here? Did Jesús make this up, too?"

"Not at all," Early said, lying without hesitation. He didn't mind her being there in the least, and there was no use in causing duress by letting her know that she was an uninvited guest. "We talked about it, and he and I were planning to drive down together to get you next week, or the week after, at the latest. But I was going to be the one driving. I guess he got in a hurry. You know how youngsters are. Boys will be boys, and all that."

"I will speak to him about this," she assured her new host.

"Well, you're his mama, so you have to do what you think is best," Early said. "He's in some trouble with me over this, but we'll work it out between us."

Isobel nodded. "That sounds very fair," she said. "I want to thank you again for helping us." There were tears of gratitude in her eyes as she hugged Early. Then she went down the line, hugging Ivey and Charnell. After the embraces, she boarded the bus. Jesús started the engine and motored slowly down the row of cabins toward Philip.

"Well, Ivey, I just told a whopper," Early said. "Let me have it."

Ivey looked at her brother for a moment as she appeared to consider her words. Then she spoke. "'God, You make me a person that has understanding of the times, to know what I ought to do.' First Chronicles 12:32." She stepped to her brother and hugged him tightly. "I'm proud of you for taking Isobel in," she said.

"Wait a minute. I'm not in trouble?"

"Not this time." She stood on tiptoe and kissed him on the cheek. "But don't get used to it."

"No, ma'am." A thought came to him. "What did you mean when you told Isobel that you had been expecting her?"

"Oh, that. Do you remember the vision I had right before Millie moved in? The one where we were swimming at the falls?"

"I do remember it."

"The black-haired woman that was swimming with us, the one I didn't recognize? She was Isobel Jiminez. Her boys were there, too. I knew who she was as soon as I stepped out and saw her just now."

"You're kidding," Early said. His jaw had literally dropped.

"I don't kid much," she said. Then, without another word, she went back into the Big House to get the supper started.

"She *doesn't* kid, much," Charnell confirmed, as if there had been some doubt on that score. "And she let you off light. Even I know you're not supposed to lie. I hope she's not lowering the bar around here. If she's dropping her guard, we'll all be in hell in no time."

"No, she'll be her old self at supper. You'll see."

Later, at the table in the kitchen of the Big House, the newest incarnation of the ever-growing extended family in Willingham Valley sat down to their first meal together. Present were Ivey and Early, Charnell Jackson, Millie Donovan and her three girls, and Isobel Jiminez and her three boys. The table was not full by anywhere close to half, but still it sat more hungry family members than had graced it in a long time. Ivey asked Isobel Jimenez to say the blessing. Isobel prayed for all who were present and some who were not, and by the time she finished the prayer, the assemblage at the table was ready to dine. Ivey had made meatloaf, mashed potatoes, fried okra, creamed corn, and hot biscuits, and they ate, and talked, and ate still more, right up until the moment when the last bite was gone.

Chapter Fifteen

By the time the year waned into fall, twelve live souls resided in the long valley, and the number of the departed that floated in the autumn breeze was beyond count. As October ushered in the bright reds and yellows on the mountain slopes, the legion of the living at Camp Redemption included Early and Ivey Willingham, Jesús Jiminez, Millie Donovan and her three children, Isobel Jimenez and her additional two youngsters, Charnell Jackson, and Hugh Don Monfort. Of this group, Hugh Don was the newest resident and had only been at the camp since the final day of September. His arrival was the unintended result of a round of cost-cutting measures he had been forced to implement due to the impact of hard times on Cherokee County in general and on the beer joint in particular.

"No one could be that damn stupid," Hugh Don groused over a Pabst Blue Ribbon as he, Early, Charnell, and Millie warmed beside a small campfire down by the lake.

"Who?" Early asked. "Burton Turner?"

"No, I'm talking about me." Hugh Don shook his head and popped another top. "I knew better than to do it. Hell, Charnell *warned* me not to do it. But I did it anyway. No one could be that damn stupid."

Hugh Don's crime had been to reduce the amount of his weekly payoff to the county sheriff, Red Arnold, Jr., also known as Little Red. He had lowered the weekly stipend as one remedy for his dwindling cash flow, which had been more like a cash trickle for some months. He was selling more beer than ever, but most of his sales were credit transactions. The sawmill had shut down during the summer due to the sour economy, and no one was sure when, or even if, that mainstay of local employment would again saw timber and make wood chips. And all of the employees of the other main source of paychecks in the area—the cotton mill—were down on short time. So even though a large number of the beer drinkers in town had more time in which to drink, they ironically had less cash with which to pursue this activity.

But regardless of the sound financial theory behind Hugh Don's attempt to reduce expenditures, the fact remained that when Little Red's bass boat fund got cut in half, he remembered almost immediately that he was entrusted with the safety and welfare of the entire population of Cherokee County—including the non-beer drinkers, about whom he had been somewhat neglectful for many years—and he shut down both of Hugh Don Monfort's beer joints in a single afternoon.

"His daddy wouldn't have done it," Hugh Don noted in a morose tone. "You just can't count on the law anymore."

"His daddy would have shot you, rolled you over, reached in your pocket, removed your billfold, and gotten his money," Charnell pointed out. Early nodded. Red Arnold, Sr., had been the county sheriff for many long and fruitful years, and he had been notorious for being a man of action, a constable who took matters into his own hands. The local icon had abruptly retired about fifteen years previously when a methamphetamine lab he had discovered over on the Dogleg Road exploded and carried both him and its owner, Johnson Burdette, to a better place, or at least to a better place than the Dogleg Road. Little Red had assumed the mantle of authority shortly thereafter.

"Well, yeah," Hugh Don conceded, "but he wouldn't have shut me down." He sighed. He hadn't been unemployed in several decades, and the shame of the condition was heavy on him.

"Why don't you just give him his money?" Millie asked.

"I tried that once I saw that he was taking the whole damn thing personal, which it wasn't. He said that one hundred won't do it anymore. Now he wants two hundred. He said that every week I wait, it goes up another hundred dollars."

"You shouldn't have pissed him off," Charnell said.

"Tell me something I *don't* know."

"Pay him," Charnell advised.

"I can't afford it!"

"Hugh Don," Early said, "everyone knows you have more money than God. Just give him what he wants, and he'll leave you alone."

Hugh Don seemed to consider this suggestion for a moment. Then he frowned and crossed his arms. "Naw, I won't do it," he said. "It ain't legal what he's doing, and it ain't decent."

"Hell, the hundred wasn't legal!" Charnell exclaimed, in case his friend had somehow missed that fine point of the law and was considering legal remedy.

"No, but it was decent," Hugh Don concluded. "Early, do you mind if I stay here a while longer? Once Little Red tries living on his own salary, he might decide to give me another chance. That one hundred might start looking good to him again. Hell, I might even get him down to fifty, like I was trying to do in the first place."

"I don't mind it a bit."

Hugh Don had arrived with the clothing on his back, a paper sackful of crumpled cash, his pistol, and a Chevrolet Cavalier loaded with beer. Early couldn't be happier.

"What about Miss Ivey?"

"You heard what she said yesterday. As long as you don't sell beer while you're here, and as long as you go to church on Wednesdays and Sundays, you're welcome to stay as long as you want. I think she's looking forward to the challenge of saving you. To her, you're kind of like the Mt. Everest of sin. She wants to climb you because you're there." Early thought of a potential snag. "She doesn't know about the trunkload of beer in the Cavalier, and we probably ought to keep it that way."

Hugh Don nodded. Early knew he could see the wisdom inherent in this suggestion. "You reckon she'll back off that church rule after I go a time or two?" he asked. As a general rule, Hugh Don Monfort would rather be shot and robbed by Red Arnold, Sr., than to go to any type of religious service. As his poor, sainted mama had once noted, he just wasn't the churchgoing kind.

"She'd be more likely to let you start a whorehouse in one of the cabins than she would be to let you off the hook about going to church," Early said. There was no use in getting Hugh Don's hopes up. Ivey had him where she wanted him, and she wasn't going to relinquish her grasp. Early clapped the old bootlegger on the shoulder. "Think of it as rent," he advised.

"*Steep* rent," Hugh Don groused.

"But cheaper than two hundred dollars per week to Little Red," Early replied.

"If you say so," came Hugh Don's reply. But he stayed, so apparently he thought so too. He established residency in a vacant bedroom in the Big House and began to live the reformed life, at least when Ivey was around.

So the twelve inhabitants of Willingham Valley continued to gel into a family unit. The days of October passed slowly and pleasantly, and each one brought the people at the camp one step closer to being kin. Their routines solidified as well. Weekdays, all the children went to the camp school, including the two newest arrivals from Apalachicola, who slipped in beside the other students without a single ripple. Isobel went to school as well, but she attended in the role of teacher. The one gap in the curriculum previous to her arrival had been foreign language, but now all of the students were afforded the opportunity to learn the intricacies of Spanish, whether they wished to or not.

Three times each day, the dinner bell outside the Big House clanged, and they all gathered together at the table for their meals. Some days Ivey was the head chef. On other days this position was filled by Millie, and on still others, Isobel wielded the spatula. But mostly they all worked together, because feeding twelve people was a great deal of work. The men in residence didn't cook much, outside of the occasional breakfast, because they were extremely poor hands at the task. But they and the children all pitched in and did the remaining chores associated with meal preparation. They set and cleared the table, cleaned the pots and dishes, and did the shopping.

And, of course, on Sundays and Wednesdays, everyone at Camp Redemption regardless of religious persuasion or political affiliation attended services at the Camp Church. Some came for the message. Some came because it was the right thing to do. One came to pay the rent. But come they did, all of them plus others, and together they worshipped and prepared for the rapture.

The second Sunday in November arrived blustery and cold. Early awakened before dawn, and after dressing he walked from the Big House to Nathanael. Once there, he stoked the fire in the fireplace until it roared, so that the Donovan family would awaken to a warm cabin. Then he walked to the Jiminez household and helped Jesús build a warm, cheerful blaze in the fireplace in Philip. After that cabin began to warm, the pair walked together to the church to get the fire going in the wood heater there. Lighting the fires had become a habit for them since the weather turned cool.

At the chapel, they fed the fire with sticks of pitch pine until it became self-sustaining. Then they piled on dry hickory and green oak until the belly of the stove began to glow with the heat. They worked efficiently and quietly, comfortable in each other's company. A small rift had developed after Jesús helped himself to the bus, and it had set their relationship back a few days, to be sure. But they were truly fond of each other, and their friendship had quickly healed. Indeed, Early had faced the realization that he might have done the same if he had found himself in the boy's shoes.

"That ought to burn fine until we get back," Early said as he closed the door to the stove. He stood and dusted the knees of his jeans. "Come on. Let's go see what Ivey has scratched up for breakfast."

"You don't think it's too hot?" Jesús asked. "The stove's turning red. Maybe I ought to stay and watch it."

"No, it's fine. I wish I had a dollar for every time I've seen this old stove glow red." Once the mainstay of the kitchen in the Big House, the stove had been used as the principle source of heat there during Early's boyhood years, long after its usefulness as a cook stove had passed. "When we get back, the whole church will be warm. You'll see."

They set out for the Big House. The wind fairly shrieked across the valley from the west. It tugged and poked at their coats and caps, trying to find and overwhelm even the smallest sources of warmth. Snow spat from the gray sky and blew about the valley floor like confetti mixing in with the dried, fallen leaves. Early heard a popping noise in the distance, like a gun being fired, and he figured that they had just lost a pine tree. He hoped it hadn't fallen on one of the buildings.

"It's cold," Jesús shivered. "I think I'll skip breakfast and go back to the church."

"We're already halfway to the Big House," Early said. "It's the same distance either way now, and you know Ivey will have hot cocoa on a morning like this. If I were you, I'd make for the cocoa." Early removed his hands from the pockets of his old flannel coat and blew on them. Then he shoved them back in and shivered. The cold weather bothered him more now than it had when he was young. He supposed this was an indication of time's inevitable march. "You're right about one thing, though," he told Jesús. "It's damn sure cold out here."

It was the coldest November he could remember. He believed in the fact of global warming, but he would be hard-pressed to prove his point today. As he neared the back porch, he could hear Ivey's blue porcelain wind chimes raising a fuss as the delicate doves danced in the wind. He recalled his mother telling him years ago that the ancient Chinese used to believe that wind chimes kept away evil spirits. He stepped up on the back porch, opened the kitchen door, and stood in the doorway. It occurred to him as he unbuttoned his coat that it was awfully quiet for that time on a Sunday morning. Ivey should be cooking breakfast by now, and a variety of helpers ought to be setting the table. Then he raised his head and saw the reason for the silence.

Later, Early recalled that he experienced the odd sensation that an old-fashioned filmstrip was being shown in the kitchen, one scene at a time, one frame per wall. There were several individual images around the room, all vying for his immediate attention, each crying out for a look. Additionally, there was an audio component accompanying many of the images, a tinny, crackling sound like an old 78rpm recording.

First and foremost, he saw Ivey. She was prone on the kitchen floor behind the table, as unmoving as a burial mound. Through the table legs he could see that her eyes were closed, her color was bad, and her chest was still. Behind him, out of sight, he heard Jesús whispering *oh shit, oh shit, oh shit* as he slowly backed up and away. To his left, Charnell Jackson sat at the bottom of the staircase in a white shirt and tie, boxer shorts, and black socks. His pale, bony legs were almost white, and he rubbed his chest at a spot directly over his heart. He did not look well. Millie and her two youngest kids were there too—across the room, over by the wall, and to the left of Charnell. Millie was dressed in blue jeans and a sweatshirt, and she had herded her children behind her like a mother duck. One of them cried softly, and Millie was whispering *it's all right, darlin', Mama's here,* over and over. To Early's right, Hugh Don Monfort lay crumpled in the floor like a discarded puppet. Blood oozed from a bullet wound in his torso, and his breathing was labored and raspy. And finally, to Early's far right stood a small man with a dark complexion and black hair. He brandished an ugly pistol at the crowd. There was a mean look in his eye, a crazy glint that indicated that he was well aware of the fact that just dropping the gun and walking away was probably no longer an option.

Early started across the kitchen toward Ivey.

"Stop!" cried the man with the gun.

"Who the hell are you, and what the hell have you done to my sister?" Early replied as he kept his course.

"I did nothing to her! She was like that when I came in! Stay where you are, or I will shoot you!" The man tracked Early across the room with the pistol.

Early ignored him and continued to his sister's side. He dropped to his knees and looked her over quickly. She didn't appear to be shot, which had been his first thought, and there were no marks on her. He checked her for a pulse and found none. He experienced a sinking feeling as he noted that her body was already cooling. He sighed as he gently raised her eyelids with his thumbs. Her left pupil was fixed and dilated. Her right was the same, but the white of that eye was blood red. Ivey was dead.

He made as if to rise, but then he gave up on that notion for the time being and sat back down, hard. Ivey was dead. His big sister had caught the train to glory. She had gone home. In theory he had known this day would someday come, that his sister was just like everyone else when it came to owing one death, that even her unique status as one of God's special people would not spare her the trip. But now that the moment had arrived and the reality of it was stretched out on the floor before him, he realized that he wasn't ready. The sad old world had suddenly become a little older and a lot sadder. He looked to his right and saw his coat. Apparently he had carried it with him across the room. He gathered it up and carefully arranged it over Ivey's head and torso. "Goodbye, Ivey," he whispered. Then he stood and looked in Millie's direction.

"She's gone," he said quietly. He heard Millie gasp.

"Oh, Christ," Charnell Jackson said. He leaned against the newel post. The love of his life had left him behind, just an old man in his drawers on a cold morning in Georgia.

"Charnell, are you hanging in there?" he asked. Charnell nodded.

Early turned and faced the man who held the gun. "You son of a bitch, you killed my sister."

"I told you before. She was like that when I got here."

"I don't think I believe that," Early said.

"I do not care what you believe. Stand there or I will kill *you.*"

Early did believe that, so he stayed put while he considered how best to proceed. He directed his attention toward Hugh Don Monfort. He hadn't forgotten him, but he had prioritized the downed people in the room that morning, and Ivey had come first.

"Hugh Don, can you talk?" he asked.

"Yep."

"How're you doing?"

"I've been better."

"What happened?"

"This Mexican cocksucker shot me."

"I figured that much."

"Enough of this talk!" The Mexican cocksucker yelled as he waved the gun to and fro.

"Buddy, what do you want?" Early asked quietly as he eyed the distance he needed to cross. Twenty steps. It might as well have been a mile.

It had occurred to him that the man was crazy, perhaps, or maybe strung out on drugs. He had apparently already killed Ivey, and Hugh Don wasn't looking so hot, either. For that matter, Charnell Jackson seemed as if he could use a trip to the emergency room. His other hand had joined its mate, and now both were holding his diseased and broken old heart. Early looked at their assailant's eyes, and he knew in that moment that he would not hesitate to kill them all. With one already dead and two others at some stage of dying, the man had little to lose. He was already in too deep to back up, in up to his shoulders at least, plenty deep enough to consider the efficacy of eliminating witnesses. Early's next thought was for Millie and the kids. He could no longer help his sister. She was gone, and he hoped her destination was everything she had bargained for. As for Hugh Don and Charnell, they were currently on their own, but while he drew breath, he would not allow harm to come to Millie and her children.

"I'll ask you again. What do you want?" he repeated.

"You know what I am here for."

"I don't have a damn clue what you're here for. But whatever it is you want, take it! Please! Just take it and go."

"I see your bus outside," the man said in an almost conversational tone.

"You want the *bus*?" Clearly, the man was insane. "Be my guest. It's full of gas, and the keys are in it."

"I have seen the bus before."

"Okay, you've seen the bus."

"I have seen it at my home. In Apalachicola."

Understanding began to drift over Early like blown sand. "You're Roberto Jiminez," he said.

"I have come for my family."

"I don't know where your family is," Early replied. Technically, this was true, especially if Jesús had the good sense that Early hoped he did and had gone to roust them—and Lisa Marie as well—and to convey them all to a place of hiding, preferably in the next valley if not the next state. If he had managed to do that while also getting hold of Austell Poe or the state police, then so much the better.

"You have them here. I know it. I saw them leave in your bus. I waited for her to return. I thought she would change her mind and bring my two sons back to me, but she did not. So now I have followed her to your door."

"Two sons? What about Jesús?" For the remainder of his life, Early would lament the stupidity of this question. What did it matter if the man claimed two sons, or three, or even ten? Early eventually chalked it up as a direct result of stress.

"Jesús was wild like his mother," Roberto Jiminez said, but there was a faraway quality to his voice, as if he were talking on a ham radio. "He ran away."

"Surprise, you lying son of a bitch," Jesús said from the darkness behind his father. He cocked Hugh Don Monfort's big pistol as he stepped from the the living room into the light of the kitchen and placed the tip of the barrel against the back of Roberto's head. "I really *did* run away."

Confusion appeared on the face of Roberto Jiminez. He began to turn.

"Jesús! I—" Roberto began.

"Stand still or I'll blow your head off!" Jesús yelled, sounding exactly like the scared kid he was.

"Early, no!" Millie hollered as Early leapt for Roberto Jiminez. His only weapons were surprise and the knife he had found beside Ivey on the floor, and the knife wasn't that sharp.

"Shoot him, boy!" Hugh Don shouted to Jesús. "Pull the goddamn trigger and put him down!"

The next few seconds were chaotic, and only later during the investigation by various law enforcement agencies were they able to reconstruct the chronology of events. After Hugh Don insisted that Jesús blow Roberto away, Jesús lowered his aim by half a man and pulled the trigger. The gun boomed like a cannon in the enclosed space, and pain of being shot in the back of the thigh caused Roberto Jiminez to lose his grip on his automatic. The firearm fell to the floor and discharged once before skittering in the direction of the reclining form of Hugh Don Monfort. The slug from the nine-millimeter struck Early in the right shoulder and spun him sideways, causing him to sling his kitchen knife toward Roberto's feet. A brief moment after Roberto picked up Early's knife and began to turn once again toward his oldest son, Hugh Don recovered the dropped pistol and unloaded the remaining seven bullets into their attacker. Roberto slumped over on his side, dead enough for several.

Later, in response to why he had shot Roberto Jiminez seven times, which the detective from the state police considered overkill, Hugh Don replied in a no-nonsense manner.

"Because that's all the bullets I had."

"So if you had twenty bullets," the detective continued, "you would have shot him twenty times?"

"Hell, if I'd had a thousand bullets, I'd *still* be shooting the son of a bitch."

After the gunplay quieted in the kitchen, there was a stunned silence for a moment as everyone who was still alive confirmed this fact. Then, Millie ran to Ivey. Charnell, too, walked slowly and painfully to his departed beloved, knelt beside her, and cried. Jesús fell bawling into Hugh Don Monfort's arms because he needed to go somewhere. And the soul of Roberto Jiminez stumbled barefooted down the rocky path to hell, where a room with a view surely awaited.

Several additional facts were ferreted out and pieced together during the police inquiry. As it turned out, Ivey had died of a brain aneurism, which, to Early's way of thinking, was not to say that Roberto hadn't killed her anyway, just as surely as if he had put a gun to her head or slipped a knife between her ribs. It was Early's view that Ivey had been frightened to death. He knew it in his heart just as certainly as he knew he was a Willingham. The only two witnesses to the crime—Ivey and Roberto Jiminez—were both dead, so the actual facts of the incident were forever hidden, but Early could see the events in his mind's eye as clearly as if they were being projected on the screen down at the Blue Sky Drive-in.

He was certain that his sister had been the first to arise that morning, because she always was, and he had heard her bustling around on his way out to light the fires. After he left, she had without a doubt come down to the kitchen to get breakfast started, which she always did. But when she entered the room, she had discovered their unwelcome intruder, and the shock of it had ended her life. There was no other explanation that fit the facts. Early just hoped it hadn't been a painful end. He thought he remembered hearing that a brain aneurism was a quick way to go, just a boom and a flash, and then nothing. He hoped he had heard correctly.

Millie was the first eyewitness on the scene that morning. She and her girls—Iris Anne and Bliss—went to the kitchen to help Grandma Ivey make the biscuits. When Millie first entered the room, she was busy removing coats and mittens and was unaware of the danger until the intruder stood up.

"You, move to that corner with those children," he had said, pointing his gun at her.

"Oh, my God!" Millie had said, her voice somewhere between a whisper and a croak. The fear of the moment rendered her nearly speechless. "What did you do to Miss Ivey?"

"Do as I say, and make no noise, or your little ones will have no mother." He gestured with the pistol. Millie placed herself between the man and her girls. Her eyes never left him as she slowly eased them across the room.

The next to enter the room was Hugh Don Monfort, who came down the stairs nursing a headache courtesy of the twelve cans of Pabst Blue Ribbon he had consumed the night before. He had drunk the first six beers while working up the courage to ask Isobel Jiminez for a date, and he had sipped the last half-dozen while contemplating the sad fact that she had said *no*. When he arrived at the bottom of the steps, he spied Millie backed up in the corner in front of her girls.

"Damn, Millie," he said, "you look like you've seen a ghost. What's wrong?" She pointed slowly and carefully toward Roberto Jiminez, who had gravitated in the direction of the living room, although he was still in the big kitchen area. Hugh Don turned his head and saw the man standing there with the gun. During his lifetime, Hugh Don had been on the wrong end of a variety of firearms, but in spite of his vast expertise, he had never quite acquired a taste for the experience. In fact, it generally made him angry when someone threw down on him, which is the wrong frame of mind to be in while standing on the barrel side of a projectile weapon. Thus, even though the sight of an armed stranger holding Millie and her daughters hostage surprised him, his primary reaction at that moment was anger bordering on outrage.

"Who's the big man holding the gun on helpless women and children?" he asked of no one in particular.

"Hugh Don!" Millie whispered loudly. He turned back toward her, and she cut her eyes in the direction of Ivey's prone form. From his vantage point at the bottom of the stairs, all Hugh Don could see was the top of her head, but that was enough.

"You sorry bastard," he said as he took a determined step toward Roberto Jiminez.

"If you wish to stay alive, you will go to the corner with the woman."

"Fuck you," Hugh Don said quietly as he advanced.

"I will shoot!"

"Naw. You won't shoot. You don't have the balls." As it turned out, Hugh Don was incorrect, and Roberto's balls were just fine. He shot Hugh Don square in the chest. Hugh Don looked surprised as he dropped to his knees. He had been angry before. Now, he was angry and his chest hurt. "My advice to you is to finish me off right now, you son of a bitch," Hugh Don said as he fell forward. From his new position on the floor, he added, "Because if you don't, I guarantee you I'll kill you for this."

Charnell arrived at this point. "What was that noise?" he asked as he came down the stairs. Then he saw Roberto Jiminez, Hugh Don, and Millie and her children. And finally, he saw Ivey. A pain hit him under his breastbone, and he sat down hard.

Early and Jesús arrived a minute or two after this scene played itself to a standstill. When Early stepped through the door and into harm's way, Jesús had caught a glimpse of the scene over Early's right shoulder. What he saw, in profile, was the angry face of the man who had left him for dead in Tate's Hell forest. So he had backed up quietly until clear of the back porch. Then he had run as if the hounds of perdition were nipping at his heels, hurrying to warn the remainder of the inhabitants of Willingham Valley to stay clear of the Big House. After calling the police on his mother's cell phone, he gathered Isobel, Lisa Marie, and his brothers together and hid them in Philip.

Raymond L. Atkins

"My father is at the Big House," he told them. "He has a gun, and he has a look on his face I've seen before." He looked at his mother. "You've seen it before, too."

"He'll kill us all," Isobel whispered, so that only Jesús could hear.

"Keep them quiet, and don't let anyone turn on the lights," he said to her. "I'll be back in a minute."

"Where are you going?" she asked, terrified.

"I'm going to get Hugh Don's car and drive you all out of here. You said it yourself. You know what he'll do if he finds you. Or me." She nodded. She knew all too well.

Jesús ran from building to building and tree to tree as he made his way back to the church, where Hugh Don had parked his car. His plan was sketchy, but it was better than no plan at all. He intended to drive the Cavalier down the access road that ran behind the cabins until he arrived at Philip. Then he planned to rescue the women and children and transport them as far as the state highway. Once they were relatively safe, he figured to wing it from that point. He knew he ought to stay with them, but he was torn between that and coming back to help Early defeat his father, even though he was unsure what he could do in that respect.

Jesús's plan changed when he reached Hugh Don's Cavalier. While rummaging under the driver's seat for the spare keys, he found Hugh Don's pistol, the big .45-caliber revolver he called his cowboy killer. Jesús pulled it out and looked at it with a feeling akin to reverence. Then he checked the cylinder. The gun was loaded. He knew then what he had to do. He ran back to the Big House and peeked through one of the windows in the living room. His father was standing with his back to him, highlighted in the glare from the kitchen. Jesús waited for the moment between one gust of wind and the next, and when it arrived he gently eased himself through the front door. Then he held his breath as he made ten quick and silent

261

steps across the front room. This trek placed him directly behind his father, who was talking to Early Willingham.

"Jesús was wild like his mother," Roberto Jiminez said. "He ran away."

"Surprise, you lying son of a bitch," Jesús replied. "I really *did* run away." And the rest was history.

The fallout from that bleak day brought many changes to Willingham Valley. The biggest of these, of course, was that Ivey's absence left a hole in their lives that could not be filled, a fissure deeper and colder than the largest of the many caverns in the valley wall. She had been the matriarch of their clan, the cornerstone of their family, and the founding pillar of the Camp Church. There was no one who could even remotely assume any of these roles, so the breach remained. The faithful were still that, and they continued to gather Wednesdays and Sundays at the church. But even though both Isobel Jiminez and Avis Shropshire turned out to have the knack for lay preaching, it wasn't the same, and the parishioners all knew that it never would be again.

The bullet with Early's name on it had broken his right arm and shattered his right shoulder. Five months later, in May, he had not yet regained the full use of either, although there was a fair chance that he would over time, God willing. Early was certain that Ivey had been lobbying this outcome on his behalf since the day of her arrival on the fields of Elysium. During his long recovery, he spent a fair amount of time thinking about the past, about time gone by and all that he had lost when Ivey passed. He was the last of the Willinghams, and if that bullet had traveled a slightly different trajectory, he wouldn't even be that.

He spent an equal amount of time considering what was to come next. He was disabled and unemployed, and his lack of prospects was a constant worry to him. But even as he puzzled over how to fill the days ahead, those same days were busy taking care of themselves. From March through May, over forty reservations came in for the upcoming camp season. Early didn't know what to make of it, but Millie did.

"It's a miracle," she said. "It means that Miss Ivey is still watching over us, and that Camp Redemption is supposed to carry on."

"You're starting to sound like Ivey," he noted. "A lot of folks thought she was crazy, you know."

"No, she wasn't crazy. *Crazy* is when you use a steak knife to try to disarm a man with a gun."

"That is pretty damn crazy," he agreed. When she was right, she was right. He touched his shoulder and grimaced.

"So, do you want me to help you run the camp?" she asked.

"Sure. What else do I have to do?" It was becoming his standard answer.

Hugh Don Monfort survived his wound as well. He was now married to Isobel Jiminez, that Latin beauty he had been attempting to court even before he had shot her husband excessively. As it turned out, she had been as interested in Hugh Don as he was in her, but, being a traditional Catholic, she had felt herself bound by her marriage vows and thus unable to follow her heart. But once Hugh Don Monfort had put seven bullets into Roberto Jiminez, the gateway to love opened wide.

Ironically, the relocation of Isobel's abusive husband from the quick to the dead had proven her instinctive fear of policemen to be prophetic. During the investigations following the shooting, it was revealed that Isobel was an illegal alien, and once this information came to light, it was no time at all before she was in real danger of being deported, thanks mostly to the zeal of an INS employee by the name of W. Bookman Ingle, who just couldn't seem to find it in him to look the other way and let the offense pass. Luckily, however, Hugh Don loved

Isobel, so he solved this issue by marrying her, thus making an honest and legal woman of her. He then offered to put W. Bookman Ingle out of his misery with the cowboy killer if he ever came around those parts again. W. Bookman faded from Willingham Valley like a bad dream on a sunny morning, leaving the Monfort family—Hugh Don, Isobel, Jesús, Fernando, and Diego—to live their lives as best they could.

As for Charnell Jackson, he had indeed suffered debilitating angina on that turbulent morning, but no physical reason was ever discovered for the pain. Millie maintained that it came from a broken heart, and since a more precise diagnosis did not present itself during three days of tests, the doctors released him from the hospital in time for Ivey's funeral. It had seemed at the time as if her interment would be delayed due to the official need for an autopsy, even though the doctors at the hospital over in Rome were confident of the cause of death. But Early didn't want one performed, and neither did Charnell. It seemed a poor way to treat her, there at the end of her days.

"I don't want her cut up," Early said. "It's just a stupid legality. She's dead, and the son of a bitch who scared her to death is dead, too. What good will an autopsy do? It damn sure won't bring her back."

"Let me make a call or two," Charnell replied. Not surprisingly, he knew a guy who knew a guy, and at the cost of a few old favors being cashed, the need for the postmortem disappeared.

Thus they buried Ivey on a cold and rainy November day. She moved into the family plot opposite Vester and Clairy Willingham. Her service was attended by her family and by the many neighbors and friends who had known her and loved her. Brother Rickey Lee asked to preach the funeral, but Early declined on his sister's behalf and instead officiated himself. He talked of her goodness, her mercy, and the likelihood that she would indeed dwell in the house of the Lord forever. Then amid tears and sorrow, Ivey was lowered into the cold Georgia ground. She had loved Willingham Valley all the days of her life, and her mortal remains would rest there now until the trumpet sounded and the faithful were called home.

The following day—after a brief search and a strong hunch—Early and Millie found Charnell Jackson sitting in the family plot. It was a bleak morning, and their breath steamed in the rainy air. Charnell leaned against Vester Willingham's grave marker, facing the raw earth mounded over his departed love. He was as cold as Vester's stone. He had apparently died sometime during the night.

"Ah, shit," Early said. There was way too much dying going on to suit him.

"Poor Charnell," Millie said. "Should we call the police?"

"We really should," he said, but there had been too many police around lately to suit him as well. So instead of notifying the authorities, they decided to take care of matters themselves. Charnell was family, after all, and he was where he wanted to be. They enlisted the aid of Jesús and Lisa Marie, and those two plus Millie dug the grave. Then they combed his hair, slipped him into his nicest suit jacket, and managed to get him into his new home without dropping him, which was a small miracle, considering the rain. Afterward, Jesús planted a cross at his head. Constructed of pressure-treated two-by-fours, the cross bore one word that Early wrote in black indelible marker.

"We'll get him a real marker as soon as we can," he said.

"I kind of like that one," Millie replied.

Early considered his chosen word, *LAWDAWG*. Then he nodded. He figured Millie was right.

Epilogue

Early sat on his bench beside the lake and puffed on the Dr. Grabow. The springtime air was heavy with the intermingled scents of wisteria, rhododendron, and azalea. Millie sat beside him, straight as a fence post. In light of all that had happened, they had implemented a designated-adult program, wherein only one of them at a time could enjoy herbal remedy for the stresses of modern life. By this method, if an emergency were to arise, such as a broken water pipe or a gunman taking hostages, at least one of them would be equipped to handle it. So she did not indulge, although she did have the occasional sip of Schlitz malt liquor. They sat quietly, comfortable in each other's company. Presently, Early dozed.

When he opened his eyes, he was confused as to the time of the day. It had been bright daylight when he closed his eyes, but now the world had acquired a sepia tone, as if a cloud had blown over the sun or twilight had arrived. He turned to ask Millie how long he had slept, but she was gone. In her place sat Ivey. She smiled and gave Early a joyous hug.

"Ivey?" he asked. Her features were distinct, but her outlines were hazy, as if she were out of focus.

"I used to be Ivey," she said. "Now I'm something else." Her voice had a slight echo, as if she were speaking in an empty room.

"What the hell?" he mumbled.

"You've been cussing a lot more since I left," she noted with disapproval. "You know it's a sin."

"Sorry," he said absentmindedly. He had been backsliding, for a fact. "Is this a dream?"

"You're asleep," she said. "But this isn't a dream."

"So I'm crazy," he concluded.

"You're no crazier than I was whenever Mama or Robert Corntassel came to see me," she assured him.

Early grimaced. "Thanks," he said. He wasn't much relieved.

"I have some things I want to tell you."

"Why aren't you talking in Bible verses?"

"That part is sort of optional. Bible verses were always a comfort to me, so I always received my messages in verse. You like your talk straight."

"Is this all written down somewhere?" He thought maybe there was a manual or a rulebook.

"Don't blaspheme."

"Sorry. What did you want to tell me?"

"Roberto Jiminez didn't kill me."

"I know that. He just scared you so bad that an artery in your brain blew out. It was the same thing as killing you."

"You've got that part right. I *was* scared to death. And don't you let anyone tell you it's a painless way to die, either! I still had a headache when I got to heaven. But it wasn't Roberto Jiminez who caused it."

"I don't understand. Millie told me she saw him standing right next to you. Hell, he *shot* me and Hugh Don Monfort!"

"There's that *h* word again."

"Sorry."

"And I'm not saying he wasn't an evil man. He's gotten what he deserved, for sure. And he'll continue to get it for several millennia to come. But he wasn't the one that caused my aneurism to pop."

"Well, if it wasn't him—"

"It was Brother Rickey Lee."

"What?"

"It was Rickey Lee. He came out to the camp early that morning to talk to me about changing my will back to the way it was, so that the church would inherit my property instead of you. He came into the kitchen right after you left. One thing led to another, and before I knew it, I was dead."

"How did he even know you had changed the will?"

"Candace Shellnut told him. She overheard you and Charnell talking about it at the diner."

"Why would she tell Rickey Lee?"

"Brother Rickey has been...conducting private prayer meetings...with her for several years now," Ivey said with disapproval.

Candace was married, of course, as was Brother Rickey. Early considered the information his sister had delivered. One thing was for sure. Candace had received the last tip she would ever get from him. And it was a mercy that Charnell had already gone to his reward. Otherwise, this development would surely kill him.

"Why are you telling me this?" he asked. "Do you want me to borrow the cowboy killer from Hugh Don and go take care of Brother Rickey for you?" He had been hankering to get his hands on Rickey Lee ever since the Avis Shropshire incident. He had never actually considered shooting the man, but if it was divine will, well, what could he do? He would have no choice in the matter.

"No. I want you to let go of your hate before it poisons you. Roberto Jiminez is where he belongs. Brother Rickey will be joining him in less than a year. Some kind of cancer. I don't know all the details."

"How do you know Brother Rickey will be joining him?"

"I have friends in high places. But the point is, you don't need to worry another minute about either one of them. Or about me. It was all bound to happen. Remember my dreams."

"Your dreams?"

"Betrayal. Death. Conspiracy. Marriage. The wrath of children. It was all foretold. Don't spend any more time hating

Roberto because I'm dead, and don't go after Brother Rickey with the cowboy killer now that you know the truth. What happened was supposed to."

"You were supposed to die?"

"I would have died soon, anyway. That aneurism was a trip to heaven waiting to happen. It had been for a long time." She gently touched his cheek. "There's something else I came to tell you. Something I should have told you while I was alive. I'm not your sister."

"I *knew* I was adopted," Early said.

"No, you're a Willingham, born and bred. You're *my* Willingham. I'm your mother."

That was the last thing in this world or the next that Early had expected to hear. "What?"

"You're my son. I had you when I was eighteen years old. Vester and Clairy were my parents, but they were *your* grandparents. They just claimed you as theirs."

"Why would they do that?"

"It's different now, but back when I had you, it was a scandal for an unmarried woman to have a baby. It just wasn't done. Your real father and I were in love, and he wanted to marry me, but he was killed before we could marry." She sighed then, as if the pain from that sad time had somehow traveled with her to the new country. "His name was John Palmer. He never even knew you were on the way."

Early mulled the sad tale. Oddly enough, it struck him as truth. All but one small piece.

"For a minute there, I thought you were going to tell me that Charnell was my father."

"No, I met Charnell not long after I had you. In church, of all places. He was a good man, and he was pretty persistent." Early nodded. He could well believe it. His mother continued. "Eventually we fell in love, and he wanted to marry me. He wanted to be my husband and your father. But I was young, and I felt that I had committed a terrible sin with your real father. I thought I deserved punishment, and I believed I could atone for my transgression by denying myself something I really wanted." She smiled a sad, knowing smile as she looked at him. "It was a foolish idea, but I was still only a girl, and that was how I thought things worked. So I swore to never marry Charnell, and Mama and Daddy claimed you as theirs. But I raised you like my son, and I have always loved you the same way." Her features became blurred and indistinct.

"You're my mother," Early said. He didn't know what else to say.

"And you're my boy." She gently touched his cheek. Then she began to dissipate, like a cloud nudged by a summer breeze.

"Can you still hear me?" he asked.

"Hurry," she said. Her voice had a hollow, distant quality to it.

"Did Charnell make it to heaven?"

"He's here with me now," she said from a thousand miles away. Then she was gone.

Early startled awake. He sat on his bench by the lake. Millie was by his side. The Dr. Grabow was cold in his hand.

"Have a bad dream?" she asked.

"I don't know what I had," he replied.

"You were talking in your sleep."

"Did I happen to be speaking English?" He hoped he hadn't been talking in tongues.

"You were mumbling. I couldn't tell."

"Probably just as well."

"Want to talk about it?"

"I do." He shared the details of his experience. "What do you think?" he asked once he had finished.

"I'm glad that Charnell made it to heaven. Miss Ivey was so worried he might not."

"So you think it was real?" he asked.

Millie shrugged. "If Brother Rickey Lee passes away from cancer sometime during the next year, then we'll know. In the meantime, we've got a Bible camp to run. We know *that's* real."

Early considered her words. She was right, of course. He stood, and together they walked toward the Big House.

****

Your boy seems content, Robert Corntassel said as he mingled with the mists that rose from the falls.

He does for a fact, Ivey replied as she drifted in the gentle spring air. *I told him long ago that he was doing what he was meant to do. But he had to come to that on his own.*

He'll be all right, Robert remarked.

I think so, Ivey said. *You'll keep an eye on things while I'm away?*

I'll be right here, he assured her. But she was already gone, and he was talking to the wind.

—The End—

271